GUN MACHINE

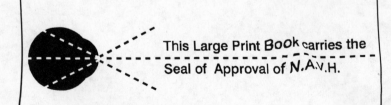

This Large Print Book carries the
Seal of Approval of N.A.V.H.

GUN MACHINE

WARREN ELLIS

THORNDIKE PRESS
A part of Gale, Cengage Learning

GALE
CENGAGE Learning·

Detroit • New York • San Francisco • New Haven, Conn • Waterville, Maine • London

LE
NGAGE Learning®

Thorndike Press® Large Print Crime Scene.
The text of this Large Print edition is unabridged.
Other aspects of the book may vary from the original edition.
Set in 16 pt. Plantin.

LIBRARY OF CONGRESS CATALOGING-IN-PUBLICATION DATA

Ellis, Warren.
  Gun machine / by Warren Ellis.
    pages ; cm. — (Thorndike Press large print crime scene)
  ISBN-13: 978-1-4104-5892-6 (hardcover)
  ISBN-10: 1-4104-5892-X (hardcover)
  1. Private investigators—Fiction. 2. Serial murders—New York (State)—Fiction. 3. Cold cases (Criminal investigation)—Fiction. 4. Large type books.
  I. Title.
PS3555.L61717G86 2013b
813'.54—dc23   2013004460

Published in 2013 by arrangement with Little, Brown and Company, a division of Hachette Book Group, Inc.

Printed in the United States of America
1 2 3 4 5 6 7 17 16 15 14 13

For
Ariana and Molly
and
Lydia and Angela
and
Niki and Lili

ONE

On playing back the 911 recording, it'd seem that Mrs. Stegman was more concerned that the man outside her apartment door was naked than that he had a big shotgun.

A 911 call is the pain signal that takes a relative age to travel from the dinosaur's tail to its brain. The lumbering thunder lizard of the NYPD informational mesh doesn't even see the swift, highly evolved mammals of phone data, wi-fi, and financial-sector communication that dart around the territory of the 1st Precinct under its feet.

It was a good seven minutes before someone realized that 1st Precinct detectives John Tallow and James Rosato were within eight hundred yards of naked shotgun man, and called upon them to attend the scene.

Tallow wound down the passenger-side window of their unit and spit nicotine gum onto Pearl Street. "You didn't want to do that," he said to Rosato, watching without interest as a cycle courier in lime Lycra gave him the finger and called him a criminal. "You've been bitching about your knees all week, and you just responded to a call at the last walk-up apartment building on Pearl."

Jim Rosato was recently married, to a Greek nurse. Rosato was half Irish and half Italian, and there was a pool on at the 1st as to which of the two would arrive at work wearing the other's skin as a hat within the year. The Greek nurse had prevailed upon Jim to improve his health, an emergency-scale program that included Jim jogging before and after each shift. In the past week, Jim had been lurching stiff-legged into the 1st with a face like a bulldog chewing a wasp, declaiming to any and all witnesses that his knees had fused solid and that he had only days to live.

When Rosato swore, his Dublin mother's accent spoke through him from the grave. "Shite. How do you even know that?"

The backseat of their unit was a shale formation of books, papers, magazines, a couple of e-readers, and a cracked gray-market iPad. One or the other of them often had to put a boot to it to create enough space to slide a suspect into the back. Tallow was a reader.

Rosato slapped the wheel, crossed traffic, and pulled the unit in beside the apartment building on Pearl Street. It was a grim gray thing, the squat building, a fossil husk for little humans to huddle in. Every other building on this side of the block had had, at the very least, dermabrasion and its teeth fixed. Two stood on either side of the old apartment building like smug Botoxed thirtysomethings bracing an elderly relative. Many of them looked empty, but nonetheless there were flocks of young men in good suits and bad ties with phones nailed to their heads, and rainbows of angular women stabbing out texts with sharp thumbs.

The shotgun blast from inside the old building made them all clatter away like flamingos.

"This was your idea," Tallow said quietly, popping the door. On the street, Tallow compulsively lifted and reseated his Glock in its holster, under his jacket. Rosato moved stiff-legged to the apartment building door.

Lots of cops married nurses, Tallow knew. Nurses understood the life: murderous shiftwork, long stretches of boredom, sudden adrenaline spikes, blood everywhere. Tallow almost smiled as he followed his wincing partner into the apartment building. He made sure the door closed as silently as possible, and only then did he draw his firearm.

The hallway parquet crackled under their feet. It was cratered, here and there, exposing rotting-newspaper backing. Tallow recognized a masthead from the fifties poking out from under the parquet by the south wall. The plastic wallpaper was slick with ancient nicotine stains, the air was warm and wet, and the staircase handrail looked tarry.

"Shite," Rosato said as he started up the stairs. Tallow made to slide past him, but Rosato waved him back. Rosato had had longer on the beat than Tallow before he made detective and felt it gave him innate superiority on the street. Tallow was too all up in his head, Rosato would tell people. Big Jim Rosato was a street police.

The voice of naked shotgun man was carrying down the stairwell. Naked shotgun man was apparently unhappy at the letter that had been slid under his door this morning explaining that the building was being purchased by a development company and that he had a generous three months to find other accommodations. Naked shotgun man was going to blow away any asshole who

10

tried to take his home from him because this was his home and no one could make him do anything he didn't want to do and also he had a shotgun. He didn't mention being naked. Tallow presumed that he was simply too angry for clothes.

They made the second landing and looked up. "Bastard's on the third floor," Rosato hissed.

"The guy's barely in his body, Jim. Listen to him. His voice is doing scales and he's repeating himself in the same sentence. We might just want to wait until someone with crazy-person skills arrives."

"Read him one of your history books. Maybe he'll pass out and fall on his shot-gun."

"Seriously."

"Seriously, shite. We don't know yet if that shot he took hit anyone." Rosato pushed on, flexing his fingers around his gun, holding it down by his leg.

They quietly ascended. The voice got louder. Rosato made the landing before the third floor, raised his gun, and took a step up before declaring, in a sharp steady bark, that he was police. And then he took another step up.

His knee folded under him.

Naked shotgun man stepped to the top of

11

the stairs and fired down.

The blast tore off the upper left side of Jim Rosato's head. There was a wet smack as a fistful of his brain hit the stairwell wall.

From his vantage, three steps back and to the right, Tallow could see Rosato's eye a good five inches outside Rosato's head and still attached to his eye socket by a mess of red worms. In that single second, Tallow abstractly realized that in his last moment of life, James Rosato could see his killer from two different angles.

Rosato's eyeball burst against the wall.

The thick air pulsated with shotgun reverberations.

The sound of Jim Rosato's killer racking another shell seemed to go on forever.

Tallow had his Glock in a two-handed hold, fourteen in the clip and one in the pipe. He'd taken first pressure without knowing it.

Jim Rosato's killer was a bodybuilder gone to burgers and long days on the sofa. He was trembling all over. Tallow could see the dim echoes of his muscle under the flab. The top of his head was bald and seemed too small to contain a human brain. His cock sat atop his pouchy balls like a gray clit. The name *Regina* was badly tattooed over his chest, stretched by his hairy tits.

John Tallow could not in that moment see any reason why he should not just fucking kill him, so he put four hollow points through *Regina,* and a stopper through the shitbag's stupid tiny head.

The stopper sent Jim Rosato's killer falling backward. A thin stream of piss described the arc of his drop. He hit the floor, retched out one autonomic attempt at a breath, and died.

John Tallow, standing still, made himself breathe. The air was thick and bitter with gunshot residue and blood.

Nobody else was in the corridor. There was a hole in a wall behind the dead man. Maybe he had randomly shot a wall to get people's attention. Maybe he was just crazy.

Tallow didn't care. He called it in.

People wondered why John Tallow didn't put a hell of a lot of effort into being a cop anymore.

TWO

John Tallow stood while the medics scraped up and lifted and bagged and took away his partner of four years, and then he sat on the stairs silently so that they had to lift Rosato's killer over him to get him down and out of the building.

People said things to him. Gunfire in close quarters had temporarily dulled his hearing, and he wasn't that interested anyway. Someone told him that the lieutenant was driving out to tell Rosato's wife the bad news. She liked to do that, the lieutenant, to take that weight off her people. He'd known her to do it three or four times in the past few years.

After a while, he became aware that someone was trying to get his attention. A uniformed police. Behind him, the Crime Scene Unit techs were moving around like beetles.

"This one apartment," the uniform said.

"What?"

"We checked all the apartments, to make sure everyone was okay. But this apartment here, there's a shotgun hole in the wall and no one's answering the door. Did you check this one apartment?"

"No. Wait, what? That hole's kind of low. I don't think it can have hit anyone."

"Well, maybe the occupant's out at work. Though that'd make him kind of unique in this building so far."

Tallow shrugged. "Force the door, then."

"The door's tight. Can't imagine what kind of lock's behind it, but it don't want to give."

Tallow got up. He knew buildings like these weren't Fort Knox. But if the uniform said the door wasn't giving, it was pointless to repeat the effort. The door wasn't the thing. The hole was. He got down on one knee by the hole. The internal walls in these places weren't worth the name. Plasterboard partitions, for the most part. When this building was crammed with people, way back when, it must've been like living in a hive.

The hole was a foot across. Tallow peered through it. No light in there. Tallow shifted his position to let in ambient light from the hallway. The uniform watched him frown.

15

"Give me your flashlight," Tallow said.

Tallow twisted it on and played it through the hole. Things glinted in the dark, as if he were shining the flashlight into the teeth of an animal deep in a cave.

"Get a ram," Tallow said.

The uniform went downstairs while Tallow sat on the floor with his back to the wall, dismissing the CSU complaints with a finger. That'd come back to bite him later, he knew. CSUs loved to complain, and if he didn't listen, they'd find someone who would.

Then again, maybe he'd earned a pass today.

Tallow sat and thought about his partner for a while. Thought about never having met his wife. Having actively avoided it, if he were honest. Remembered feeling relieved that Jim and his wife had gotten married on vacation, so he couldn't and therefore didn't have to attend the ceremony. Tallow had decided, after the one time he'd had to crush a stranger with the news that her husband had died on duty with three big bullets in his gut, that he couldn't be married. He didn't want to stand at a wedding and think about being married. He didn't want to sit at Jim Rosato's table and think about being married.

16

The uniform had found another uniform, and together they had unhappily carried the ram upstairs, blistered black paint over blue metal.

Tallow stayed on the floor and hitched his thumb at the door.

The uniforms put the ram to the door. It bent and held. They looked at each other, swung back harder, and drove the ram in again. Wood splintered, but the door stood.

Tallow got up. "Take out the wall."

"You sure?"

"Yeah. It's on me. Take it out."

The ram crushed the wall in. A few dull thumps sounded from within. The CSUs cursed their mothers for the dust the strike kicked out. Three more short swings made a hole big enough for Tallow to step through. Two more dull thumps. He twisted on the borrowed flashlight and passed it around slowly.

The room was full of guns.

Guns were mounted on all the walls. There were half a dozen guns at his feet. Turning around, flashlight at shoulder level, he saw that guns were mounted on the wall he had come in through. Some guns were mounted in rows, but the right-hand wall had them in complex swirls. Some were laid on the floor on the far side of the room,

17

forming a shape he couldn't quite fathom. There was paint daubed on those.

There were scents he couldn't place. Incense, perhaps. Musks. Fur or hide.

Rippling patterns of gunmetal, from floor to ceiling. In the stale, faintly perfumed air of the room, Tallow felt almost like he could be in a church.

Nobody was in the apartment but him. He pointed the flashlight at the door. The door was reinforced with sliding metal bars and heavy locks. There was the red flicker of an LED on one of the locking devices. Tallow couldn't figure out how anyone could get into this apartment by way of the door, but he could see that a ram wasn't going to do it.

Tallow carefully stepped through the apartment, checking all the rooms without touching anything.

There were guns in all the rooms.

In the back room, there was a gap between the heavy curtains covering the sole window. A single shaft of light fell through the gap into the small gun-encrusted room. Dust motes hung in the still beam. Tallow stood for a moment without breathing. Left the room slowly and silently.

Tallow almost smiled as he put his head

back out through the hole, pointed at a CSU, and said, "Got something for you."

THREE

The situation at the apartment building quickly boiled into rolling chaos. When uniforms started jostling with a few co-opted detectives during the recanvassing of the occupants about apartment 3A, Tallow took the opportunity to slide downstairs.

The sun was already behind the long chromed arms of the financial district. He looked at the pale sky and wondered for a moment where the day went. He got in the car. It felt empty even when he sat in the driver's seat. Tallow nosed the car out into the thickening traffic and pushed east, back into the deep of the 1st Precinct.

Fifteen minutes later, he was parked outside his favorite coffee shop, the one with tables on the sidewalk and nobody to complain about smoking. He bought a pack of cigarettes and a disposable lighter from the place on the corner, sat at a metal table with a tall sleeved-cardboard cup of venomously dark coffee, lit up with hands that were not yet shaking, and began the effort to shift out of automatic and let the world back in.

Letting the world back in by stages. Letting himself become aware of that slight pinch in his suit jacket, under the arms. This was the only suit jacket he'd had cut to accommodate his shoulder holster, which meant he'd gained some weight across the chest. As he shut his eyes for a moment, he could feel little points of tightness on his scalp. Spots of dried blood stuck to his skin.

By stages. The untreated cardboard sleeve around the venti-plus cup, stamped with biodegradable inks, proclaiming the coffee shop's proud independence, the simple black printing on the flecked card making its own statement about authenticity. The shiny metal table reflecting too much light, the glare making it hard to sit there for too long during the day, especially if sitting there with a notebook or laptop, ensuring that no one hogged the sidewalk seating for too long. The taste of wood and oil on the cigarette smoke. Drawing it down, the warm comfort of it in his chest, letting the smoke bleed out of his nostrils. Chemical aftertaste on the back of his tongue. Autonomic reach for the coffee, sweet and rich, washing away the cigarette, stopping his head from going

21

too light. Tallow hadn't smoked in nine months. He hadn't started again either, not in his head. This was medicinal. He'd toss the pack and the lighter when he left the table, he'd decided.

More stages. The music leaking out onto the street from the open coffee-shop door. Brooklyn glo-fi, a couple of summers old, kids on the edge of Park Slope imagining California beaches. Two girls on the other side of the window, in fauxhawks and sleeveless hoodies framing unfinished sleeve tattoos. The more unfinished of the two was the better one. That girl had less money but a finer eye for an artist.

Behind them, a printer rattled on a trestle beside the countertop, an automated print vendor coughing out a POD paper, the New York Instant, or an aggregation of social-network capture.

Stages. A bus growled by, the dynamic display strip down its side scarred by a black rash of dead pixels. Advertising some CGI thing starring three different versions of Arnold Schwarzenegger, one of them from his twenties and another from his thirties. A car jumping impatiently behind it, sparkling new and fresh off the lot but proudly sporting 1950s fins. Candy-apple red and spikily sporty, driven by a man closing on fifty in a candy-striped shirt with sleeves carefully furled to show a maintained forest of gray forearm hair.

Stages. Jim Rosato was dead. Nothing was getting rid of the copper taste that kept jabbing Tallow's tongue, as if he'd aspirated some of Jim's atomized blood when the shotgun blasted half his partner's head off. Tallow had blocked everything, and now the screens were down, he couldn't help but see Jim's death on high-definition replay.

Tallow choked on smoke.

"I knew you'd be here. Mind if I sit down?"

His eyes snapped up. The lieutenant was standing by the opposite side of the table. She had a coffee in her hand. Tallow wondered how long he'd been sitting there replaying Jim's death and not noticing anything else at all.

"Please," he said.

She had a manner of moving like an intricate folding machine when she sat or stood, a slow precise compression, her head and shoulders remaining quite still. Her black suit creased perfectly. She flicked out legs in boot-cut pants. Her father was a tailor who knocked her out bespoke clothes at cost. Tallow knew to avoid her on the days she wore a new suit, because the collection

23

of it was a traditional event in which she was berated by her father at length for becoming "top pig."

The lieutenant was watching Tallow with those sharp glacial eyes, clever glass scanning him with mechanical precision.

"I spoke to Jim's wife," she said, prying the lid off her coffee with clear-polished nails.

"I left something out when I talked to you," Tallow said. "His knee gave out when he was taking position. All that jogging. Didn't want you to mention it to her."

"You can leave that out of your typed statement too," she said, with an attempt at a smile. The lieutenant had strong, handsome features. When she smiled, Tallow thought he could see a little girl peeking out from behind that hard face, from under the efficient cap of black hair. "Your shooting's going to be ruled good, of course. I spoke to people. You'll still have to go through a formal interview and appearance, but no one's going to give you any trouble."

"I wasn't worried."

Her eyes flickered over Tallow's face, looking for something. When she didn't find it, she let out a disappointed breath and raised her coffee to her lips.

Tallow took a last draw on his cigarette.

Turned to face the road and accurately flicked the stub across the sidewalk and down a drain. Swilled some coffee to wash the taste of the thing out of his mouth. The lieutenant was watching him again.

"You haven't talked to me about the apartment you knocked a hole in."

Tallow sucked his cheeks in, trying to force coffee-flavored saliva over the foul taste on the back of his tongue. "Not a lot to tell. Never seen anything like it. I'm presuming it'll make an interesting news story when it gets out."

Tallow became aware that she was watching him again. "What is it, Lieutenant? Am I doing something wrong?"

"You seem further inside your head than I'd like. More than usual. I want to know that you're dealing with what happened today, John."

"I'm fine."

"That's what bothers me. I partnered you with Jim all those years ago because you were complementary kinds of crazy. You kept each other in check. I need you to not crawl back inside your own skull and watch the world with binoculars from deep cover. You've been bad enough for the past year as it is."

"I don't follow."

25

She stood up. "Yes, you do. You're at the age where the rush of the job has passed and the grind of the job is taken in stride, and this is the time when you're wondering if it wouldn't be so bad if you just stopped giving much of a shit and rolled along doing as little as possible. I'm resting you for forty-eight hours, mandatory. Come back as a detective I can use."

She paused, and then tried to fly that smile again. "I'm sorry about Jim." The smile didn't take. She left.

Tallow waited five minutes, turning another cigarette around in his fingers. Put it back in the pack. Pocketed the pack and the lighter. Walked into the coffee shop, found the bathroom, and vomited coffee and his past two meals into the toilet with a thin scream.

FOUR

Jim Rosato once commented that Tallow's apartment was where he unpacked his head.

One bedroom was stuffed with books, magazines, and paper. Its door was missing, like a failed levee, and the flow of print coursed into the living room, cresting under the table that two old laptops and an external drive lived on. Two tall speakers jutted from the surface of it all like lighthouses. The other bedroom was halfway bricked up by CDs, cassette tapes, and vinyl. A store clothes rack filched from a dumpster stood in the corner of the living room as his wardrobe, but most of the clothes that should have hung from it were slumped under it on the floor.

Tallow elbowed into his apartment with the day's magazines under his arm. Not the sheaf it would have been at the top of the month even five years ago. A lot of his favorite stuff had migrated to the web. A lot more had just disappeared over the horizon of the digital dawn, never to be seen again.

He didn't open them, just put them down on whatever stable surfaces he could find. Took his jacket off, wriggled out of the shoulder rig. Hung the rig on the clothes rack, dropped the jacket on the floor. Sat in one of his two chairs.

Tallow tried to think about the apartment full of guns. How a place like that would come to be. But all that would stay in his head was his partner and only real friend having a handful of his brain torn out by a shotgun.

Forty-eight hours. Tallow knew he was going to go crazy in here.

FIVE

Tallow's sleep was studded with unremarkable nightmares of a coppery shine. The cell phone on his bedside stack of books woke him.

The women in Tallow's life had all informed him that he habitually awoke with a form of Tourette's. For the first hour of the day, he was incapable of summoning reserve, patience, or social skills.

Tallow assaulted the cell phone and answered it with "The fuck what."

"Come into the office."

"Fucking mandated forty-fucking-eight fucking hours woke me the fuck up for."

"CSU just got done with a sampling of your guns. I'm sorry, John, I know I told you forty-eight hours, but I need you in here now."

"Fuck. All right. Yes. Shit. Give me an hour."

"Thirty minutes. And be human when you

29

get here. I'm cutting you a degree of slack right now, but I will take a big steaming shit all over your personal record if you talk to me like that again."

"Yes. All right. Lieutenant goes away now. I wake up. Yes."

"Thirty minutes, Detective."

Thirty-five minutes later, he started to run the gauntlet of sympathizers at the front door of Homicide in the 1st Precinct building on Ericsson Place. It took him ten minutes of awkward handshakes and awkward words to get to the lieutenant's office. Jim had been the popular one. No one really knew what to say to Tallow. But most of them tried. It was painful.

The lieutenant considered him sourly. "I said thirty minutes."

She was wearing a suit he hadn't seen before, in a cold slate-gray worsted.

"People kept stopping me. What's wrong?"

"I could start with you pissing off some CSUs so badly that I had to go into debt to get them to hand the sampled guns off to the night shift so I had a prayer of getting ballistics today. But I won't."

Tallow slumped into the one chair on the other side of her desk without being asked. It was hard plastic and did not invite long stays in her office, which was why she put it there. "Well, I'm glad you didn't just give me shit for that."

"Don't," she snapped. "I'm not happy, John. Did you not *detect* that?"

"Sorry," he lied.

"So. CSU ran a sampling of guns from the apartment on Pearl you aired out. Four of them. They came back two hours ago."

She picked up a thin sheaf of clipped papers, went to read from the top one, and then threw it down on her desk again. "I do not *believe* the pallet of shit you have delivered to my door, John."

"What's wrong with the guns?"

"What's wrong with them? They all killed people."

Tallow thought he could detect the beach landing of a major headache at the back of his head. "Can you be clearer, Lieutenant?"

She snatched up the papers again. "Gun one: Bryco Model 38, .32-caliber. Anomalous striation due to deliberate interference with the barrel interior. Implicated in the homicide of Matteo Nardini, Lower East Side, 2002. That's an unsolved homicide, by the way. Gun two: Lorcin .380 semi-automatic, extensively modified, test-firing matches the bullet dug out of Daniel Garvie, Avenue A, 1999. Unsolved. Gun three:

31

Ruger nine-millimeter, scarred firing pin, Marc Arias, Williamsburg, 2007, unsolved. Would you like to use your imagination for the fourth one?"

"This was a random sampling of guns from the apartment, yes? CSU didn't just lift a group from one location."

"Random grab."

Tallow stood up suddenly. Eyes unfocused, he walked around his chair, put his hands on the back of it, refocused on the lieutenant.

"That's impossible."

"No, John. What's impossible is that yesterday you found something very odd that should have amused another department in this precinct for months on end. Yesterday, it was a curiosity and someone else's problem."

"Every single gun . . ."

"That's right. On current evidence, you have reopened several hundred homicides and brought them all to my door."

"Me?"

"Oh yes. You. This is on you, Detective Tallow. You knocked the hole in that wall and just had to stick your head in."

"Oh, come on . . ."

"You broke it, you bought it. That's the rule all over town."

"You can't."

"You watch me. You found a room filled with guns, and every single one of those guns is going to prove to have been used to kill exactly one person. I'm assigning you to follow through on the ballistics and find out how these guns came to be in that room and find the owner or owners and hang every last one of these cases around their necks. Because I'm damned if I'm letting anyone hang them around mine."

Tallow did not pick up the chair and throw it.

The lieutenant saw his fingers flex. "On top of that, the squad is stretched too thin as it is. *And* I just lost my best officer to an idiotic shooting incident that should never have happened. So you're working this alone until further notice. Any questions?"

Tallow just looked at her.

"Good," she said, offering him the paperwork. Her thumb and forefinger fidgeted on the edge of the sheaf, making it hiss as he reached for it. "Now go home and get changed and then start work, for God's sake. There's blood on your jacket."

Tallow jerked, checked himself over like a leper. There was a dark speckling on his left sleeve. Particles of Jim Rosato on his left side. Jim Rosato was always on his left side.

Jim never let him drive.

Tallow had still been awake less than an hour, but he found a way to swallow some words down and left the office very quickly.

SIX

Driving back from Ericsson Place, Tallow started running the numbers. New York City took anything up to two hundred unsolved homicides a year. There were something under ten thousand unsolved homicides since 1985.

Of the three samples the lieutenant had told him about, the earliest associated homicide was 1999.

He didn't know how many guns were at the site. Two hundred? More than two hundred. Tallow told himself to start with two hundred. In a space of more than a decade, losing two hundred kills in a volume of well over a thousand unsolved . . .

Tallow had had occasion to visit the Property Office, down in the Bronx, and wander the twilit halls of the subbasement where cold-case homicide evidence was stored in three-foot-tall brown barrels, four stacks high, with reference numbers sprayed on their sides in black paint. Tallow did not intend to live there with the grave goods of the unavenged dead of New York.

Tallow needed to plan.

Being in his apartment at this time of day felt wrong, as if he were in an alien time zone. He stood in front of the big soot-edged mirror in his small bathroom looking at himself and his suit. He took the suit off. Considered. Took off the gray tie too, and the white shirt, and everything else, piling it under the sink unit with one foot. Tallow subjected himself to a scalding, painful shower, forcing himself under the burning spray and slapping flat palms on the walls to make himself stay there, braced and bunched up. Blasting everything out of him.

Tallow toweled off his stinging skin and went to his bedroom. Under the bed was a suitcase, and in the suitcase was a black suit. The suit he wore to funerals. In the living room, he found an olive shirt and a thin black tie. His old hip holster was in an Amazon.com box half stuffed with CDs (Charly Blues Masterworks issues that he'd forgotten he owned), two levels down in the stack of boxes that stood in the far corner of the room. Tallow put it on, pushed away the suit jacket with the back of his wrist, and slid the Glock into it. Lifted it half an inch and reseated it.

The suit accentuated the fact that his leanness was turning into gauntness the longer he plowed into the wrong side of thirty. He decided that he was okay with that.

Tallow went back out into the world in a funeral suit.

Seven

The hunter stood still on the street, watching them take his treasure away.

He'd known something was wrong. The day had started out badly. He was having trouble seeing both his Manhattans, and it was a wrenching effort of focus to see what he thought of as New Manhattan. Not forests but buildings. Not horses but cars. Some days it didn't bother him. Today he felt out of joint, and abstractly concerned about his state of mind. Perhaps he was getting old, and his brain was not as plastic as it used to be. Once every couple of months, he'd awake wondering if he might be genuinely ill.

He'd taken ketamine once, as a younger man, and on processing the experience realized that its first effect on him was that he was no longer worried about having taken ketamine. He never invited that loss of perception into his life again, but on those occasional weak days, there was a sick sense in the pit of his stomach that he'd spent weeks unconcerned about being unable to see New Manhattan.

The day had started out badly, and so he walked the trail to his cache, signposts and trees flickering in and out of view, to ensure it was secure. The walk had taken an hour longer than it should have, not least because of the difficulty of seeing and avoiding CCTV cameras. Sometimes his mind transliterated them into Old Manhattan elements, but today, nothing was on his side, including his own brain.

He watched the men and women in blue jackets loading his treasure into vehicles. Years of work disappearing.

He was armed. He could try to stop them. Even if he hadn't been carrying a gun, he was a hunter. He could take them down bare-handed if necessary, or fashion a weapon from whatever was available. But he would be seen.

His anger built. Parts of New Manhattan dropped out of his sensorium. He could smell oak, pine, and sweet birch. Heard a flock of plovers clatter out of the treetops in fright. Bark crawled over the fasciae of the buildings he faced, under light dappled by forest canopy. He looked down at the ground and had to summon hard strength to force the wet grass under his feet to turn back into dry sidewalk. A red-back salamander, without dewy blades of green to slip through, elided away into mist and was gone.

The hunter stood still and watched them take away the last evidence of his life. Apart from the bodies.

EIGHT

The perimeters of the 1st Precinct form a shape like a cracked arrowhead pointing out to sea. It totals one square mile of Manhattan. Tallow had to go in the other direction, away from his mile, and that never filled him with joy.

At this moment, Tallow did not feel like he had friends at Ericsson Place. Or, perhaps more correctly, he felt that any aid he'd get there would come from pity. He told himself that pity would lead to half-assed work, but in his gut there was a churn of humiliation and offendedness at the thought. And when he considered going back to the house on Pearl Street to canvass the residents, he felt sick. So he spent ten minutes with his laptop on ACRIS, the online city register, and grabbed the name and office address of the building's landlord.

It was going to be a long drive uptown. Through the narrow, coldly shaded streets of the deep 1st, just now starting to get that sweetish, sweaty scent of halal gyro and shish from the early phalanx of street vendors setting up their shiny, flimsy carts and their piss pots for their sixteen-hour workdays.

Tallow felt uncomfortable in the driver's seat. A constant juddering sense of being on the wrong side of the car. He hoped that the long drive would retrain his brain a little.

Past the holes-in-the-wall offering sixty-minute divorces, and the strangely denuded storefronts that Vice continually begged for the budget to surveil for drug traffic. Past Ground Zero, this morning sound-tracked by the gunfire snapping of badly secured plastic tarps in the breeze and the cursing of the mini-entrepreneur suckfish trying to stop their 9/11 picture postcards from blowing off their folding-card tables by the fence.

And then out, into the territories of others.

Tallow drove with the unit's radio on. He would rather have driven with music, but he'd learned to appreciate police-band chatter as its own kind of sound structure. So he rolled with the waves and eddies of crime and its management as he drove. Officer down in the Bronx, off duty and unluckily walked into a robbery at an auto body shop;

reports that when the officer took one and fell, a school safety agent snatched up his dropped gun and returned fire. Mother and daughter found stabbed to death in Sheepshead Bay, reporting officer commenting that they were so holed and smashed that they looked like ragged wet blankets. The body of a missing Bronx man found in the trunk of a stolen car abandoned in Long Island; the detectives who had been looking for him in order to hang an attempted murder around his neck had some choice comments, quickly drowned out by responders to a Midtown location where a guy had apparently doused his pregnant ex-girlfriend in gasoline and set her alight when she didn't give him whatever he had wanted.

Because it's all about what other people want, Tallow thought as he threaded his way through Manhattan and its bodies.

He was in the late West Fifties when traffic slowed to a crawl. As he edged the car along, he saw a heavy woman with gray hair dyed an unconvincing black kneeling in front of one of the sickly trees planted in the sidewalk. Her shins, in faded woolen socks, were resting on the short wrought-iron fencing that framed the square of dirt the tree was struggling to live in. There was something silvery sticking out of the back of her neck. Paramedics and cops were standing around her, clearly so wrapped up in the problem of her that they weren't bothering with the little crowd of gawkers grabbing cell phone shots. Tallow realized that the slim shaft of metal had gone right through the back of the woman's neck and out through her throat, pinning her to the slender tree trunk.

Ahead of him, the traffic broke, revealing the paramedics' rig parked beside a fat Chrysler Town & Country with one wheel on the curb, and a bike and its rider under it. The back wheel of the bike looked like it'd burst, the tire shredded and the rim hanging open like a dented letter *C*. The rider was in a couple of pieces. Lime Lycra smeared in meat.

Tallow realized that several of the bike wheel spokes were missing. He counted a few of them scattered back across the sidewalk. He knew where the last one was. Some freak of torsion must've flung it through her neck like a loosed arrow.

He considered badging a uniform or a paramedic to get the whole story but in the next second decided he didn't need it. He drove around the scene and away from a dead woman praying to a tree in New York City.

■ ■ ■ ■

West 145th in the 500s was far enough away that by the time he finally reached it, Tallow had tension pains locked across his upper back, and posture pain rammed into his lower back. He clambered out of the parked unit like a dying crab. When he tried to straighten up, important-sounding bones crunched frighteningly inside him.

He took a deep breath and got a noseful of sun-warmed dog shit for his trouble.

The landlord's office was a sliver of closet slipped between a firetrap overstating itself as a hotel and a CARIB & SOUL FOOD vendor with a frontage painted in the shade of green that reminded Tallow of hospitals. There was a rangy kid of sixteen or so in a retro Knicks shirt standing in the narrow doorway smoking a blunt. He had a deep, laid-open scar running down from the corner of his mouth to somewhere under his chin. On profile, it made him look like a ventriloquist's dummy. A switchblade handle was outlined in his pants pocket. Chocolate and mint hung on the weed smoke drifting his way from the blunt. Tallow took another look at the kid and shaved a year or two off his age.

"You a cop," said the kid without looking at him.

For far from the first time, Tallow wondered why this kind of conversation ever had to happen. He would have thought that of all the items of information that got passed from generation to generation or peer to peer, the unfortunate results of idly screwing around with a cop to feel tough would be among the first and would not be forgotten.

"Is that a problem?"

"Not if you going someplace else."

Tallow heard giggling from inside. The kid had an audience. Tallow wasn't sure if he was really in the mood for this. He preferred to be easy about these things. Jim Rosato would've put the kid's head into a wall without thinking twice.

Tallow took a few easy steps toward the door. The kid, still not looking at him, moved to block the door, puffing on his blunt. Chocolate and mint. Kids' flavors.

"You going someplace else."

More giggling. Tallow walked right up to the kid, who shifted again to block him. Tallow leaned the other way, shuffled, raising his hands and making an awkward show of clumsily trying to get past the kid. The kid couldn't help but grin as he moved

46

again. Young boys were cracking up inside the office.

Tallow stamped on the kid's instep. He shrieked and fell backward, scrabbling to clutch his foot.

"Oh my God, I'm sorry," Tallow said. "Are you okay?"

The kid was incoherent, screaming, trying to pry his Nike fakes off his swelling foot. Inside, three boys between ten and fourteen were suddenly very quiet. One of them had taken the office chair from behind the space's single desk and had been spinning around on it. Tallow watched him slowly rotate to a stop and then considered them all with a chilly study.

"It was an accident. I was trying to get past him and I accidentally hurt him. You understand what I'm telling you, don't you?"

A big voice came from the back room. "What the fuck is going on out there?"

"Police," Tallow said.

A wide man in his forties shouldered his way out of the back, one hand on his belt. He might have been a linebacker or a weight lifter once, but he'd gained some weight, probably in the past year or two, and his pants weren't staying on his waist anymore. He wasn't ready to change the way he

47

dressed or start wearing suspenders, so he walked around with one hand on his belt to continually tug his pants up off his hips and over his belly. He took in the scene.

"What the fuck, man?"

Tallow showed him his badge. "Looking for Terence Carman."

"That's me. But what the fuck is this?"

"Your boy here fell over. Isn't that right, kids?"

The children just stared.

Carman put his shoulders back and moved into the room, yelling. "You get the fuck out of here now, you little shits. Go on, move it, find some other blood to piss off. Del, stop that fucking noise and stand up, you sound like a piglet getting it up the ass from an angry horse, man. Help him the fuck up, go on, get out."

There was moving and dawdling and bitching as they left. Carman turned to Tallow with a massive shrug. "My sister's kids, man. What you gonna do, they've got to be someplace. Oh shit, would you look at that."

Tallow followed his angry glance and bent to pick up the blunt from where it had been smoldering a small brown hole in the thin carpet.

Carman watched him. "You're not going

to make a thing out of that."

"I don't know yet. You own an apartment building on Pearl Street."

"Yeah, I figured I'd be getting a visit. Just not so soon." Carman reached for the blunt. Tallow jerked it back.

"I am in a bad mood. I've just had to dance with your relatives, and I've recently had to shoot one of your tenants dead while wearing my partner's brains on my sleeve. So how about I get some open and friendly cooperation, so I don't have to balance this little thing here on top of the mound of shit I could pour through your door."

Carman looked at Tallow and gave up. He seemed to sag inside himself, the skin around his neck rucking up like a kicked rug.

"Okay, okay."

Tallow held his gaze on Carman a few beats longer. Carman sank a bit more, trudged to the front door, and, with great theatrical effort, closed and locked it. "C'mon," he said, wading through knee-deep misery toward the back room.

The room was a grimy box. Metal shelving stuffed with binders lined one side. Two ratty armchairs, a small table with two overfilled ashtrays, and a few stools stolen from unwary or uncaring drinking establishments filled it out. Carman took what was obviously his armchair and spilled into it, a hand on either arm, legs slightly apart and solidly planted. Tallow imagined that this was what passed for the patriarch's chair in Carman's world.

Tallow pressed the end of the blunt into the ashtray. Carman nodded. Tallow considered the nearest stool — the pink plastic seat covering split like an idiot grin, yellowed foam lolling out — and decided to risk the other armchair instead. Sitting, he discovered that some padding and probably a few of the springs were gone. He was lower down than Carman. Tallow wondered if Carman had cut the padding out himself.

"So you killed Bobby Tagg, then," Carman eventually said.

"Was that his name?"

"You didn't know his name?"

"It's all a bit of a blur, to be honest. So, what, we called you, or . . . ?"

"Hell no. My other fucking tenants called me. Pretty much all of them. Shit, they called me before they called you. Like I was going to do something about Bobby Tagg stripping bare-ass naked and waving a goddamn shotgun around. And then you can be damn sure they were all back on the phone when you wasted the crazy asshole."

"All of them?"

"Every last one."

"Good. Tell me about the tenant in apartment three A."

"Never met him."

Tallow looked meaningfully at the stupid weed-stuffed mint-and-chocolate-flavored cigar butt sticking out of the ashtray. "This is your friendly cooperation?"

"No, no, stay sat. I'm explaining. Because I don't want any trouble, and you're gonna see why. The rent on three A is paid annually. In cash. What happens is, sometime in March, someone calls me up and says, How much for another year on three A? And I'm like, tax time's coming up, so I take the rent, add on twenty percent for my trouble, make it a nice round number, and give them that. Next day, there'll be an envelope on the floor with the cash in. And I forget all about three A for another year."

"And that didn't smell like trouble to you?"

"Listen, people rent from me for all kinds of reasons. I got people paying me four grand a month just for somewhere to fuck three lunchtimes a week. My old dad always said, Asking too many questions gets in the way of doing business."

"What business was your dad in?"

"This one. I inherited it. The Pearl Street place has been in the family since the fifties. Inherited the guy in three A too. His original deal was with my old dad, and that too passed down to me."

"So your dad met him."

"I guess."

Tallow sank lower in the chair. "This is where you tell me that your dear old dad collected his last rent check a while back."

"Yeah. Retired, went to Disney World, died on the It's a Small World ride." Carman glanced around his shitbox fiefdom with a mirthless grin. "Yeah, there wasn't any compensation. There were hookers involved. And explosives. Anyway. No, my old dad's long gone."

Tallow took out his notebook and pen, feeling like he was about to try to screw fog but professionally compelled to log what little this meeting had given him. "So, Mr. Carman. You never met the tenant of three A. It was a long-standing arrangement with your father. How long do you think this arrangement has run?"

"Twenty years, easy. I, you know, I don't have paperwork on it to refer to."

"I figured. Have you ever been inside apartment three A?"

Carman rubbed the back of his neck.

Smiled. A smaller smile, but a real one this time. "Tried once. Back when I first took over running that building, when my dad was still around. I was younger, and I hadn't learned that one thing yet. So I wanted to know something about the invisible man, you know? Couldn't get in. He'd jammed the lock somehow. Hadn't *changed* the lock, but there were dead bolts or some shit behind the door. Never did figure out how *he* got in and out of the place. And the next time I looked? He had actually changed the lock, and added some new ones. I said something to my old dad, but he said, It's the guy in three A, leave it, it don't matter."

"What one thing? You said you hadn't learned that one thing yet. What's that?"

"Like I said, asking too many questions gets in the way of doing business. You got to learn not to ask questions all the time. That one thing is learning the right question to ask at the right time."

"Is that right."

"You'd know that, Detective. Right?" Carman sat proud in his back-room throne, having found a little epigram he'd probably heard on a TV show and offered it to his guest like an old subway token.

"Who are you selling the building to, Mr. Carman?"

"Some banking company. Vivicy. They're, like, financial services, all that weird money stuff that no one understands and that never sounds completely fucking real."

Tallow wrote *Vivicy* down and paused a moment. Made a small spiral movement with his pen, like he was stirring the fog.

"Mr. Carman. Why are you selling the building? Why is Vivicy buying it? And were you going to tell them about the man in three A who has secured his apartment door so that no one can enter it?"

Carman sucked his teeth. Tallow just gave him the dead stare.

"I'm selling it because they offered me enough money to retire on," Carman said eventually. "And I don't mean retire down to Florida, get loaded, and drown while trying to dynamite a children's ride and get blown at the same time. I mean a fucking yacht someplace, and slaves and shit."

"And."

"And the guy in three A ain't my problem. They're going to knock that place down, and if the crazy guy's still in there when it happens, then it still ain't my problem, serve him right, and I got mine. That about cover it, Detective?"

"When do you get paid?"

"When the building's empty."

"I also asked why are they buying it."

"Yeah, well, that wasn't the right question at the right time. The first day my old dad figured I was bright enough to jerk off and chew gum at the same time, he told me this. He said, The thing about land, son, is that they don't make it no more. So if you want a big shiny building in the financial district to keep your internets and your gadgets and your fucking gold treasure in, well, the financial district ain't going to grow more land for you to put it on. So you need to find an old building and knock it the fuck down and build over the hole."

"Give me the names of the people you've been dealing with at Vivicy."

Carman tensed up quickly. "Why?"

"Because nothing's getting knocked down until I say it is. Your building's a major crime scene, and not one damn thing is going to happen to it before I want it to. Give me the names."

NINE

It was getting harder and harder to find pay phones in Manhattan, and it was getting harder and harder for the hunter to see them.

The hunter did not yet wish to resort to prepaid cell phones. If cornered on the subject, he'd be forced to admit that he was not yet completely conversant with the finer points of their operating parameters. Was it easier to pick a cell phone conversation out of the air than to hurriedly put a tap on a random pay phone line?

Some days, obviously, it all bothered him less. The hunter didn't realize it, but his opinion of those days changed like the wind. Some days, when he could hear only traffic and machines and the sound of synthetic soles on sidewalk, he wanted nothing more than the condition of living on Lenape Manhattan Island.

The change for the phone flickered in his

upturned palm. One moment coins, the next moment seashells. The hunter set his jaw, clamped down on his perception, and the coins stayed coins long enough for him to force them into the thin mouth of the machine. He summoned from a recess in his memory the telephone number of the first man, and dialed it. The phone made a noise that he supposed meant that the number didn't work. He went to the next alcove in his mind and pulled the number of the second man.

The hunter listened to ringing, and then clicking, and then a woman's voice telling him his call was being transferred. A recording, he decided. The twenty-first century seemed very far from him today. The line rang again, a different sound.

On the fourth ring, the second man said, "Andrew Machen."

"Do you recognize my voice?"

An ice-pick pause. Then, through a hard swallow, "Yes, I recognize your voice. How did you — I mean, how can I help you?"

The hunter smiled. They were still afraid of him.

"Mr. Machen, I have been keeping things at a building on Pearl Street." The hunter gave Machen the building number and the apartment number. "My things have been found by the police. I have watched them begin the process of carrying them out of the building. These things are mine. And in a way, they are yours too. They are the tools of my trade. Do you understand what I am saying to you?"

Machen's breathing had been speeding up as the hunter spoke. Now he was fighting to fill his lungs enough to get through a full sentence. "That building. I'm buying it. My company's buying it. The police killed someone there. Yesterday. Some shut-in lost his shit when the current owner gave the residents their eviction notices. What have you been keeping there?"

"Think about it. What have I been keeping there? I told you a moment ago."

"Oh no. Oh no. You can't have."

"And now you are telling me that this is your fault. That you have bought the building that contained my things. That you have precipitated their capture."

"I didn't know! How could I know? You weren't supposed to tell us! Hell, you weren't supposed to keep the fucking guns —"

"You had no rights over them. They were mine. They were sacred. They had done powerful things and were not to be tossed away like used toys the day after Christmas."

The hunter smiled when he said that to Machen because he had a strong feeling that he had not remembered the existence of Christmas for some weeks.

"Well . . . what am I supposed to do?"

"Fix it," said the hunter quietly. "You must understand, Mr. Machen. If the other two men decide that you have become an impediment to their success, you must understand what I will be asked to do."

The hunter hung up the phone. He went to cross the road but saw a CCTV camera hung from the entrance to a bank on the far corner. So instead, he turned left, down an alley, and melted into an imaginary forest.

TEN

Vivicy was housed in the top ten floors of a 1980s skyscraper that looked like a spaceship standing on its launch gantry. A spaceship that had been staging, melancholy, since that decade's recession, waiting for someone to come along who could afford to fuel it up for its leap to the sky. It was oddly sad, seeing the city soot barnacled to the clamps and pylons affixed at the building's edges as an architect's smiling decorations.

Its launch date was as long past as the days of the three-martini lunch in the financial district. Midafternoon, and the people still on the street were darting toward buildings with panic in their steps, chewing the last woody lump of a power bar or quickly stamping out a half-smoked cigarette.

Tallow, back in the 1st Precinct, had smoked

a cigarette for lunch as he considered the building. He'd placed the phone calls to Vivicy he'd needed to on the long drive back downtown but had decided to reinforce a few points in person.

Inside the building, the spaceship metaphor held. A mother ship's cathedral, with huge aluminum pipes for pillars and a burnished metal floor. Magnesium or something, Tallow thought, as he walked on it; it was sprung, or suspended on joists somehow, so that his feet lifted a little as he moved. A floor for Masters of the Universe that put a spring in their steps on the way to the elevators in the mornings. Inside, the building didn't feel like an unfueled article on an abandoned launchpad. It felt like it was just waiting to fill up with all the world's money before it took off for new maps.

Recessed golden spots attempted to throw Constable-like shafts of God's light into the hall. The near-ambient background music was clever. Waiting in line at the security station, he realized the music swelled to a little climax every couple of minutes. Some Muzak-laboratory mutation of the theme to *The Big Country,* where the orchestral strike was muted and the motorik beat of German Krautrock from the seventies flowed under and past it. When the metal buttresses of this church were first flown, the music had probably still sounded like the future, he thought.

Tallow badged through the security station. The guards, bearing on their black shirts the embroidered brand of a firm called Spearpoint, nodded at Tallow in the conspiratorial and collegiate manner of those security employees who consider themselves brothers and sisters of police. Tallow nodded back, just to make life easier. He took the elevator with a man who was compulsively raking the base of his thumb with bitten fingernails. Hard enough to raise tiny red blooms from between the flecks of old scarring.

Tallow got off at Vivicy's first floor and, along with a grim-looking courier, quickly took the second-stage elevator that serviced it and the top nine. The courier ground his teeth. It sounded like paving slabs being rubbed together. At the building's top floor, Tallow stepped off and found a helpful map screwed to the wall by the elevator that laid out the office territory for him. Tallow waited until the courier was deep in hot negotiation with the harried receptionist and glided through the main doors into the main part of the floor.

People looked up as he moved down the middle of the space toward the corner office he wanted. They didn't look at him so much as sniff the air, decide that they didn't detect the kind of predator they feared most, and return to work.

The corner office was crewed by a personal assistant at a brushed-steel desk. Behind her, the big doors to the office she guarded. Tallow broke his stride — his Rosato-stride, the stride he'd learned to keep up with and then emulate, relentless Rosato like a ton of boulders rolling down a slope toward you. It'd been too easy to roll along with it.

Tallow took twenty seconds to observe the personal assistant. Japanese American woman in her twenties. Beautiful eyes, bitten lips, short black hair. She touched it. Pushed at it with her nails. False nails, but small and neat. Touched her hair again, caught herself doing it, made herself put her hand flat on her desk as she wrote with the other. Tallow had seen the hint of a tattoo under the hair. Her head used to be shaved. The hair was growing back, and she was managing it, but it still bothered her. The clothes bothered her. The clothes were good, business wear chosen with some taste, but cheap. A warm day, even under the air-con, but she had long sleeves. He watched her stop at the document she was annotating, turn to a battered little notebook, and refer to something. Her own notebook. She wanted to hold on to the job so badly that she was preparing for everything it could throw at her.

Tallow put his police face back on, walked to the desk, and badged her.

"Detective Tallow, 1st Precinct. I need to talk to Andrew Machen."

She looked at his badge like it was his gun.

"Mr. Machen is, uh, he's not available right now, Detective. If I can, can, take a number from you, I can arrange a meeting just as soon as he's, you know, he has an emergency right now, and —"

Tallow dropped his voice. "He's in there, isn't he?"

She raised her voice, clearly hoping it was loud enough to be heard through the doors. "No, sir, Mr. Machen is not in his office right now."

Tallow made a move to the doors. She came out of her seat, fear and tears pearling her eyes.

Tallow touched a finger to his lips. Smiled. Put out his hand to calm her. Said in a loud voice, "This is a homicide investigation, ma'am, and I'll go wherever I like, and if

you don't get out of my way and stop block-
ing these doors, I will arrest you and then I
will arrest him. Is that clear?"

She sat back down, a little smile timid on
her face. Tallow smiled at her again as he
opened the doors.

Andrew Machen said, "Did she really
block the doors?"

A big man rose from an Xten Pininfarina
chair that looked stolen from a starship's
bridge and very deliberately put a cell phone
in an African blackwood case down on a
Parnian desk before walking around its
curve to meet him. His charcoal shadow-
check suit was cut to accentuate his wide
shoulders. He was a product of that
Hollywood-gym regime that gave a man a
wide chest, a long abdomen, and snake hips.

"Yes."

Why are your fingers shaking? Tallow
thought as Machen reached for a hand-
shake.

"Detective Tallow, 1st Precinct. May I
have five minutes of your time?"

"Seems like you already took it. Apologies
for" — Machen waved that oddly trembling
hand at the doors — "all that. Very busy
time. Obviously I want to put myself at your
service, but what we want, limitations on
our resources, you know . . ."

Nothing in the office matched, Tallow noticed after a moment. There was no unifying approach, no theme at work. No taste, Tallow supposed. Just a collection of very expensive things that didn't go together. Except, presumably, by the scale of their price tags.

"I know all about limitations on resources, yes. I have a few questions."

The visitor's chair — singular — was of the same make as Machen's chair but cheaper, with two long curved runners instead of wheels and with a different color trim. Machen gestured to it, walking back around his protective curl of a desk.

"Whatever I can do, Detective."

Machen's hand seemed to shake less once he was in his space throne behind his absurd zebrawood desk.

Tallow gave him the address on Pearl Street. "You're buying this building, yes?"

"Yes, I believe so. I mean, I don't have direct day-to-day oversight of that purchase, but yes, I remember something about it. Possibly it's not me you should be speaking to."

"You do own Vivicy, yes? You did found this company and continue to own and control it."

"That's right."

"Then it's you I should be speaking to, Mr. Machen. What are your plans for that building?"

"I don't have —"

Tallow let a little steel into his voice. "I think you can help me, sir."

Machen simulated relaxing back into his chair. The thing seemed almost to close chrome arms around him. "Let's say I can." He smiled.

"Your plans for the building, sir?"

"Knocking it down."

"Why? To build offices? Seems to me you have plenty of space here."

"Ah, well, Detective, here we enter the dark arts of financial wizardry. And this is something I do actually employ a wizard for. Pingback."

Tallow decided to take out his notebook. "I don't really know what you're referring to there."

"It's what my wizard calls it. The time it takes a bit of information to go from my computer to the New York Stock Exchange and back again. Any kind of financial trading has to take into account the speed at which an opportunity can be observed and a deal can be executed. The Pearl Street location has particularly good pingback."

Tallow scratched down some notes, and

then paused. "Wait. Aren't we closer to the Stock Exchange here than we would be if we were sitting in that building on Pearl?"

Machen clapped his hands. Tallow had the sudden feeling that Machen practiced this routine for dinner parties. "Aha. And that's why I keep a wizard. Because the pingback on the Pearl location is actually better than it is here. Even though we are physically much farther away. Working this out is almost like feng shui." Machen mispronounced it. Tallow let it go.

"My wizard," Machen said, "tells me that it's due to maps, utility services, history, even ground conditions. The maze of wires under our feet wasn't all put there just to serve us in the financial sector. Otherwise, all lines would lead to Wall Street, right? The wiring we use to reach those computers aren't laid down in a direct fashion, and they're not all of the same quality. Jumping from fiber to copper and back again, or even from wireless to fiber to copper, and trunks going around the block when you just want them to cross the road . . . all of this affects pingback time."

"Sure, but not so you'd notice."

"But the computers notice. The databases notice. Fifty milliseconds' delay in our information flow can be the difference between getting rich like pharaohs that day and checking the package of ramen at the back of the cupboard for green bits that night."

"Really."

"Well, not really. But it does decide who gets to close deals on a minute-by-minute basis all damn day. Pingback location is the new real estate in Manhattan, Detective. So, yes, I'm going to knock that tenement down and put a big shiny office on it with lightning pingback, as I've been instructed to by my wizard, and make a lot of people a lot of money. Which is what we're all here for. Right?"

Tallow was trying to write it all down. "This is insane."

"It's where we live now. The real maps of the great cities of the world are invisible. They're underfoot, or they're wi-fi fields, or they're satellite links. On a global basis, the financial markets' biggest problem is the speed of light. I read a paper last year that said, quite bluntly, that what was holding back the efficiency of the global financial system was most often light-propagation delays. I know a guy in Bonn who thinks he can make a killing by floating an artificial island in the Arabian Sea and putting an uplinked trading center on it, bypassing six different choked systems and the delays inherent in their light cones."

Tallow looked up at Machen. "This isn't just your job, is it?"

Machen laughed, short and explosive, and some tension seemed to rush from him. "I love it. I love doing this. You know, some days, I don't even see the buildings when I walk to work. I just see the networks, the flow of money and instructions and ideas, huge invisible shapes and zones and lines. It's the biggest game in the world, and to win it I have to do battle with the forces of relativity itself."

He laughed again, more quietly and easily this time. "And I know what I sound like. And you have to understand that I don't take myself quite that seriously. But at the same time, nothing I've said is a lie. It's just fun. It's the life I always wanted."

Tallow watched him. Machen's happiness faded by inches. When Tallow judged him to be back at his starting point, he said, "I want to make something very clear. That building is the center of an extremely serious investigation. I am here to impress upon you that that building is not to be touched by anyone until our investigation is done."

"Well," said Machen, "that does make things . . . complicated. We have exchanged contracts with the owner of the property, but the money hasn't yet been transferred, and . . ."

"Execute the contracts. Transfer the money. And then hold the building intact until the conclusion of our investigation."

"I'm not certain, Detective, that you have the power to demand that," Machen said. It seemed to Tallow that Machen then thought twice about having said that, rubbing a knuckle against his lips, his eyes going somewhere distant.

"I think it would be time-consuming for both of us if I were to attempt to find that out for you, sir."

Machen stirred. "No. You're right. I apologize. We'll complete the sale and hold the building as is for a period. Can I give you my personal number?"

Tallow nodded, and Machen produced a silver card case from a drawer of his desk. With thumb and forefinger, he extracted from it a slim stainless-steel business card and reached across to hand it to Tallow. It, acid-etched in a Neville Brody font Tallow recognized from magazines, read:

MACHEN@VIVICY.LIFE
824-6624
@MACHENV

71

"Nice," Tallow said. He slipped it into his breast pocket, wondering if it was going to interfere with his cell phone reception, and for one distracted second amusedly regretful that the card was too thin to stop a bullet in the fairy-tale manner of a luckily placed cigarette case or brandy flask.

"So," Machen said, "this is all about the naked man who got killed?"

Tallow gave him a look. Machen spread his hands, grinning. No shaking now, Tallow saw. "I admit, I have been overseeing the whole process of obtaining the location. Observing. So naturally I was informed of the incident fairly early on. Does the man have any family?"

"Not that I'm aware of at this time. Why do you ask?"

The grin became rueful. "Should I feel guilty? I feel a little bit guilty. It does appear that the purchase of the building is what set the guy off. I mean, we weren't just shoveling these people out into the street. We were paying good money and taking care of all our obligations while remaining well within property law. But from all accounts, this poor guy just saw someone taking his home away and it sent him over the edge. I feel like I need to do something more."

Tallow stood. "If I find out, I'll let you

know, sir. Thank you for your time."

Machen rose again, offered his hand again. "And you'll stay in touch about the building?"

"Of course. Once we're done with it."

Tallow felt a little tremble travel down Machen's arm, through Machen's hand, and into his own. "Perhaps," Machen said, "more frequent updates?"

Tallow smiled and broke the grip. "I'll do what I can."

Tallow left the office before Machen could say anything more.

Outside, he whispered to the personal assistant, "You're going to be fine."

She beamed at him with relief, a stunning blaze of a smile.

Tallow left.

In the elevator, he reviewed the last minute of the interview. Machen had played the part of a charming, empathetic, understandably reticent but ultimately fair man reasonably well.

Except that if Machen knew Bobby Tagg was dead, then he also knew that Jim Rosato was dead. While Machen would have no reason to know that Tallow had killed Tagg and that Rosato was Tallow's partner . . . why, if you were playing nice guy, would you not take the chance to commiserate with a policeman about his dead col-league? That rang wrong.

Why was Machen shaking? He had put down his cell phone, presumably his personal phone, when he stood up. What had just been said to him?

Perhaps he was in fact keeping his distance from the deal. He'd assigned it to underlings to complete. That would make sense, Tallow supposed. Perhaps he'd literally just heard about what happened. Perhaps it'd taken a day for the information to ping from the bottom to the top of Vivicy. Light-propagation delay.

ELEVEN

Tallow knew he could expect a phone call from the lieutenant before the end of the day. He had to show that he had at least covered the basic underpinnings of the investigation, such as ensuring the crime scene wasn't demolished tomorrow. To be replaced, Tallow now sourly dreamed, by some shimmering half-real wizard's castle.

Covering the bases meant driving out of the 1st again, to One Police Plaza.

Crime Scene Unit was still, against all logic, located at One PP. Yet it covered the whole of Manhattan. Some of its responsibilities had been delegated to Evidence Collection Teams, one of which he knew had been working at Pearl Street today. But the heavy lifting of forensics was all at One PP. An overworked, under-resourced, and, in Tallow's opinion (back when he'd cared to voice one), under-vetted department. How anyone had thought problems with CSU and chain of evidence would be solved by creating ECTs was beyond him. They just added more links to the chain and were staffed mostly by people who were both under trained and virulently pissed off with their lives.

CSUs, by contrast, tended to be simply insane. Cops still talked about the CSU supervisor who had sort of accidentally opened fire on his staff during a demonstration, and there was the legendary CSU from twenty years ago who was famous for telling any people who asked how to effectively and untraceably dispose of a body, in return for the price of a bottle of Smirnoff and/or a go on their wives. CSUs were hated, and they hated in return. Their hate was corrosive and shameless. They had simply "lost" the evidence on the shooting of four officers a few years back, and they dared anyone to do anything about it. There was a lot of political noise, denouncements, and public apologies, but in the end, every CSU who had been at One PP before it happened was still there afterward.

Tallow was nervously aware that his name was on the worst cold-case dump CSU had ever seen. He was not looking forward to having them look at him and judge by eye exactly how much his organs might be worth on the black market.

He realized he was standing by his car staring into space and lifting and reseating his Glock in its holster. Tallow scowled at himself and got into the car. And then got out again and got into the driver's seat, even angrier with himself.

One Police Plaza was in the orbit of Pearl Street. Pearl Street left the 1st Precinct and curled around One PP before heading for the Brooklyn Bridge and then on to the tip of the island. A brown, Brutalist block of a thing that still looked like it'd been helicoptered in by an occupying force to act as a base for some provisional authority. The tangle of fencing, checkpoints, ramps, and bars around it did nothing to dispel the illusion. Invading long-lost cousins in blue, here to force civilization on their barbarous island relatives from behind their monolith perimeter.

But they'd been here too long, and the invaders in their original Brutalist ship had seen some of their number go native. Whenever he went to One PP, Tallow had the notion that everyone there could tell from his spoor that he was a regular police from the 1st; that people weighed him by look and judged that he was not the sort of Major

Case guy they make TV shows about. Somewhere else that Tallow didn't belong.

He found an elevator and descended into the dungeons of the castle of his distant tribesmen.

The elevator doors opened to reveal a very large man brandishing a bloodstained antique phone receiver in a plastic bag and proclaiming, "I found this up him!"

"You know," said Tallow, "I really have no response to that."

The very large man's face fell. "Sorry," he said. "I thought you were someone else."

"I figured. Where can I find your boss?"

"I thought you were her."

Tallow had to ask. "You found that up someone's . . . ?"

"The body's seventy-eight years old and thin as a whip. You wouldn't have thought it'd even fit up there without dislodging his heart." The very large man looked at the phone with a new thought. "Although I guess that would have killed him quicker."

"Listen, I need to see your boss."

"She went out for coffee. At some point."

"How long have you been waiting outside the elevator?"

"Don't judge me."

"I really need to see your boss."

"Why?" He waved the phone handset.

"What could be more important than this?"

"Okay. How about you tell me who's handling the Pearl Street cache?"

"Oh. That." Tallow was fairly sure he hadn't just admitted to sexually tampering with kittens, but you wouldn't have known it from the look in the large CSU's eyes. "You're that guy."

"I am in fact that guy."

"I'd move into a hotel if I were you, guy. Don't tell anyone which hotel. And buy armor."

"I'm going to need body armor now?"

"Maybe like a suit of armor. And a human shield. You're on Scarly's shit list until you're literally a fossil and the sun's turned into a red giant."

"Oh God. All right. Who's Scarly and where do I find them?"

Down a dirt-smeared corridor lined with wooden doors to offices barely big enough to rate the term. Latex paint in some dismal government shade of green was peeling off every vertical surface he looked at. Tallow followed the raised voices coming from the open door at the end.

Scarly was a birdlike woman in her mid-twenties in the process of yelling, "Of *course* I don't care if you're bleeding! I'm fucking *autistic*!" at an ill-looking man with five

79

years on her whose appearance wasn't improved by the absence of a chunk of left ear. As she continued to berate the man, she scratched involuntarily at her forearm, exposed by a T-shirt she'd lost weight since buying. The forearm was wrapped in plastic that was fixed on by duct tape.

"You know what, Scarly?" the bleeding man said, flapping his arms. "There's a letter in my apartment that says that if I'm found dead at work it's going to be your fault and you probably did it deliberately." He wore a lab coat that he'd dyed black, which gave him the look of a sickly, oil-covered seabird trying to take flight.

Tallow knocked on the doorjamb, scanning for a second what seemed to be the feculent office of a crazy hoarder who really enjoyed the scent of month-old used burger packaging.

Scarly rounded with an acid "What do *you* want?"

"It's the police, Scarly," the other man said, pressing a grimy towel to his ear. Tallow could smell the chemicals on the towel from the door and winced at the thought of that residue cocktail leaking into the man's bloodstream. "They've come to take you the fuck away."

"Of course it's the police, you moron.

We're all police. We work in the police shop."

"Detective John Tallow, 1st Precinct."

"You," said Scarly. "I hate you so much my dick is hard."

The other rounded on Tallow too. "You. This is your fault." He took the towel off his ear and turned his head to show it to Tallow, bobbing up and down. "You did this to me."

Tallow sagged in the doorway. "How did I do that to you?"

"Because I had to test-fire some fucking archaeological handgun that Wilkes fucking Booth probably discarded as too old and rusty to kill Lincoln with, and the chamber jammed and the firing pin shot out of the back of the fucking gun and ripped off a chunk of my fucking ear! A handgun that *you* found. Jesus Christ, what were you thinking?"

Tallow just looked at him. Looked at him until the other man was silent and unsure. Tallow could feel the woman's eyes on him, but he kept his gaze on the man with the ruined ear. And then Tallow said, quite quietly, "I don't know. I was half deaf from gunfire in the field and wearing my partner's brains on my face at the time. I am very sorry that I was not thinking of you. Now, I'm supposed to be on leave, because I saw

81

my partner get his head blown off and I killed the man who did it. You should probably also be aware that I knew that man was dead before I took careful aim and shot him through the brain. But I've been ordered to conduct this investigation, without a partner. And it hasn't been a cool day for me so far, and I am sick of threatening people and staring people down and trying to get people to behave like useful humans. So what I'm saying to you is that if I lose my temper, which I try very hard not to do but obviously I'm not having a great week, then whatever happens afterward will be explained away as the actions of an officer suffering from PTSD. I am really not available for any of the usual CSU bullshit. I understand my lieutenant has already begun to make amends to you for the situation. Therefore, while I am very sorry about your ear, I have to tell you that if anyone decides to make my life more difficult . . ."

Tallow took a breath, and smiled. "Well. I don't want to get off on the wrong foot with you people. Your name's Scarly?" he said, turning to the woman.

"Scarlatta," she said.

"Hello. I'm John. And your name?"

"Bat." On Tallow's chill look: "Hey. Parents in the eighties. What're you going to do?"

"Go back in time and kill them before they breed," Scarly suggested.

"She's not really autistic, by the way," Bat said. "She just thinks people will bug her less if she says she is. And, um, we're sorry about your partner."

"Yeah," said Scarly. "That does actually suck."

Tallow leaned on the doorjamb, buying a moment to take in their office. One work-bench, a chair on either side. Two laptops, one ruggedized, the other with a few gouges in the brushed aluminum. Plastic shelving up on all the walls. Inflatable speakers hung around the room, their wires vanishing into stacks of files, jars of strange powders, boxes, and containers of alchemical and likely illegal things Tallow chose not to recognize. Whatever wall space was not covered by storage was papered over by printouts and clippings, a riot of black-and-white imagery that probably made sense to no one but these two. Food wrappers, disposable coffee cups, and pill packaging formed a small mountain under the work-table. He spotted an old black plastic bucket filled with wellworn paintballing gear in the far corner of the room and wondered if the red on the back of one gun's butt was paint or old blood.

"You're not the CSUs who were originally on the job," Tallow said.

"No," spat Scarly. "It got handed off to us. Which makes perfect sense, because what you really want on a job like this is as much confusion in the evidence chain as possible. And I guess me and Bat hadn't eaten our ration of crap for the year. So here I am, with a career-ending job and a working partner with the magical talent of making guns shit themselves in his face."

"So," said Tallow, "tell me how I can make your lives better."

"Seriously?"

"Seriously. I know my boss did something, like I said . . ."

Bat sniggered. "Yeah. Your boss made some disciplinary paper on our boss fall into a memory hole."

"But that wasn't enough to get you two off whatever hook she'd decided you deserved?"

Bat gave Scarly a meaningful glare. "Guess not."

Tallow pointed at Scarly's arm. "You were getting a tattoo when you were maybe supposed to be processing the shootings at Pearl?"

84

Bat made a face. "Her wife insisted. Switched her cell off and everything."

"You know," said Scarly, "if I'd known marriage was this much trouble, I never would have joined the protests demanding the right. You straights can fucking keep it."

A great tiredness draped its boughs across Tallow's shoulders. "Could we maybe continue this near some coffee?"

They led Tallow to a small conference room a couple of corridors away and persuaded a coffee machine to grind out a tarry paper cup full as he spilled into a worn plastic spoon of a chair and tried to marshal his forces. The CSUs sat opposite Tallow. Scarly dropped a folder of photos on the tabletop and pushed him the cup as Bat finished swabbing his ear and tossed the stinking towel on the table too.

"So. Seriously. Where are we right now?" Tallow asked. Not really wanting the answer. He tried to close a hand around the precious coffee but had to jerk his fingers away, sharply enough that his wrist popped painfully. Tallow wondered if the other end of that coffee machine was slurping water out of a lake in Hell.

"The ECTs are moving the guns in small batches," Bat said. "We're making them take

85

so many photos that one of them asked if she was being trained to shoot porno." He opened Scarly's folder and fanned out the photos, all from apartment 3A. "They're coming back here, we're logging them, matching their locations in the apartment to the floor plans and the previous coverage the other CSU team took. And right now, we're picking weapons at random to test-fire and do ballistic matches on. When the fucking things don't explode on firing."

"And that wasn't even the oldest one," said Scarly.

"I refused to test-fire the oldest one we've seen so far. Look what the fucking Bulldog did to me."

"How old?" said Tallow.

"You're interested?" Bat leaned forward. His large eyes widened disconcertingly, to the point where Tallow worried that they might fall out of Bat's head and into his coffee. Where they would boil and possibly explode.

"I like history," said Tallow, gingerly sliding his cup to one side.

"Stay put. I got something to show you." Bat flapped off into the corridor.

"What was the gun that exploded?" Tallow asked Scarly.

"I think it didn't explode so much as come

86

apart like rotten cheese. Once our guy used a gun, he put it in his little room and seemed not to touch it again. They all just rusted out on the wall or whatever. There's paint in some of them."

"But the firing pin flew out?"

"That's what he says. I haven't looked at the gun since he fired it. An old Charter Arms Bulldog .44. Cheap-ass gun gussied up to look like a serious gun. Wouldn't be surprised if a chunk of the hammer had flaked off and blown back."

Tallow tried the cup again, and this time it didn't burn. He sipped the coffee. Corpse mud and cloying sweetener. He drank more anyway. "Why do I know that brand? I can't put my finger on it, but it . . ." He grimaced.

"Son of Sam." Scarly smiled. It might have been the first time he saw her smile. "Son of Sam used a .44 Bulldog."

"How would you remember that? You a gun freak?"

"I'm a CSU. We're all gun freaks. And Son of Sam is still an open case around here. Of which some grim asshole reminds us every six months. Like it's our fault or something. I wasn't even fucking born when he was arrested."

"You're kidding me. I thought the new DA closed the case."

Scarly laughed harshly. "And give up a stick to beat NYPD with? Listen, you, me, and anyone else without a brain tumor knows Son of Sam was a lone gunman. But if you're crazy, and you squint at it, and you've maybe got something the size of a golf ball sitting on the part of your brain that you use to put your underwear on properly in the morning — then, hell yes, you see evidence of a magic devil cult helping the guy blow complete strangers away before going home to hump Rosemary's Baby or whatever Satanic people did for fun in the 1970s."

Bat swept back in, cradling a gun in a clear plastic bag. "You're going to love this." He grinned.

Bat laid the package in front of Tallow.

"What the hell?" said Tallow.

"I know, right?" Bat was delighted.

"It's a *flintlock.*"

"It is in fact an Asa Waters Model 1836 flintlock pistol, which sold new at a hefty nine dollars. The last flintlock sold to the U.S. government, in fact; a .45-caliber, muzzle-load. Based on the kind of naval boarding pistol that you could load with shrapnel, nails, or any other thing that was lying around."

Tallow picked it up, turned it around in

his hands. "It's not in great shape."

Bat frowned. "You're not getting it. Everything we know right now suggests that every gun in that apartment was used to kill someone. So what you're looking at is a pistol nearly two hundred years old that our guy *restored* to where it'd make a reliable murder weapon and then put it up on the wall to rot. He found it God knows where, rusting out and probably near water, and got it to the point where it'd work. In fact, I'd lay odds that all that damage and scoring up around the muzzle? I bet that wasn't him."

It was gorgeous, Tallow had to admit. The voluptuous curve of the thing, and the rich dark wood that had clearly been polished lovingly at some moment in the recent past. The metal had lost its luster now, and there was some light pitting here and there, but, again, you could see where the metal had been pared and deeply cleaned. It did not look its age. On one of its plates was an insignia of some kind, a little too blurred by the years to be clear, and a word that might have been *Rooster* above it. Not *Rooster.* It was a longer word, but the incising had grown too shallow.

"You're not going to test-fire it?"

"Hell no. Pointless, anyway. Our guy

would very probably have had to make his own slug. What we need to do is run a query through the computer for any body in the past twenty years that was found with a soft lead bullet pancaked inside it behind a .45-caliber hole. I mean, who knows. What I really want to do is cut the barrel open and get a look inside."

"Amazing." Tallow laid the gun down with more reverence than when he had picked it up. "Thank you for showing me. So, you're shooting the scene, matching the shots to the floor plan, taking them out . . ."

"Yeah," Bat said, moving the gun back toward him, loving it with his wide eyes. "Some of them have paint on, as you would have seen. We're going to process that, see if it gives us anything."

"But it won't," said Scarly.

"Listen," said Tallow. "Do you have, maybe, a big spare room around here that we could colonize? Like an incident room we could all use. But different."

"I don't know what that exactly means," Bat said, frowning, "but, um, I think there's space on the next floor down. We just shipped a shitload of evidence barrels out to the Bronx. But I don't know if we could use that without our boss —"

"My boss just did your boss a solid. And

my boss can undo it fast enough, if need be. I want that space."

"No offense, buddy," said Scarly slowly, "but don't you have rooms and shit at Ericsson Place?"

"Sure. But that's not where the case is going to get solved. It's going to get solved here."

Scarly folded her arms. Leaned away from Tallow. Everything about her, in fact, seemed to Tallow to be closing up. "This ain't getting solved, Detective."

"You think?"

"If this guy was gonna be caught," Scarly said, "he would have been caught already. You know what you did when you put a hole in that wall? You interrupted the career of a genuine fucking bogeyman, some crazy-ass ghost-dog serial killer who filled a room with his fucking trophies to jerk off over. He's never going to go back there. And you know what else? He's going to start killing again, probably more and more quickly than before, so he can generate another trophy room slash jerking pit. Not only is this not getting solved but more people are gonna get killed because of it, and we won't catch him after those either because this guy is just too damned good. All you did, Detective, is find the home address of the Devil in New York City, and now he's moved someplace else.

"Look at these. Look at these photos. He's arranged this shit. These are patterns. They mean something to him. Look at this one here, this sort of whorl of guns. The ones around it are finished shapes. This one doesn't have a closed circle. You see that? There are still spaces to be filled. He wasn't done. Look here: some of these shapes look like cogs. They look like they fit together. The whole fucking room is the trophy. A cross between a church and an engine. And now he's going to start all over again. Because he has to. This is a life's work.

"You know what I see when I look at you, Tallow? I see a cop who's nine parts dead already. I see guys like you shuffle through here all the time. You stopped giving a shit about the job or yourself years ago. Look at you. Your fucking suit doesn't even fit. And for all your big talk about the bad week you're having, you're not even angry. You're just tired. Five bucks says your partner was carrying you, and ten says your boss laid this case on you because she didn't want to waste two actual police on it. This case ain't getting solved by you, and me and the Bat here are collateral fucking damage. You're already dead, and this guy here? He just got reborn. So, yeah. Thanks a lot. You are not making our lives better. Use someone else's house to pretend to work the case in, yeah?"

The room went icily, awkwardly quiet. Bat studied the ceiling. Tallow looked at Scarly. She looked at him right back. Neither of them broke the hard gaze for a full minute.

Tallow took out his phone then and checked the time.

"First," Tallow said, "I want every photo from the scene blown up to one-to-one and matched to the floor plan. If you can score some spare whiteboards, or plasterboard or something, and have them moved downstairs to whatever large empty space you've got, that'd be great. I'm going out to the scene, and by eight I'm going to be at the Fetch on Fulton. Meet me there. I'm going to feed you and get you drunk, and you're going to talk to me."

"Why?" Scarly said, shaking her head as if she were suddenly disoriented.

"I guess I didn't make myself clear," Tallow said. "You two are my new partners. And we're solving this case. Because you know what? The one crumb of comfort I have today is that when my boss told my partner's wife he was dead, she also told him that I had killed the thing that did it. There are hundreds of people who got told that their loved ones were dead but never heard that we'd done a damn thing about it. So we're solving this. Am I clear now?"

Scarly peered at him. "You don't believe that for a second."

"Does it matter?" said Tallow, and left.

A short drive got long, Tallow trying to find a clear shot through the tangle of traffic, aiming for the Brooklyn Bridge.

The police radio was on. Tallow let the city keep him company for as long as he could stand it. Guy in Stuyvesant Heights came home, found his tires slashed, walked to the bodega on the corner to find out if anyone saw it happen, got shot through the left eye. Nobody saw anything. The Upper East Side's "serial groper" had struck again, kicking a twenty-five-year-old woman to the ground and grabbing her crotch before she managed to set off a rape alarm that scared the shit out of him. Lexington and East Seventy-Seventh, and somehow no one saw a thing. And a sudden burst of chatter about a beat cop in the Bronx who had just got pulled by IAB after reports of his whipping a kid's face with his badge got out. The burst of chatter being cops who claimed to have been right there and hadn't seen a thing.

Tallow snapped the radio off, his mind wandering again to that gun: 1836. His interest in history was persistent but patchy. There just never seemed to be the time to delve into any one topic he was interested in, and he always ended up skimming it and moving on. But 1836. He wondered. Pearl Street had its name because it was once paved by crushed oyster shells — mother-of-pearl. Was it paved in pearly shells in 1836? He wondered if he wasn't traveling the same route as whoever had brought that gun into Manhattan in 1836. There was a time when Pearl Street was the water's edge, he knew.

The headlights of passing cars in the gathering dusk took on the glow of slowed, smeared, time-loose ghost lights in his imagination. He shook the thought off.

Tallow pulled up a short distance, and on the opposite side of the street, from the house on Pearl Street, just in time to see the ECT pull away with their latest hoard from the gunmetal trove in 3A.

Tallow got out and stood on the sidewalk, just looking at the place for a while. It took him that long to realize he had company, of a sort. An older man, leaning against a signpost. A heavy coat, suede or some other skin, roughly patched with mismatched leathers. A hide satchel over his shoulder. Soft shoes, like moccasins, just firm enough to be relatively new but already sooty from street wear. His hair and beard were all rust and snow. Tallow noticed that, for an obvious street guy, he didn't smell terrible. *Still,* he thought, *there's all kinds of crazy.*

Which brought back the image of screaming naked Bobby Tagg and his shotgun.

Tallow didn't register his having taken out and lit a cigarette until the second drag. He glared at the thing, annoyed with himself. Wasn't he supposed to have thrown the pack away?

"Tobacco?" said the street guy.

"Um. Yeah."

"Spare one?"

"Sure," said Tallow, locating the pack and pushing one cigarette out for the street guy. Tallow saw his fingers, callused and hatched with tiny scars. A man who had worked with his hands, a carpenter maybe, before whatever happened to him happened. Tallow had worked streets long enough to know that it didn't always take a big thing to send someone to the point where it seemed to him that the best option was to live outdoors and eat out of garbage sacks.

The street guy pulled the filter off the

cigarette with a hard, fast pinch. Tallow saw him pocket the filter as he gestured for a light. Tallow flicked his lighter and saw something between disappointment and contempt flick across the street guy's face before he resigned himself to lighting his smoke off the flame.

"Thanks."

"No problem."

The street guy drew smoke, held it in his lungs, and let it creep out of his mouth and nose. He wafted his hand through the smoke as it rose, cupping it, dancing his fingers through it.

The man licked his lips. "Not the way it used to be. Too many, what's the word . . . additives." The tip of his tongue seemed to be trying to gather residue from his lips. "Honey. Benzene. Ammonia. Can't you taste them? Even copper."

"I'm going to quit again soon," Tallow commented.

"Good," the street guy said. "Tobacco should be used only on special occasions. Smoking it all day just cheapens its value and reduces its effect." Exhaling again, he pushed his fingers up into the smoke, as if helping the silver curls up into the sky.

Tallow's immediate thought was to ask the man what today's special occasion was. He held the thought. He didn't have the strength for a conversation with a street crazy. Instead, he stamped out his own smoke, said "Good luck" to the street guy, and started across the road to the building.

"That's what I'm praying for," said the street guy to Tallow's back. "Just a little good luck."

TWELVE

The hunter drew on his tobacco and sent his prayers to heaven, watching the man in the black suit enter the building that contained his work. At first, the hunter had been furious with himself for not going in as soon as the thieves in the truck drove away with more of his tools. Now he was calmer, knowing that if he'd gone straight in, he likely would have been discovered and possibly even cornered by the man in the black suit, whose walk and jacket draping betrayed the presence of a firearm on his hip. Now the hunter had the upper hand. His prey was in sight and had no sense of being stalked.

The hunter did not, however, have a correct tool for the job. Nothing with resonance. He briefly fantasized about finding the right tool in his bag: an old snub-nosed police .38, perhaps, or some weapon that enjoyed infamy as a cop killer. But all he

99

had was a hunting knife.

He considered that the shoes he'd made in the summer were sufficiently broken in to give him woodcraft stealth. If he was very careful, if he ensured that he would not be caught in the large open spaces of the building . . .

The hunter husbanded his smoke before casting it skyward, watching the foot traffic thin out and reading the seconds off his pulse. In his peripheral vision, ancient branches gathered.

THIRTEEN

It took a conscious effort for Tallow to keep his hand off his gun as he walked up the apartment building's stairs. There was no threat here. He told himself that with every step. But every step held memory.

He got to the landing where Jim Rosato and Bobby Tagg had died, and it was there, standing in the space that for him still reverberated with blood and black powder, that Tallow realized his brain hadn't been working properly all day.

He'd killed a man. He should have been taken off the street no matter what. He should be on paid leave, whatever the caseload was. His sidearm should have been taken from him. He should be talking to counselors. He should be talking to the Internal Affairs Bureau, and probably someone from the DA's office. No one was going to rule it a bad shooting, and the fact that it was the shooting of a cop killer doubtless made some of the usual complications go away or get "lost" in paperwork. He'd heard of some guys who'd had to wait years for their shootings to be ruled on. In Tallow's case, he could be fairly sure of a good ruling within a couple of days of the process starting. But regardless of all that, he shouldn't have been out on the street.

Unless he was being placed in the way of something. Unless he was actually being used to write off this case.

Tallow leaned against the wall, next to the patch where Jim Rosato's brains hadn't quite been scrubbed clean from the plaster, and almost laughed.

The lieutenant was hedging her bets. She'd ordered him to solve the case Or Else. But in her back pocket was *The only warm body I had to cover the case was a useless detective whose partner had just gotten killed and in any event he had untreated trauma from the shooting.* Or even *We couldn't have made the case anyway; Tallow was on administrative leave and shouldn't have been working it.*

Every variation he came up with had the indelible mark of "John Tallow's all done."

He wondered when he'd disappointed her so badly that she'd felt it so easy to hang apartment 3A around his neck and drop it

102

and him both into the Hudson and out of sight. At least out of sight until next year, a nice clean calendar without a couple of hundred unsolved homicides on it.

Tallow had been clanking and buzzing up and down Manhattan all day like a good little police robot and not thinking. He wondered if maybe he did have some real trauma that he wasn't admitting to himself or not even perceiving.

"I'm an idiot," he said to himself.

He didn't hear anyone express a need to argue the point with him.

Tallow stepped forward on to the landing and stood over the place where Bobby Tagg had fallen. Tallow hadn't even known his name until Carman the landlord told him. Tallow didn't know a thing about him other than one day his world fell apart and he figured the only way he could force life to make sense again was to walk out into the hallway naked with a shotgun and scream. It doesn't always take much to make that happen. This time, just a letter shoved under the door.

Tallow's vision got blurry. He was foggily aware of his jaws clenching, and of an empty feeling in his chest.

He turned his attention to the hole in the wall of 3A, now enlarged to a door-size

103

entrance next to the actual door. It seemed that that door's elaborate locking mechanism was still giving people trouble. There had been a half-assed attempt to affix police tape across the hole. He crouched down by it so that two of the yellow strips created a frame for him to study the main room through. First, though, he closed his eyes and inhaled through his nose. He was there to refresh his sense-memories before the apartment was thoroughly deconstructed. Tallow, accepting in this still moment that he was a killer, wanted to close his eyes and breathe the air of a killer's temple.

The hunter carefully tore off one end of a paper sugar packet, lifted from the condiment tray of a coffee shop that unwisely left such things outside. He tipped the packet into his mouth and sucked the crystals down.

The hunter slipped the empty paper sleeve back into his pocket and waited. Waited for the sugar to start fires in his muscles. Waited for the street to get just a little quieter.

Tallow, hunkered down, just breathed and listened. Trying to recapture the scents he experienced when he first entered the room. Dissipated now, flattened or scattered by

ECTs and airflow, but still there in trace enough to reactivate sense-memory.

He just wished he could identify them all. He knew, or at least made an educated guess, that there had been herbs in the room. Tallow was a city boy. He didn't learn until his early teens that herbs did not actually originate in bottles through the power of Science. He thought maybe he recognized sage. Grass. Something that reminded him dimly of root beer. Something else, almost identifiable, its nature dancing just outside of his sight, like an animal slipping behind trees in the forest.

Tobacco, maybe?

The hunter shifted his bag so it rested on his right hip and pushed his right hand into it. He found the grip of his knife easily. The hunter pressed his thumb to the lip of the sheath it lay in. When the time came, he could lift the knife out smoothly with his right hand, already pushing the sheath back. His left hand would grab the sheath and pull as the blade passed upward and free. A disabling strike up the face should his prey be turning to him. The presage to a downward strike under the base of the skull if not. The modern man in him was calculating the blow already. Putting the blade between the C2 and C3 vertebrae would see its tip emerge from between the prey's teeth. The shock alone could sometimes make a clean kill of the strike. If the prey turned toward him, then the upward slash would make him clutch at his face, creating the space and time for a hard punch between two ribs, driving up through intercostal muscles toward the opposite shoulder and into the heart.

He did not prefer the knife. But perhaps his prey deserved only an animal's death.

He could gather some of his more prized tools. Hamper the swift theft of more. Create new opportunities to return and rescue other pieces. Buy time for Machen to do whatever he could.

The sugar was working. The street was as quiet as it was likely to get. The hunter started across the road, holding his knife inside the bag.

Tobacco. Or almost tobacco; somewhat related to, if not direct blood of, cigarette tobacco. Tallow almost smiled. Maybe the crazy street guy was right about the additives.

He opened his eyes and studied the main room as best he could in the early-evening light. The suspect had never lived here. That much was obvious. The church analogy that first struck him held firm on a second visit. This was a place, Tallow knew, that the killer came to. A place of worship. It occurred to him now that some of the other scents could easily be old incense. He breathed again, and this time he identified something that might be cedar, or juniper.

The killer never lived here. But Tallow was more certain now that the solution to the entire problem was here in this apartment. That the solution *was* the apartment.

The hunter reached the other side of the street. He looked both ways again, for pedestrians. There was no one to see him enter the building besides a few drivers, and none of them would pay enough attention to be of use to anyone. The cars didn't matter. He could barely see them anyway. They flickered in his vision like deer in the deep forest. He let the cars fade away entirely, until the sounds of them became nothing but hooves, birdsong, and heavy weather overhead. The hunter took a breath, held it, and then gently, gently opened the door as if it were the weighted leather flap on the front of a lodge, and purification and the future awaited him within.

■ ■ ■ ■

Tallow decided that, for all his robotic fulfillment of the basic checklist today, he'd mostly done the right things. If the CSUs did the blow-ups and the matching he'd asked for, then tomorrow he could begin thinking properly about this whole thing.

He had, however, forgotten to call the lieutenant. Given her mood at the start of the day, Tallow figured that not checking in would probably not be the wisest decision he could make. Tallow put hard fencing around his thoughts and made them snake into a serpentine line of some order. He needed to arrange the day's actions in terms of effect.

Tallow stood, wincing. Apparently he was no longer flexible enough to stay down on his haunches for that long. He shook his legs as he walked. Standing on the landing with his back to the stairwell, he took out his cell phone.

The hunter moved through the ground floor hallway slowly, as if there were brittle twigs beneath his feet. Each step cautious and exact, taken after examination of the immediate terrain.

■ ■ ■ ■

The lieutenant sounded empty with exhaustion. The sort of exhaustion that comes from a day of being blazingly angry. Her voice had the dry crackle of the worthless embers that remained, and the echo of a space filled with nothing but bitter smoke. She asked Tallow for a report on the day's activities, but he knew from the sound of her voice that the heart of her had already gotten up and gone home and that he was talking to a propped-up husk left behind to feign engagement.

"I'm at the Pearl Street scene," Tallow told her. "I've spoken to the landlord, and to the guy whose company is in the process of buying the building. The landlord's been taking anonymous cash payments on the apartment, and that all started when the landlord's father was running the business. The guy whose company is buying the building, he's planning to knock the place down as soon as he can. So I've made sure that's not going to happen for now, and I'll tickle the landlord again at a later date. I've touched base at One PP, and I'm seeing the two CSUs I've got on the case later tonight for further discussion."

"Tell me," murmured the lieutenant, "what do you know now that you didn't know this morning?"

Tallow thought about that. She sounded used up. It wasn't the time to share his more recent conclusions. "I know our guy's a planner. I think he's going to kill again, and soon. And when he does, we'll know it's him."

"How?"

"I was thinking about this on the drive back from One PP. I have this feeling that our guy chooses his guns very carefully. At least, for some of his kills. The ECT pulled a flintlock out of here today."

"A what?" The voice of a woman starting to fight her way through smoke.

"A flintlock. Seriously. And the CSUs say that it was clearly restored to the point where it'd fire reliably, and after it was used, it was put up on the wall here to rot. I can buy a revolver off the Internet for thirty bucks if I'm just interested in killing someone. This is something else. I can't shake this feeling that, for at least some of his kills, he's selecting weapons for very specific reasons."

"Like what?"

"I'm not there yet. I'm setting up at One PP tomorrow. They're finding me some

110

space to work through material as they process it. Oh. Yeah. If their boss calls you tomorrow about that? If you could threaten to undo whatever extra favor you promised them, that'd be really useful."

"Jesus, Tallow. Anything else?"

"That's all I have for now, Lieutenant. Like I say, I'm meeting the CSUs in a little while, see what else I can glean from them. Also," he added, another thought drifting across his mind as if on the breeze, "I need to do some reading tonight."

The hunter froze in his tracks when he heard the voice. He held his position and listened for a second voice. None. The hunter clenched his jaws, tightened his stomach muscles, physically forcing himself into the present. He was not climbing a wooded slope. He was on stairs. The prey was speaking on a cell phone.

He would have to wait, or the person on the other end of the line would hear his prey's death. Sometimes that was a suitable outcome. The hunter did not wish it in this instance. It would reduce the amount of time available to him after the killing.

The hunter moved to the next staircase. He would be ready.

The lieutenant was awake now. "Reading? John, I told you, I need you to not disappear into your head."

"Look," said Tallow, "tomorrow I go over the unsolved homicides we already have matched to weapons. But tonight I want to be able to just think about this thing. I haven't been able to catch my breath until now. I'm going too fast. I'm not even supposed to be working this case."

There was a pause. Tallow grimaced. He had told himself he wasn't going to let that slip out. But now it was done, and he supposed the response might be interesting.

"John," she eventually said. "You know how shorthanded we are. And I made some calls. IAB and the DA's office are on board with the idea of you continuing work, and I have the promise of a good signature under a letter explaining that all relevant parties decided it was better to allow you to continue working this case."

"I don't know how legal that is, Lieutenant."

"If all the right police say it's legal, then it's legal, John. And all the related paperwork and data entry will shortly be lost, so nobody will have cause to question it. I know you've had the worst week it's possible to have, but I need you to be right where you are now. Okay?"

For twenty seconds, Tallow concentrated on keeping his breathing regular and easy. Even over a cell phone connection, a bright listener can hear the respiratory tell of someone getting angry.

"Okay, Lieutenant. I'll be by tomorrow, once I've got more from CSU."

The lieutenant gave a guarded "All right, John." And then: "Anything else you want to tell me?"

"No," Tallow said.

The hunter heard the electronic noise of the cell phone call ending. He continued to move. Carefully craning his neck around, he could just make out the prey's shoulder. He was standing with his back to the stairs. The hunter would be at a height disadvantage. Perhaps a strike through the base of the spine, paralyzing the prey. It would buy time for a more precise killing strike. He could pick a blow that would create the least blood spill.

The hunter withdrew his knife. Thumbed the top of the sheath. His left hand began to pull the sheath away. The hunter smiled at its soundlessness. The moment was beautiful.

Tallow's head jerked around at a terrible sound.

The hunter stopped as the noise of people and equipment crunching through the building's front doors thundered up the stairwell. Very swiftly, knowing which steps made more sound than others, he took great light strides down the staircase on his toes, turned the corner, and was halfway down the next before stopping to look.

Two men in overalls were banging through the doors with carts and plastic boxes.

"Would you for fuck's sake hold the fucking door open? It's like trying to kick a pig through the eye of a fucking needle here."

"Yeah, that's what your mom said."

"You want to give me shit when we're going to unpack a roomful of guns? That's what you want to do here? You want me to test-fire some of those bitches and see if they're still loaded?"

"You can't even open a fucking door and you think I'm worried about you operating a gun? I could just stand there and watch you shoot yourself in the fucking face."

"Hey. Hey, buddy. Little help here?"

The hunter had replaced his knife and now walked down the stairs as if he lived in this building. He strode across the foyer and held one of the doors open wide, allowing the Evidence Collection Team to get their equipment inside. The hunter still had good eyes, and he could read the print and insignias on their coveralls from above.

"Hey," one of them said to the hunter, "you know if the elevators are working yet? I mean, there's gotta *be* elevators here, right? It ain't fucking human otherwise."

"Sorry," said the hunter, "I was just visiting a friend, and I always use the stairs."

"Meh. Thanks anyway."

"You're welcome," said the hunter, and slid past him and onto the sidewalk.

Tallow jogged down a couple of flights of stairs to find two guys trying to drag two container-laden two-wheeled carts up the steps.

"ECT?"

"Yeah. We're on the 'fuck you, you don't get to eat dinner' shift. You Tallow?"

"Yeah."

"Then fuck you too, buddy."

"Thanks."

Outside, standing by the police truck he

115

hadn't seen approaching, the hunter drove his two fists into the top of his head, again and again. Everything was wrong. Everything around him was an eye-stinging kaleidoscope of Old and New Manhattans. Trees shuddered and budded streetlights. The mailbox on the other side of the street grew a partially muscled skeleton, the tin under it flexing like lungs to produce an awful whistling scream. The road rolled and cracked as precolonial island terrain tried to force itself up into the low dusk light. His breathing was deep and labored, like a wounded animal at bay. He struck his own head again, and again, squeezing his eyes shut so tightly that pain flared across his forehead and down both sides of his neck.

When the hunter opened his eyes, he was facing the car that the cop in the black suit had arrived in. Shaking, he staggered across the street to it, battling to keep it present in his vision. Not taking his eyes off it, he groped in his bag for a stub of pencil and a scrap of coffee-shop napkin. He commanded his hand to cease trembling, and, with exaggerated care bought with a rising headache and unsettling bleached flares in his eyesight, he wrote down the car's license plate number, make, and model.

FOURTEEN

The Fetch used to be the Blarney Stone. Or, at least, one of the Blarney Stones. At any given time there seemed to be at least four bars in the Five Boroughs called the Blarney Stone. This one, possibly the most greasily plastic Irish bar of them all, had been sold a couple of years ago. The new owners wanted to retain the PVC Irishness of the place — although, naturally, they had never gotten closer to setting foot on Irish soil than buying a bag of peat from a garden center in Brooklyn — but thought that the place might be one Blarney Stone too many.

So they called it the Fetch. Either because one of them had a genuine interest in folklore or because someone told them it was an Irish Thing, like shamrocks and beating your wife with a bit of tree. Tallow always suspected the latter, as the name was up on a flat sign over the front door and written in the windows in big goofy green letters, slick and cheap as processed ham.

Tallow knew that a fetch was the Irish version of a doppelgänger, a supernatural copy of a living person whose manifestation usually meant imminent death for the original. What a great name, he believed, for a place that people lurched out of at night while seeing double.

He was lucky enough to get a spot across the road. He reached into the alluvial deposits in the back of his car and pulled up a tablet device, an e-reader, and a compact wi-fi router and put them into an old laptop bag whose crushed handles he had seen lolling limply from under the passenger seat. He also slipped the paperwork the lieutenant had given him earlier into the bag. Getting out of the car, he felt a clattering landslip of aches and pains tumble from his shoulders down to his knees. That and finding the evening was warm decided him on the awkward process of popping the belt fastener on his hip holster and wrestling it and the gun into the bag unseen.

Crossing the street, Tallow couldn't help but peer into the narrow alley to the right of the Fetch. Local legend had it that, in wilder times, bar-fight victims would just be thrown down there like garbage sacks. It was said that the police wouldn't even run them in because it was crueler for them to awaken in a pile in the morning, all soaked with one another's beery urine.

There may have been new owners, but there wasn't new money in the Fetch. Everything in the place seemed to creak — the door, the flooring, the cracked and scabby fake leather on the booth seats — as if all were installed in the husk of something old and tired and hunched.

Tallow went to the bar and did what he always did. Looked at all the taps and then ordered a pint of cream ale. Looked at the food menu, front and back and specials, and then ordered a cheeseburger and onion rings in beer batter. Tallow asked the bartender if he knew if there was a spare table outside in the smoking area, which there was, and asked for his food to be taken to him. The bartender's bored assent was smothered by a yell from the guys in the back of the bar, where there was a big flatscreen TV that justified the old window lettering that called the place a sports bar. A cheer shot through with shouts of something like *"Oshidashi!"*

Tallow frowned, dimly recognizing the word. *"Oshidashi?"*

The bartender's face broke open into a big yellow grin. "Sumo. It's saving my life."

119

"How?"

"Got the big-ass TV. Got the satellite feed. But those guys, there just ain't enough football and baseball in the world to keep them docile. And soccer just don't do it. There ain't enough happens in soccer. It's like watching twenty-two hair models kick a ball around for what seems like six months and then one of them falls over and the ball goes in the goal. And then I found this channel does big-ass edited-highlights sumo specials. So I say to the guys: You got these two big-ass guys, none of this kiddie wrestling shit, they look like two linebackers been locked in a Burger King for five years, they run at each other like two eighteen-wheelers in loincloths, they beat the *shit* out of each other, and the winner gets a plate of fucking money right there in the ring. Two days later, the guys are crack whores for sumo. I got big Irish guys yelling at the TV in Japanese and they're not giving me shit anymore. Saving my life. Gimme like twenty minutes for your burger, okay?"

Tallow went through the bar and out into the smoking area, shaking his head. The smoking area was an old service yard that'd just been stuffed with tables and chairs, probably from a garden center in Brooklyn, and a couple of metal buckets for cigarette butts. He didn't intend to stay out here all night, but a smoke before and after some food sounded good. It sounded better, in fact, than the idea of eating, but he knew from experience that if he didn't force something in there now, he'd wake up feeling sick and empty.

It was warm. He took his jacket off, fished the cigarette pack and lighter out of it, chose a table at the far end of the yard, and folded the jacket over the chair before sitting down. His back was to the rear fence. He wanted to stay facing the entrance to the smoking area so he could keep an eye out for the CSUs.

The cream ale was the color of maple syrup topped with an inch's fall of apple blossom. It tasted much as he'd expected it to. He lit a cigarette, and although he paused at how it already tasted like cigarettes had when he was a heavy smoker, it still tasted much as he'd expected it to. He smiled slightly, briefly, and pushed curls of the smoke up toward the darkening sky. He began to relax, just a little bit.

Tallow looked for an ashtray, and found it: an old seven-inch record that had been melted to form a cup. The spindle hole looked like it'd been plugged with Silly Putty. Tallow frowned at it. Clamping the cigarette between his lips and squinting one eye against the smoke, he turned the ashtray around in his hands. He figured it'd only been suffering this abuse for a few weeks, but it was still no way to treat a record. He didn't find the telltale gouge of a record yanked out of an old jukebox that could justify turning a piece of music into a bad flowerpot. Someone had just decided that, hell, it's only a bit of vinyl.

He found a tissue in his left pants pocket, wadded it, moistened it with a little beer foam, and gently sponged away at the record label. Someone had stubbed out a cigarette hard in the middle of what some wiping revealed to be a butterfly motif. That and the exposed white *C* meant the label was Chrysalis. A fossil brand. Chrysalis Records had gone away long ago, a pretty little butterfly that got eaten by a business spider that got eaten by a corporate bird that got eaten by a big multinational cat. Tallow kept cleaning, determined to solve this one little mystery, exposing as much of the ravaged pale blue paper as he dared. He tossed his cigarette into the nearest metal pail. It was distracting him. He wanted to do this. It felt like archaeology to him. He immersed himself in it, making small passes with the tissue until he could see the type

122

above the spindle hole.

Tallow could feel himself actually grinning. The record was "Heart of Glass" by Blondie. He hadn't heard it in years. He remembered when he first heard it, as a kid, and had giggled because Debbie Harry said "pain in the ass."

He remembered that, and a lyric about being lost in illusion, and nowhere to hide.

Tallow was pretty sure he didn't have that album on CD and resolved to buy the MP3 when he got home, as tribute to the record's sacrifice. He replaced the ashtray on the table. He knew he'd *use* the damn thing as an ashtray, and it was too late to save the record now, but it didn't sit right with him. You just don't do that to a record. Then again, he thought, chances are that no one in the vicinity of the record that day owned a device to play it on. Tallow himself didn't know anyone apart from himself who possessed a turntable for home use.

That said, Tallow had to tell himself, he didn't actually know that many people.

His food arrived. He looked at the label he'd unearthed, smiled, and took a bite of his burger. It tasted a bit better than he'd expected.

After the first few bites, he reached down into the laptop bag propped next to his chair, flicked on the wi-fi pod — he knew the machine well enough to do it by touch — and pulled out the tablet device. He tapped the search string *tobacco prayer* into the web browser and, as he worked through his meal, got a shallow education in Native American tobacco use from a handful of horribly designed websites using color schemes that should have earned the sites' creators a night in the cells. Crazy street guy was right about the use of tobacco, it turned out. Two of the web pages he looked at featured large flashing links to quit-smoking sites and help lines, declaiming that the casual and heavy use of tobacco was un–Native American.

Tallow washed the last of the burger out of his teeth with a mouthful of ale and, on the ground that he wasn't Native American, casually lit his second cigarette. Somewhere in the middle of the meal, his body had decided that it was actually hungry, and now he was a sated and sedate mammal.

He let his head lean back, and he blew smoke at the sliver of moon in the evening sky and two pigeons swimming along the light breeze. He relaxed.

And then, as certain as if he were going to throw up: *Oh God, I'm going to cry.*

Tallow sat up straight, eyes wide, breathing gone jerky and ragged, chin creasing and mouth twisting, unable to feel his feet on the ground. He watched his right hand tremble around the cigarette, his head too distant from it to make his fingers obey him. He clenched his left hand into a fist, hard enough that after half a minute he could feel white blazing crescents in his palm from his fingernails. Tallow gathered it all and tried with every internal guard he could muster to push it all down into that awful gaping hollow sensation in his chest.

He was almost to the end of his cigarette before declaring victory. The more he pushed it down, the more he started to feel angry. Tallow had unclenched for maybe a minute. All he'd been trying to do was relax before reviewing the day so far. He was angry at everything and nothing, because he couldn't find anyone to conveniently blame for the fact that he apparently didn't get to relax for one minute before losing it. If he tried to live like a normal human for a minute, he'd end up bawling like . . .

. . . like a trauma victim.

"No," said Tallow, and stubbed his cigarette out in the ashtray, directly onto the gray putty covering the spindle hole.

"No what?" said Bat.

"Nothing. Thinking out loud. Thanks for

coming."

Bat and Scarly stood in front of his table. He hadn't seen them coming, which made him angrier at himself for no rational reason. Scarly held a pint of stout, and Bat a long glass of ice water. A slice of something that was either a bad lime or a really bad lemon was stuck to the inside of the glass. Tallow waved at them to sit down.

"Is this your regular bar?" Scarly asked.

"I guess," Tallow said. "Two or three times a week for the past few years. Why?"

"The bartender didn't know you. I had to describe you to him, and he guessed that you were, well, you. The guy out back."

"And?"

"I don't know. Just seems weird that for a place you've been using two or three times a week for the past few years, the bartender didn't know your name or say, you know, Oh yeah, that guy."

"I keep to myself. Will you let me pay for those drinks?"

"You can pay for the next round. One pint is going to be less than a fucking Band-Aid on the gaping wound of the day I've had, Detective."

"Okay. How about some food? Can I buy you some food? Bat?"

Bat winced. "My stomach is like this sort

of bag of horror that I put food into and that then empties the food out largely unchanged three hours later. Me and food don't get along. I don't, as a rule, eat food."

Scarly took a swig of beer and muttered something about eating only once a day, something about a warrior's diet.

CSU crazy talk. Tallow pulled another cigarette from his pack with a sigh, and offered the pack to them. Bat considered it with shining eyes, but when Scarly waved it off, he did too. "Okay. Did we get the use of that floor space?"

"Hell yeah," said Bat, and with that aspirate Tallow could tell that it wasn't water but vodka in the long glass. "I don't know what your boss said to our boss, but once again, it worked like magic. I really kind of want to meet your boss. I think she might be a wizard."

Tallow's hands were still shaking. He tightened his finger muscles until they stopped. It hurt. Tallow was okay with that, so long as his hands did as they were told.

"Lots of those around," Tallow said.

"So," Scarly said, "we're doing what you asked for, right now. Got some people making copies and moving whiteboards and shit. I don't know what it's going to achieve, but we're doing it. What we need from you,

Detective, is for you to work the cases we give you evidence on."

Tallow raised an eyebrow.

"You asked us what you could do to make our lives better. It's this. Work these as individual cases. If we deal with a couple of these right off the bat, the pressure's going to come off us for a while."

Tallow shook his head. "How can I close them? It's all one guy. We close all of them or we close none of them."

Scarly drank off some more stout. "You said *close.* I said *deal with.* If we've got to work with you on this, then I don't want you getting lost in the woods. When we give you ballistics and shit, I can't have you staring at the big picture and not seeing the individual cases."

"What she means," said Bat, "is that if we get a couple of these to the point where all we're missing is the identity of the killer? That's enough to show we're making progress."

"Oh God. You're both insane."

"What?"

Tallow took a sharp breath to forestall an explosion. "Everything but the killer? Make the case with everything but the case? You're —"

Tallow stopped.

128

Scarly waited, and then said, "You told us you like history."

"We're just proposing a methodology here," said Bat. "We don't want you sitting in a simulated crazy-killer room trying to do cop voodoo, is what we're saying. Work up a few of the unsolved to the point where the killer is the only thing missing from the picture. We do that often enough —"

"— and we start to see the killer by inference," said Tallow. "By the shape of the hole he leaves. Okay. Weird way to put it, but I can get behind that." He flicked ash into the ashtray and smiled at it. "I keep thinking about that flintlock you showed me. Why would the word *Rooster* be scratched into it? Was that a name? I mean, I saw *True Grit* and all, but I didn't think there were really people called Rooster back then."

When Bat frowned, his eyes seemed to slide forward out of their sockets by a quarter-inch. *"Rooster?"*

"Sure. There was a badge or, I don't know, a heraldic device maybe, and the word *Rooster* above it. I like history, but my interests kind of jump around, and that sort of thing's nothing I've ever done a lot of reading about."

"It didn't say *Rooster*," said Bat. "It said *Rochester*. It was kind of blurred and fucked up, but, yeah. *Rochester.*"

"Huh," said Tallow, and sat back, considering.

"Why were you thinking about that?" Scarly asked. In the periphery of his pensive gaze, he could see she'd almost drained her pint.

"Something you said about the .44. It was like the one Son of Sam used. And the level of restoration you figure the guy lavished on that flintlock to get it to fire reliably. What if the revolver meant to our guy . . . what if it meant exactly what we think it meant? And if it did . . . then what did the flintlock mean? Rochester. Rochester."

"Well," said Bat, "like I said before, it won't be hard to fish out of the records. There won't be too many bodies in the last twenty years with a homemade .45 slug in them. The search will probably pop something in the morning."

"What kind of history do you like?" asked Scarly, finishing her pint just as a long girl in her twenties approached the table with a tray. The girl, all runner's legs in purple tights and long fronds of candy-apple-red hair in some nineties anime cut, collected his food plate and Scarly's glass. "Can I get you anything else?" she asked.

"Another pint of the cream ale, and

130

whatever they want, would be great, thank you."

"Also your cell number," said Scarly.

The long girl inclined just a little and tapped Scarly's wedding ring with one red fingernail.

"Another pint of the stout would be great, thanks," Scarly said.

"You are fucking disgusting," said Bat as the girl left. "Don't you think for a moment about your wife's feelings?"

"I'm fucking *autistic*," said Scarly.

They sat in awkward silence until the waitress came back with a tray of drinks. And her number written in pencil eyeliner on a napkin.

"Fuck you," Scarly crowed.

Bat poured a little of his drink over the napkin. The numbers smeared like dark tributaries in scabland.

"Fuck you!" Scarly yelled.

"Keep it down," said Tallow. "I may want to come back here again."

Scarly made a deflating sound, scrunched up the napkin, and tossed it accurately into the nearby metal bucket. "Doesn't matter where I get my appetite from so long as I eat at home. You didn't answer my question."

"Hm?"

"What kind of history do you like?"

"Oh, lots of different stuff. I like New York history. City history. Yesterday, when all this started, I told my partner we shouldn't respond to the call because he had bad knees and it was the last of the old walk-up apartment buildings on Pearl."

Tallow sipped his beer, knowing that he probably shouldn't have ordered it since he intended to drive home. "And I know that Pearl Street was called Pearl Street because the first paving used on the road was crushed oyster shells. Mother-of-pearl. The Dutch called it that, I think. Hold on a second."

Tallow leaned to the side and saw that his wi-fi pod was still working. The tablet was still on the table. He poked it out of sleep mode and pulled up another search engine page. "That flintlock. From 1836, you said."

Bat nodded assent.

Tallow pecked in the words *Rochester NY Murder 1836.* It threw up nothing of interest aside from someone's thesis on "crime and deviance in early Rochester."

"It was made in 1836," said Bat, leaning over and reading upside down. "Doesn't mean it was used in 1836."

Tallow replaced *1836* with *1837* and ran the search again, wondering. "It's just tickling something at the back of my head," he explained. "Something I read, some-where . . ."

Bat laughed. "Would that be your car parked across the street? With the library landfill in the back?"

"Yeah," said Tallow, and stopped. Five results down: *The first murder victim in the city of Rochester, NY.*

He read it aloud to Bat and Scarly.

"Seriously?" said Bat.

Tallow skimmed the text. " 'In the case of William Lyman, murdered October twenti-eth, 1837, by one Octavius Barron . . . with a pistol he stole from the premises of a Mr. Passage, a local baker.' "

Scarly grunted. Her beer seemed to be evaporating alarmingly quickly. "Makes sense. A baker would be fairly well-to-do. You know what that mark on the gun could be? A militia badge. I can see him spending the extra couple of dollars to get it en-graved."

Tallow kept reading. " 'Barron first claimed to have been asleep at home when the murder was committed, but his own mother told the authorities that he was lying.' Nice. Ah. Listen to this. 'In his confession, Barron explained that he'd had to beat a homemade bullet into shape and

133

hammer it into the muzzle of the gun.' "

"The fucked-up muzzle," said Bat, and then thought better of showing interest and threw his hands up. "No. Not buying into this."

"Go on," said Scarly, intent.

"Hm. Told a priest he didn't do it, his accomplices had, and that's why he wasn't found with the pistol or the dead man's pocketbook. The pistol was in fact never found. And this report does expressly call it a pistol. The assumption seems to be that Barron tossed it in the river."

"I bet you it was found and quietly passed back to Mr. Passage, who probably put it in a trunk for the day the British came back. He was in the militia, and he was a baker, so he knew everyone." Scarly grinned. "This is good. But would it be the river? It'd be the bay, right? I bet there'd be a Rochester naval militia."

"Unless they meant the Erie Canal to the Hudson. That might have been open by then."

Bat, exasperated, waved his hands between them. "Hello? Are you really saying that this gun we found was the mysteeeeeerious lost gun that killed the first murder victim in Rochester? Guys, the guns we've processed so far have been married to kills in Manhattan. If you're looking for connections, then you're saying that he took his show on the road and we're going to turn up guns applying to homicides all over the place."

"Not necessarily," mumbled Tallow, going through the text on his tablet screen for more information. "Maybe it means he committed a homicide in Manhattan that had connections to Rochester." He looked up at Scarly. "You know what that might mean about your .44."

"What?" said Scarly, before her brain caught up to what he meant. She laughed. "Nah. Can't be."

"Can't be what?" said Bat, irritated that he wasn't keeping up with the increasing altitude of what he had determined was an idiot flight of fantasy.

"Can't be Son of Sam's actual gun," Scarly said, sipping stout.

Bat sat back. "Christ. Of course it can't. Because —"

"Because," said Tallow quietly, "Son of Sam's gun would be in an evidence storage barrel in the Bronx, right?"

"Oh," Scarly breathed, eyes widening. "Oh. That's . . . that's interesting."

Tallow turned his gaze on Bat. "Our guy's been killing people and going undetected for twenty years, even when he did something as crazy as go to Rochester and recover a lost gun and restore it to the point where he could efficiently kill someone with it. Do you really think he did that without any help at all?"

"Dude. You're saying some cop fished Son of Sam's own gun out of an evidence barrel and gave it to a crazy asshole who used it for one of his umpty-hundred kills. That's crazier than he is."

Scarly huddled into the table, her face more animated than Tallow had ever seen it. "No. No, I'm liking this. So you think this is a crew?"

"No. It's too single-minded to be anything more than one guy making the plans and committing the homicides. I'm thinking he had some kind of network. Maybe not a big one. But people who owed him favors, people he paid, people he could somehow trust just enough to get him the things he needed. Maybe, yeah, maybe someone did get him a gun he liked out of an evidence barrel. You didn't stop to think for a minute how someone could commit several hundred homicides in Manhattan over God knows how many years and not get one of them hung around his neck? Not *one*?"

Tallow had come to that junction on his train of thought only about thirty seconds ago, but he didn't feel the burning need to tell Bat that. It didn't matter. Tallow felt like he was thinking well again. He felt like his brain had kicked in since that afternoon's visit to Pearl. It occurred to him that this might be his most energetic thinking in years.

"So some kind of network. Some people who could find him the right tools for the job. Like a flintlock from Rochester. If the search on that kill is going to be so easy, Bat, then I'll bet you ten dollars right here that the kill on that gun is going to have some special relationship with the first recorded murder in Rochester."

"I'll take that," said Bat with a curl of the lip. It revealed very narrow, keen teeth and gray gums. "What about the Bulldog .44?"

Tallow looked at Scarly. She gave him a twisty grin of complicity.

Scarly said, "I've got ten that says that if you didn't manage to massively fuck up the ballistics through your ricockulous magic trick of making it shoot backward, then it's Son of Sam's gun, and we have a much bigger and scarier case than even we thought."

Bat laughed, a short yap that said more about discomfort than joy. "So I'm twenty bucks richer and I didn't even have to buy the drinks first. Win. You're both nuts, by the way."

"All right," said Tallow as Bat chugged a quarter of his vodka. "You tell me why our guy had a flintlock in his cache."

"How the hell should I know? I'm not some lunatic who built a church out of guns."

Tallow smiled. "And that's why I wanted the storage space. I take your points about not getting lost in the forest and ignoring the trees. But cop voodoo can be strong too. We need to be in that apartment, as best we can, and understand why he kept those guns and what he was thinking. That apartment was part of his plan too. Scarly referred to him as a serial killer. If that's true, then he must almost permanently be in totem phase. Totally high on the adrenaline of being surrounded by his trophies."

"Aha!" yelped Bat. "No! Because if you think he's matching weapons to targets that carefully, then he's not experiencing trolling phase, is he? He's not walking around looking for juicy kills. He's aiming specifically at specific people. So no!" He pulled a face at Scarly. "Wrong!"

"Oh," commented Tallow. "You're on board with our idea now, then."

"Yes. No. Yes. What? Fuck you."

Scarly cracked up.

"Fuck you, *John*," Tallow gently said.

Bat put his hands up, laughing. "All right, all right, John. So he's not a serial killer, and he's not in totem phase, and we need to work out exactly what his deal is regardless of whether I win twenty bucks or not. You win. Can I have another drink?"

"Sure." John stood up and pulled twenty dollars from his wallet. Scarly yanked the two tens out of his grip hard enough to leave the ghost of a friction burn on his fingertips.

"I'll go," she said, getting up. "What do you want?"

"Better get me two of those energy drinks they keep in the fridge with the bottled beers."

"Done." She took off at a clip.

"She's really married?" Tallow said to Bat.

"Yeah. Talia's like this Scandinavian Amazon who can break rocks with her boobs. She could fit Scarly in her armpit. Sometimes I think she likes Scarly just because she was the most portable lesbian available."

"So her wife could kill her. So she plays away from home. Well, that makes sense."

Bat smiled. "Scarly just wants the phone number. She'll leave it in a prominent place at home. Talia will see it. Talia will go in*sane*. I mean, anger, screaming, tears, smashing stuff up, the works. And then she will fuck the shit out of Scarly for twelve to twenty-four hours. She'll fuck Scarly until she can't walk, ice water in the face if she passes out, punching, kicking, choking, you name it. Like a wolf pissing on its territory, right? Only with more strap-ons. Scarly will come into work afterward — and it's funny how it always seems to happen when she's got a day off booked — she'll come in looking like she's been dipped in crystal meth and tossed to a Canadian hockey team. Which was what she wanted. Which was what the whole thing was about. It's the one thing about Talia she can control, and she loves it."

Tallow thought about this for a few seconds, and then raised the last of his beer. "To the secrets behind a happy marriage in New York City."

Bat cackled and tapped Tallow's glass with his.

FIFTEEN

The hunter moved down the block and curled up in the doorway of a small, abandoned retail unit that had previously been a Christian bookstore. Its weathered signage and faded, skewed window posters pleased him. He felt like he was sheltering in the lee of the corpse of some strange dead animal that had made its way to the island from foreign climes and died before reproducing or polluting the ground.

Content, he drew his knees up to his chest and let the modern world collapse back into Mannahatta. The buildings on the other side of the street tumbled away as if gently shoved by heaven's giant hand, re-forming into the foothills and slopes of shore-side Old Manhattan. Stands of broad pignut hickory arose from the inclines, their catkins unfurling. If he looked closer, with concentration, he could see the long tears in the hickory trees' bark where black bears had eaten, and detect the scent of rich dark sap where it bled from the exposed wood. Allegheny hawkweed sprang from around their trunks like scattered flakes of amber. The hunter closed his eyes, listening to the calls of ring-billed gulls. He was close to the water here. A short walk would have brought him to the permanent, ever-growing piles of shucked oyster shells on the narrow beach where the catch was always best.

There was the rasp of starved panic grass in the breeze that he always somehow found so soothing. He could close his eyes for an hour. There was time to kill.

When the hunter awoke, the cement under him was chill and damp, and ghosts from the hated future leered at him through cloudy store-window glass. He stood, flexed to pop the stiffness from his spine, and looked up at the sky. He could judge his position and the hour even from the miserly, bare starscape afforded him in modern Manhattan. There was plenty of time for him to make the journey to his night's last destination.

He started walking, slipping a hand into his bag for his travel notebook. The walk would take him some two and a half hours. He could have done it in less than two hours quite easily, save for the slow emergence of security cameras in the city. The hunter preferred not to be seen. His travel notebook was filled with maps he'd drawn himself indicating the locations of CCTV machines and their estimated fields of vision. The operation of the notebook would have been arcane to anyone else, of course. And that, too, was intended. The hunter's intent was always to leave no trace on the island. Save for the bodies of his prey. In the unlikely, unlucky event that he was killed in the process of the hunt, there was nothing on his body that would mean anything to anyone. And his only regret in death would be that he would not be correctly buried. There would be no food left by his body to fortify his spirit in its walk across the Milky Way to heaven. There would be no one to cry his name, and indeed no one to close his or her lips in mourning and never speak it again. That, he reflected, wasn't so bad. No one knew his name to speak it while he was alive now. His name could not die with him because it was already dead, and, in a way, so was he.

It was said that the spirit stayed close to the corpse for eleven days after death. Perhaps he might find a way to kill people even while disembodied. It was a thought that brought a thin smile to his lips as he walked.

He grubbed around in his bag as he progressed past Grand on his way down the Bowery, walking in the glow from the electric showrooms of the many lighting stores fringing the street. He had a few pieces of dried squirrel meat in there, wrapped in plastic and cloth. The hunter, working by touch alone, claimed a small piece and reclosed the wrapping. He bit a morsel off and chewed, slowly and methodically, matching action to footfall. The flavor was somewhere between chicken thigh and rabbit. There was better squirrel to be had farther up the island; the animals in Central Park inevitably took in enough pollution to render their meat blander, and sometimes more bitter, than it really should have been. But it kept him moving, and it kept the saliva flowing, so that he avoided thirst and didn't deplete his physical reserves.

A little under two hours later, the hunter entered Central Park by Fifth Avenue and East Sixty-First.

He continued moving north. Up by the Seventy-Third Street parallel, paths became dark tangles wending around nighted looming woodland. This was the Ramble. The hunter took one last reckoning by the sparse stars above, gripped the knife in his bag once again, and glided into a stand of American sycamores.

Here and there, he caught glances from men standing alone or in pairs who kept to the edges of the paths, occasionally drifting mothlike to the trail lampposts. The hunter had no issue with the men, whom, more than twenty years ago, he had learned should be called two-spirits. There had been a two-spirit of the Crow Nation whom the hunter admired, a man whose true name translated as "Finds Them and Kills Them."

When they met the hunter's eyes, they turned away. He was not here for them. When they met his eyes, they were glad he was not.

Orbiting a great mountain of a Kentucky coffee tree, the hunter saw the one he had come to the Ramble for. The timing was quite exact. Not a tall man, but stocky, giving a sense of size and solidity even without great height. A man who looked like he worked with his hands, and with weights. Military boots that struck the hunter, mired as he now was in the modern day, as somewhat science-fictional. A black running suit, the hunter supposed, though the fabric and cut more suggested stealth fatigues. The jacket unzipped to show a blazingly clean white T-shirt. Thick dark hair that could have been a grown-out Marine cut. Walking with a soldier's bearing. Walking a dog. An absurd, white fluffy dog that stood less than two feet high. It put the hunter in mind of a wolf that had been crossbred in a laboratory with a cuddly toy.

The man walking the dog had a gun in a shoulder holster under his left armpit. Something snub-nosed and easy to draw fast, judging by the fold of his jacket around it. The weight the man was offsetting suggested a heavier gun than necessary. A .327 Federal or similar, a snub-nosed with the punch of a .357 Magnum, bruising recoil, and a thunderclap muzzle blast. The gun of a man who wanted to exert serious muscle power to keep the gun aimed through the recoil, who considered himself tough enough to shoot without ear defenders or shades. The gun of a man pretending that his personal protection was discreet and concealed and "just in case."

The hunter swung back around, passing through a thatch of some pea-like shrub that didn't belong on the island, and darted through a planting of fragrant yellowwood to reach another gray curl of trail paving. He knew precisely where he was going. Central Park had been his foraging ground for a very long time.

He stepped from the pitch-black into enough ambient light that his face could be identified right in front of the man with the dog.

The man stopped walking. He clearly recognized the hunter instantly, looking straight through the years since their last meeting. The dog's lead was in his right hand. He flipped the lead to his left hand, deftly. The hunter raised his own right hand, showing it as open and empty.

The hunter looked at the dog. The dog met his eyes and wagged his tail. The hunter put out his raised hand, palm down, and slowly lowered it. The dog sat. The hunter lowered his hand a little more. The dog lay all the way down, head on his paws, entirely at peace.

The hunter placed his attention on the man. "You are Jason Westover. Do you know who I am?"

Jason Westover nodded, once, slowly. He turned his left palm to face the hunter and released the dog's lead.

The hunter took one pace forward, limiting Westover's available movement space even further. "You are very probably armed. I am most definitely armed. Do not assume that you can move faster than I can. Do not assume that anyone will hear you if you shout. Nor that they'll care if you do. The Ramble has its own reputation."

"You planned this," said Westover flatly. Not a question. The hunter appreciated the implication of respect.

"I have always made a point of being aware of where and when to find you should it be necessary. You have a schedule for walking your dog —"

"My wife's dog."

"— your dog that has proved quite inflexible over the last two years. You are often visibly unhappy when doing so. You choose the Ramble, and at this time of night, because you believe the confluence to be inherently dangerous. This is why you are armed. Perhaps you think it helps keep you sharp after a day at your desk. Perhaps you're looking for trouble."

"If you're here to kill me," said Westover, "then, please, let's get on with it. If you're here to talk to me, then say something interesting. If you want my help with some situation, then stop fucking around and ask for it."

The hunter smiled. Westover visibly, involuntarily shivered but kept his spine straight and his arms in preparatory position by his sides.

148

"You always did treat me with less overt deference than the others."

Westover didn't move.

"No response?" said the hunter, raising an amused eyebrow.

"Nothing you'd be interested in hearing. How bad is it, that you've had to contact me directly in the middle of the night?"

The hunter took a breath. "All the things I have done for you. All the work undertaken. Each of those acts has a thing associated with it. Each of those things was stored in a single special place. It was well secured, but, as I'm sure you know yourself, no security is perfect. The place was breached. The things within it are now in the possession of the police."

Westover frowned, shook his head. "I swear, over the years you've only gotten more fucking schizophrenic. I have no idea what you're even talking about."

"Think about it," the hunter whispered.

Westover did. The hunter could almost see Westover's heart rise into his mouth. "Oh God. You're crazier than I thought."

"Is a man crazy for going to church? For tending the earth that gives him food?"

"All right. All right. I can't do anything about that. I appreciate the warning. Tell me what you need to secure your silence.

149

What can I get you? Plane ticket? Passport?"

The hunter's hand was still in his bag. He judged Westover's position. Westover, distracted as he was, remained ready for violence. "I am taking something from my bag. It is not a weapon."

The hunter extracted the scrap of napkin he'd written on earlier, reached over, and passed it to Westover's fingers.

"I want," said the hunter, "to know who that car belongs to, and where the owner lives. That, I'm quite certain, is in your power. I have noticed, not always with pleasure, how broad the reach of your security company has gotten over the years."

Westover looked at it. "Who is this?"

"A police detective, I believe. I want this information ready for me by this time tomorrow, at this place. I would have called you, but your telephone is no longer in service."

"I change numbers regularly these days," muttered Westover, still looking at the napkin. "A cop. Why are you talking to me about this? I'm not the one who —"

"I believe it would be more efficient for you to do this," said the hunter. "I want to keep that man in reserve, for now. Also, I believe he would refuse me, and that would start us down a short and nasty road. Don't

150

you think?"

Westover nodded. "Okay. I can do that. Not as tricky as it used to be, in fact. What will you do with the information?"

"My ultimate goal would be recovery of as many of my tools as possible," the hunter said. "I don't wish to start all over again. But I will if I have to. Removal of this man may help disrupt the police process. Or it may just be a new beginning for me. So . . . I haven't decided yet. Nor have I decided how it would be done. The information you find will help me with that too."

"How?"

"I told you, Mr. Westover, back when we started down this path together. Never ask me about my methods. You don't need to know. And I don't want you to know. It is not for you."

Westover pocketed the napkin. "All right," he said once more. "Tomorrow night. You'll have a name, an address, and whatever other details on the man I can have pulled. What happens then?"

The hunter took stock of Westover again for a few seconds. "Why don't you have a dog walker?"

"What?"

"You're a wealthy man, Mr. Westover. I know that very well. I did, after all, help

151

that happen. And I've kept my eye on all of you, over the years. Also, I spend a lot of time here in Central Park, and I know full well that wealthy people in this city pay people to walk their dogs. So why don't you have a dog walker? Is it just the illicit little thrill of the notion that one day someone will try to mug you and you'll gun them down? Or is it something else?"

Westover shifted on his feet. "I want to know what happens then. I want to know what I personally have to protect against, and what I have to prepare for."

"Answer me first."

"It gets me away from my wife for a while. Simple as that. As to the other thing: I run a security company. I wouldn't do that job well if I were not aware of my personal security."

"Why would you want to get away from your wife? She hasn't looked well over the past year or so. I would have thought you would want to take care of her at night. Unless you pay someone to do that."

Interesting, thought the hunter. Westover's right hand wanted to go, in that instant, not to the gun but to the small of his back, above the top of his pants. The hunter was fairly sure he hadn't missed the tells of a second gun. A knife, then. Probably something almost weightless, like titanium or surgical steel. Probably something short. Probably a folding blade. The look on Westover's face. He instinctively went for something that had to be used close in, with savagery. With punching, ripping, stabbing motions. With hate.

Westover's lip curled. "My wife. She is. Was. A smart woman. She developed questions, over the years, about the success of my business. There was a bad night. Over a year ago. We were fighting. I wanted to —"

Westover looked over into the trees and the night, biting his lip. His eyes were oddly bright in the ambient glow from the trail lights.

"I wanted to hurt her. To scare her. To make her shut up. She's smart, but she, I don't know. She's not worldly. The fight got ugly. And. Well. Like I said. So I told her."

"You told her." The hunter kept his voice flat and uninflected. It was not how he felt.

"I told her everything. To frighten her into shutting up. Into not fucking picking at it all the time." Momentarily unconcerned about keeping his hands in view and moving slowly, Westover almost convulsively passed his right hand across his eyes. His head bobbed, and the hunter could see tendons working in his neck. The hunter waited.

"Well. It worked," Westover said with a forced, sick laugh. "I scared the shit out of her. She, um. She had a bit of a breakdown. So, no, you *cunt,* she hasn't looked well for the past year or so. I don't know if she's ever going to be well again. And I walk her stupid fucking dog at night because I can't stand her eyes on me all night every fucking night. All right? So now I want to know what happens after I get you this information. Are you going to keep coming back here to find me? Do I have to give your description to the guards at my apartment building?"

"That," murmured the hunter, "wouldn't be the most clever thing you could do tonight."

"Answer my fucking question."

The hunter pinned down his sudden need to instill in Westover a new and bloody wisdom about using that tone with him. He pinned it down and placed it in a far copse in the back of his mind, for now, secreted against future opportunities, like a nut stored for the winter. The hunter took a step back and said: "I'll answer your question. I will continue to protect you, and take your tribute for the hunt, as I have always done.

I intend to recover my tools, if at all possible, and to make any investigation into them too difficult for the police to pursue. It is my hope that very soon my work and our relationship will return to normal. The one thing I can comfortably predict is that you and the others will never be satisfied with your places in life, no matter how elevated your perches may be. However, we must take into account the possibility that I may become seen and known."

Westover cocked his head and narrowed his eyes, trying to keep the hunter's own eyes in his line of sight. The hunter turned to the side by ten degrees, away from what little light there was, the darkness gathering on him.

"Should that happen," said the hunter, "should everything I've achieved since we first spoke be lost forever and should I lose the freedom of my island? Then you will have to die. And now, so will your wife. Do you understand that?"

"Nobody has to die," said Westover.

"Somebody always has to die," said the hunter, and took a second step back that had him swallowed by the trees and gone.

Sixteen

Tallow, Scarly, and Bat tumbled out of the Fetch sometime after eleven. Tallow wasn't drunk, and he was quite deliberately not completely relaxed, but he felt better about the world than he had when he'd entered the place. Bat and Scarly were, however, in states of reasonably confused refreshment.

Scarly put her hands in her pockets and smiled up at Tallow. "We are going home now. I am going home to my wife, and Bat is going home to his whatever Bat does when no one is looking."

"Save the phone number for the night before your next day off, will you?" Bat giggled.

"You incredible fuckbag. That's it. You're paying for the cab, and the cab will drop me at home first."

"Whatever," Bat said, still giggling as he started off down the street. "Let's find a fucking cab, then. G'night, John."

"Night." Tallow smiled and watched them stagger away. Ahead of them, he could see a man in pink denim pants and a knitted cape and hat half limping, half skipping toward the pair, singing something Tallow couldn't make out. Another street guy. Mismatched sneakers. Obviously mentally ill and, from the way his limbs jerked, probably also physically ill. Scarly must've given him her scary glare, because Tallow watched the poor man dance around her and Bat like they were on fire.

Tallow laughed, quietly, and stood there for a moment more, in front of the alley, and looked up at the sky. A few stars had poked their way out through the scattered cloud and light pollution. He wondered, briefly, about those places he'd heard about, where you could see all the stars at night. People had told him about being able to see the Milky Way. He could never imagine how that was even possible.

These were stars enough for him.

He felt a hand yank at the laptop bag in his fist.

The man in the pink pants and knitted cape was next to him, trying to drag the bag away from Tallow with one hand. His mouth was fixed in a snarl, and Tallow smelled ethanol and eucalyptus panted out through the gaps in his teeth. He was shockingly strong. He pulled again, and Tallow felt his fingers give around the handle of the bag.

Which still had his firearm in it.

Tallow then saw, in the man's other hand, a short green plastic children's ruler, a wedge snapped off the end to make it into a point, looking like it'd been roughly ground against curb or sidewalk to sharpen it. For a millisecond Tallow noticed and registered a cartoon Indian chief's face printed on the plastic, just above the man's grip, smiling and giving the peace sign.

At which point, Tallow stopped thinking. He got his other hand around the back of the man's neck, used the man's momentum from his yank at the bag to spin him around and drive him face-first into the alleyway wall. Tallow heard the shattering of the man's teeth and the crunch of his nose crushing inward. The man made a noise like a snorkel trying to suck air through tar and collapsed.

Tallow heard Bat saying "John?" closer than he'd expected. He turned to see that Bat and Scarly had run back to him.

"My gun's in the bag," Tallow said, breathing fast. "I took it off when I went into the bar."

"Shit," said Scarly, looking at the pile of

man in the alleyway mouth. Tallow wondered why she sounded impressed.

Tallow's brain kicked back into gear. "You see any CCTV around here? I don't want to have been seen."

Bat found the green shank. He didn't touch it, just poked at it with his shoe. "Jesus, look at this. Why does it matter if someone saw you? The asshole could have killed you."

"Because my firearm wasn't secured, because the asshole has no face now, and because I've been put on the Pearl Street case to fail. I'm being set up so they can take me off the force for PTSD." He was suddenly cold, and his heart rate was up like a runner's, and he was saying too much. It wasn't good enough. Tallow held a breath and closed everything down, looking at his unconscious assailant. *That was a Jim Rosato move right here,* he thought.

Scarly was already looking up and down the street. "No CCTV coverage. But the longer we stay here chatting like morons, the better the chance of someone else coming out of the bar or just wandering by."

"Give me your lighter," said Bat. There was a sharp snap of professional appraisal in his voice that made Tallow hand it over without question.

"It's just a disposable," Tallow commented.

"Good," said Bat, prying the top off with surprisingly strong fingers. "You only touched him at the back of the neck, right?"

Tallow nodded. Bat emptied the lighter fluid over the back of the man's neck. He then kicked the shank back into the man's potential reach.

"You're going to set fire to his neck?" Tallow asked, not completely certain that he wanted to ask that of a CSU or get an answer.

Bat tossed both parts of the lighter as far down the alley as he could. "No. The butane will fuck up any epithelial cells you might have transferred to the back of his neck. Just in case anyone gives enough of a shit to check him over."

"Go home, John," said Scarly. "Now."

And Tallow would have, were he less fascinated by the abrupt transformation of his companions.

"What do you think?" asked Bat, stepping back to survey the picture.

Scarly leaned to one side, squinted. "Kick his head around so it's facing away from the street. It'll look more like he's sleeping rough."

Bat used his toe to shift the man's head.

The man gurgled. "Fuck it," said Bat, and kicked him in the temple. The man's head turned; now he was facing the alley.

"Good enough. Go home, John. And if you take your gun off again for any reason I will shoot you myself and then we'll make it look like you committed suicide. Am I making myself completely clear here?"

"Yeah," said Tallow.

She gave him a shove in the shoulder to start him across the street. "We'll see you in the morning. C'mon, Bat, let's find that cab."

Tallow stopped, turned to them, and, with nothing more useful to contribute, simply said, "Thank you."

Bat gave his weird grin. "Hey. We're partners now."

Tallow went back to his car and started for home, having decided once and for all that CSUs really were completely insane.

SEVENTEEN

Tallow parked, pulled a few books out of the back of his unit, and went inside.

His apartment, on his return, smelled oddly musty. As if there had been no living man occupying it for years. He spent minutes walking around his place, looking at the megaliths and barrows of CDs and books like a confused archaeologist happening upon some ancient settlement unseen by human eyes since before God was a boy. He wasn't sure if he didn't spend enough time here or if he just didn't spend enough time fully present here.

He started his laptop, launched his usual music service, and bought a 320k MP3 of "Heart of Glass." He set it to repeat and let it loop through the room as he found a big atlas that would serve as a desk, rested it atop a thick stack of books, and unpacked the contents of his jacket onto it. The books from the car and the tablet from the bag went next to his notebook and cigarettes. He pulled his chair over and sat in front of it all. And then got up, scowling, to look for a drink and an ashtray. He found a can of iced coffee moldering in the back of his small fridge, and an empty foil food container, still crusted with discolored rice, in the trash. Tallow sat down again, ready to think, and then realized he'd given his lighter to Bat.

He sat back, absently patting the insides of his thighs, debating the problem. He had decided, he told himself, that he didn't want a cigarette. It would stink up his apartment. He would exert control and ignore that his feet were now tapping, heel to ball and back again.

He then went to the kitchen, precariously got his cigarette lit off the stove, forced the small kitchen window open, and leaned out of it like an indecisive suicide contemplating the drop, puffing away disgustedly. He was going to toss the pack in the morning. After all, he reasoned, he didn't even have a lighter anymore, so there was no use in keeping the cigarettes. He would toss them now, but they'd go stale in the pack as they lay in the trash and, again, stink the place up. Tallow was pleased with his reasoning, and smoked.

Sitting back down, he tore open the iced coffee, took a swallow, and decided that if Mother Teresa had ever served iced coffee in the depths of Calcutta, it probably wouldn't have tasted quite as bad as this. He took a second swallow anyway and turned to the reviewing of his notebook. He woke his tablet and copied some drawings of tobacco prayer ties into the notebook, scratching a reminder to himself to ask Scarly and Bat about the composition of the paints found on some of the guns.

He also copied down what he hoped were the salient details on that historical Rochester slaying. Hands flicking across the tablet, he pulled up a couple of generic summaries of the Son of Sam killings and did the same for those. Right now, both events were part of the same flight of fancy. Tallow knew he was nowhere with the case, but even the consideration of these other cases made him feel like he was still thinking, and if his mind was in motion, then he would be in a condition to trap the real details when they presented themselves.

Tallow went back to the laptop bag. The paperwork the lieutenant had given him this morning was still in there. He hadn't properly reviewed it yet.

The first processed weapon. A Bryco

Model 38, .32-caliber. Basically a Saturday night special, small, cheap, and distributed in bulk. Nothing special about it at all. Except that the report said the inside of the barrel had been interfered with. Tallow made two notes: he wanted to see pictures of the bullet, and he wanted to see inside the barrel. Maybe Bat could cut it open at the same time as he fulfilled his little wish of splitting the barrel of the flintlock.

The dead man associated with the gun: Matteo Nardini, Lower East Side, 2002. Nothing immediately jumped off the paper. Tallow put that sheet to one side.

Next was the Lorcin .380 semiautomatic. Tallow had encountered Lorcins on the street. They were thirty-dollar guns, more for posing with than for using because of their incredible unreliability. For a few years, they'd been known in the department as broke-pimp guns. They were made out of a zinc alloy that would snap like a cracker if you looked at it funny. He remembered one such poverty-stricken pimp who was carried into the precinct house because he'd had the idiocy to open fire on police with a Lorcin, only to have the slide mechanism shunt right off the back of the gun and into his forehead, smacking him unconscious.

The report noted that the weapon had

been extensively modified. Again, his guy had taken a gun that no sane person would use for a killing and rebuilt and restored it until it would guarantee a result. Which indicated that, again, the use of this particular gun had meant something to his guy. But a Lorcin? What was he missing about a Lorcin?

"No sane person," Tallow said to himself, and gave a little joyless half-laugh.

Chewing his lip, he put the make of the gun into the search on his tablet and skimmed the results. One sentence leaped out at him. *A common street handgun, due to legendarily poor security at the manufacturing plant over a number of years.* Tallow knew that — Rosato had once told him that, in fact — but seeing it there put it into a new context for him.

Tallow read down and discovered that Daniel Garvie, found on Avenue A with a bullet in the back of his head in 1999, was a previous customer of the New York Police Department. Convictions for petty theft.

Tallow sat back and told himself a little story.

A stolen gun to kill a thief.

Tenuous.

But it sort of fit the fiction he'd started assembling around the case today.

Gun three: Ruger nine-millimeter, scarred firing pin, Marc Arias, Williamsburg, 2007, unsolved. Tallow wished he knew more about guns. He wished he knew whom the flintlock had killed.

Gun four: a Beretta M9. Didn't mean a thing to Tallow.

He put the tablet to sleep, and then put the laptop to sleep, and then dropped his clothes like a trail of dead and put himself to sleep.

Eighteen

[show direct message conversation]
D MACHENV: CALL ME ON A CLEAN PHONE RIGHT NOW
D WESTO911: clean phone? what am i stringer fucking bell?
D MACHENV: DO IT. I JUST HAD A VISIT FROM AN OLD FRIEND
D WESTO911: oh shit.

BBMessage [timestamp]
[JW] Call me now
[AT] Am at dinner w commish and wacko wanda among others. May have to talk about her!
[JW] We have an issue with that
[AT] wtf
[JW] I'm heading downtown. Get out of there now

Blog entry [user: emilyw] [locked]

Any interest in finance becomes an interest in power, and an interest in place, I think. When I started working on Wall Street, I was interested first and foremost in doing a good job in a high-pressure environment. But it became apparent to me, quite quickly, that I would do my job better if I took notice of the real flows of currency, and the actors and locations they gravitated to and spun around. And I think — it might even be too obvious to state! — that that leads you to a study of history.

There I was, routing around financial meltdowns the world over, not realizing that I was standing on the site of the original American financial meltdown. Wall Street itself, named for the wall the Dutch put up to fortify the New Amsterdam settlement against the natives, a wall that eventually extended out to what is now Pearl Street, the old shoreline. It was here on Wall Street that the smart operators of the 1600s looked to do business with the locals, the people of Werpoes and the other Lenape villages of what they called Mannahatta.

The Europeans had noticed that the Native Americans seemed to place great value on something called wampum, or "white strings." These were lengths of beading made from shells and woven together into strips or belts. They had many uses. The relative complexity afforded by shape and color meant that wampum could be used as a communications medium and as a record of events, not unlike a simple tapestry. There are surviving photos of wampum belts constructed to seal and commemorate treaties. They were used as devices to preserve and tell stories from one generation to the next, a crucial cultural aid in otherwise oral societies. Wampum had myriad other social functions. In short, there was perceptible value to wampum in Native American society.

When the Europeans arrived, they immediately looked for ways to open commerce with the natives, and when they saw the traffic of wampum, they felt sure that they'd found it. Therefore, they began to produce their own wampum. It must have been difficult at first, essentially trying to forge a currency without really understanding it, but the Europeans had one important advantage. The natives of Mannahatta were a preserved Stone Age culture. These seventeenth-century Europeans had metal tools and all the advantages of coming from a world poised less than a century from the top of the Industrial Revolution.

The natives, at first, must have found it to be some weird way of reaching out. The Europeans making wampum, rich with cultural memory and meaning, and wanting to hand it over in exchange for furs and food. I wonder if the natives felt *beholden;* if they felt they *had* to take this strange, useless wampum and exchange it for the goods the Europeans needed to survive.

Soon, of course, the inevitable happened. The Dutch flooded this tiny primitive market with fake wampum. They massively overproduced it, at great speed, and the villages of Mannahatta couldn't absorb more than a fraction of it. Wall Street caused and presided over America's first financial collapse. But the furs and the food and the other goods obtained from the Lenape with fake currency allowed the wall of Wall Street to grow until it enclosed and swallowed villages like Werpoes. It's still there now, buried under downtown, a hidden place of power. I don't think of it as subsumed into the new power of Wall Street.

I think of it as lying in wait, glowing with the half-life of its lessons learned and its vengeance pending.

I'm not supposed to go near Werpoes. If you can see this friends-locked entry, then you know there are issues in my life that I can discuss only in the most allusive of ways. But I invent new reasons, weekly, to get a little closer. Purchasing cut flowers from a certain store. Getting food from a certain café. I edge nearer, incrementally, despite the risks, because my first interest was in power. And Werpoes was the first community I know of that was crushed by the sort of financial wrongdoing that I did for a living. The living that, in fact, gave me, completely, the life I have now.

I've had to learn a lot about Native American culture since those days. I'm drawn to it, fascinated by it, and hope that what I've learned will protect me in the years to come. But I'm drawn to power, too, and there is power there.

Don't go to Werpoes. It's not safe.

NINETEEN

Tallow woke up about six a.m., feeling like boulders had been rolled over him in the night.

The shower didn't help. He endured a short but explosive session on the toilet, and when he turned to flush there was blood in the bowl. He got dressed, stuffed some things back in the laptop bag, and left.

At seven a.m., he was outside a large florist's store that he knew, on Maiden Lane. They were just opening, bringing in leafy goods from trucks temporarily double-parked on the tree-lined street. Tallow slid in the front door, past two unpleasantly healthy men in wife-beaters and jogging pants carrying pallets of heavy pots like they were cafeteria trays. A slender woman spotted him in the gap between two large and odious monoliths of vegetation that might have been triffids and said, "I'm sorry, we're not really open yet."

With a smear of regret, Tallow badged her. "I know. I just have a quick question about something."

The woman walked around to him, wiping her palms on a pair of jeans that hadn't been blue in five years. She was white like lilies, and willowy, her hair the pale glow of blondes who have worked in the sun for a long time. "What did you need, Detective? Is this quick question for a wife, a girlfriend, or your mother?"

"I didn't badge you to get special treatment, I promise. I need to see a tobacco plant, if you have one."

Her eyes said she was in her forties, but only two lines were drawn on her forehead as she made a small pensive frown. "Hm. You know, I think I do. Come with me."

She led him past four or five stages of plant life, along an aisle, and into a small jungle of shrubs. Tallow watched her eyes tick down and across three levels of shelving. She settled on a small pot containing a sickly-looking collection of sticks topped with wispy white heads. "Woman's tobacco," she told him. "The Native Americans used the leaves to alleviate heavy periods, postnatal sickness, and stomach problems."

There were so few leaves on the object

that Tallow didn't want to touch them for fear of killing the thing.

"Or there's this," she said, lifting a heavier pot filled with a vivid, vigorous green foliage that sprayed white trumpets of flowers whose mouths were a warm pink. "Your basic *Nicotiana tabacum,* cultivated tobacco, a distant relative to the tobacco seeds the Taino Amerindians gave to Christopher Columbus, which became the plants that Jean Nicot gave to the French court, where people were so goddamn delighted by the effect the ground-up leaves had on their heads that they named the plant after him."

Tallow rubbed one of the leaves between thumb and forefinger. He got a, *yes,* a distant relative of that slightly sharp scent, just barely suggestive of cigarette tobacco, that he'd detected in apartment 3A.

"That's it," he said. "I think. Maybe if I crushed it up and burned it."

"You crush and burn it, you buy it," the florist said with a smile.

"Sorry," Tallow said. "It's for something I'm working on, believe it or not. You seem to know about this stuff."

She rolled her eyes around the room. "I kind of should, don't you think?"

"Sorry. Sorry. I'm not really awake yet. Would you know if this is the sort of tobacco plant that would have grown naturally around here, way back when?"

She bit her cheek, turning the pot around in her soil-streaked hands. Her nails were longer and stronger than he would have expected for someone in her job. "Well. It's a cultivar, like I said, and some people think it has a couple of other tobacco plants mixed up in it. But sure, something pretty much like it would have grown around here. The woman's tobacco would have been local too. You would have found it on the slopes headed down toward where Pearl Street and Water Street are now, back in the days before the natives sold the place to the Dutch."

Tallow made a decision. "I'd like to buy this, um, this one with the flowers here."

"Nicotiana tabacum."

"Yeah."

She raised a skeptical eyebrow. "I don't do cop discounts. And women really do prefer roses."

"I'm sure they do. But I think the person I'm looking for prefers *Nicotiana tabacum*. And I don't take cop discounts."

Which was a damned lie, because in the past couple of years he'd done it a lot, and he knew it, and she knew it just from the look in his eye, but Tallow paid full price for the pot and a bag of plant-food sachets, and was happy to do it. He thanked her and left, dodging another weight-lifting display as he went.

Tallow's next stop was the coffee shop, where he purchased a cardboard tray of six of the morning specialty, an iced coffee, in the grotesque venti-plus, that was made with nothing but too many shots of espresso and seriously chilled cream. The half a dozen drinks came in milkily translucent corn-plastic containers stamped with a cartoon of a naked man plugging himself into main electricity through his genitals and leaping into the air with the joy of voltage. Tallow made a pit in the backseat of the car and placed the tray in it. The tobacco plant sat in the foot well of the passenger seat. It wasn't yet eight a.m. So far, Tallow had remembered everything except food. He figured he could survive until lunch and pointed the car at One PP.

Tallow walked into Bat and Scarly's office to find Bat slumped on a chair with his head on the workbench, turned away from the door, while Scarly softly sharpened an old straight razor on a worn strop, watching her partner intently.

"I don't think he *needs* his eyebrows, do you? I mean, they don't serve an immediate *function* or anything," she whispered.

"I am not asleep." Bat moaned. "I am merely resting my brain. And if you come near me with that thing I will shave your face off your skull with it. Or possibly just puke in your eyes."

Tallow laid his laptop bag against his chair, unloaded the plant on the floor next to it, and put the tray of cold coffee on the bench next to Bat's head. "Do you have space in your fridge for half of these?"

Bat's head rose slowly on his skinny neck, like a sedated hen's. He turned his head at a mechanical crawl, scanning the immediate area, until his eyes detected the coffee.

"Oh my God," Bat prayed. "I love you. I would let you have sex on me and everything. But I am very tired and would prefer not to have to move."

Scarly killed a cup lid with feral fingers and chugged a third of a container. Her eyes flexed weirdly in their sockets. "Oh, that's the stuff," she said. "That is really the stuff."

Bat was weakly pawing at the lid of the cup nearest him. Tallow reached over and took it off for him, abstractedly wondering if this was what fatherhood felt like. Bat sipped from it like a sickly Dickensian child. Tallow half expected him to whimper "God bless us, every one."

"Fuck me," Bat gasped. "It's like an angel shat ice cream–coffee rainbows in my mouth."

"Little bit," said Tallow as the momentary illusion of parenthood atomized. He opened his own cup and drank. "Did we get anything back on that Bulldog yet?"

"Nope," said Scarly, bent over and putting three of the cups inside a small fridge that had been hidden by the general crap in the office. "Couple of hours."

"Okay. Listen," Tallow said, reaching down and pulling the lieutenant's papers from his bag, "what do you know about Ruger nine-millimeters?"

"Place the papers where I may see them," said Bat. "I do not wish to burn precious caffeine molecules by moving."

Tallow did as he was told. Bat leaned his head over the paper, trying to get gravity to aid him in keeping his eyes open and working.

"Ruger nine. Scarly, what don't I know about a Ruger nine with a circular lock on the shell casing's ass?"

"That'll be the Ruger Police Service. There were Luger works in it to make it a reliable nine. They did all kinds of odd variants for a while, trying to make government sales." She stood up and looked at Tallow.

"Ruger used to have this massive reputation because of the Ruger Super Blackhawk. They used to say it was a great gun for holding up trains, because you'd fire it at the train and it'd stop. Huge goddamn thing with a seven-and-a-half-inch barrel, but really accurate and it didn't break your fingers or wrist when you shot a .44 Magnum load. So it was, you know, a special gun for police by the makers of this immense fucking elephant gun that everyone's heard of. That was the pitch."

"So this guy was shot with a police sidearm?"

"One that was marketed to police anyway. Why?"

"Thinking about what we were talking about last night. Is it possible — even just for the sake of argument — that our guy really was matching his weapons to his kills in some sense?"

"Say it is," said Scarly. "What have you got?"

"A petty thief killed with a junk gun that was probably stolen from its manufacturing plant."

"Thin," Scarly observed.

"I know. But now I want to know more about the victim of the Ruger."

"We can do that here. You want to see

downstairs first?"

"Sure. Um, probably a dumb question, but do you have smoke alarms down there?"

"Nothing that can't be disabled," said Bat, stirring. "But you probably won't be able to sneak a cigarette down there without someone noticing."

Tallow hefted the plant. "No. I want to crush some of these leaves and then try burning them."

Bat looked at it and admired Tallow's apparent loss of sanity. "Cool. You bought another lighter then, huh?"

"Oh shit," said Tallow, who hadn't.

Bat laughed. "Jesus, John. We can't let you out of our sight, can we? Relax. This is CSU. We have plenty of things that burn shit. Hell, we don't have much here that *doesn't* burn shit."

Scarly snorted. "That's true. Last month a computer power brick caught fire and set light to Brendan Foley's legs."

"And that microwave oven that went up at Christmas."

Scarly dismissed it with a disgusted wave of her hand. "Fucking Einar rolling in drunk for the eighteenth time with his 'I hate all your ice-cold American drinks, I come from a very cold country and do not wish to pour more ice in my body.' You heard what they did to his head?"

"What?"

"Well, the skin grafts took, but, you know, he basically made napalm, so there wasn't much left under it. So they injected him with this weird sort of facial caulking that swells and firms up under UV light and essentially kind of re-inflated his head. It was cool."

"Oh! And the old still exploded last summer!"

"Right! Did you see Foley's legs the other day when he was doing that fucked-up pantsless lap of victory around the main labs? Legs like a dead giraffe."

"Downstairs?" said Tallow, with just a little pleading in his voice.

Downstairs was cavernous: bare and stained cement, gray pillars holding up a blackened ceiling that had broken-down flotillas of fluorescent light tubes sailing across it in lazy waves. Walking in from the elevator, Tallow saw an arrangement of wheeled whiteboards, and great blankets of clear plastic sheeting on the floor. Getting closer, he could make out big glossy photos under the sheeting and tacked to the whiteboards.

"Oh my God," said Tallow.

"Yeah," said Scarly. "We got into work

early. Not that *he* was much use. We rounded up some help and got it done."

The CSUs had run off copies of all the photos, in a rough ratio of one to one, and arranged them on the floor and on the whiteboards according to the evidentiary floor plans. The plastic sheeting had been rolled out over the photos on the floor so he could walk over them. It was as close as could be gotten to a copy of the whole of apartment 3A, with the whiteboards standing in for walls and partitions.

There was a table over to one side, with papers scattered on it. Tallow set his iced coffee and his potted plant down there, turned, and surveyed the space. Scarly deposited next to that the things she'd brought from upstairs, excavated out of their office. An old mortar and pestle, a foil tray that'd had fossil grains of rice pilaf wiped out of it with a wet nap that was itself not young, and a small chef's blowtorch. Tallow was learning not to ask certain kinds of question about the way the CSUs operated.

"This is amazing," Tallow said, and meant it. He wasn't just taken aback at how well and how completely and how intelligently they'd done it. He was genuinely shocked that they'd done it at all. Tallow had expected to be down here all morning doing it himself, and he hadn't been looking forward to meticulously matching photos to floor plans and codes, let alone scavenging CSU offices for tacks and adhesive. Walking around the perimeter of the space, he knew immediately that he couldn't have done it as well as this. Laying this broad plastic sheeting over the photos on the floor was inspired, and Tallow wouldn't have thought of that at all.

"What's the plant for?" asked Bat, bending down and peering at it suspiciously. "I don't trust plants. Food things come from them."

"It's a tobacco plant. I had the idea that I could smell a kind of tobacco in the apartment."

Bat turned his judgmental squint on Tallow. "This is your much strong cop voodoo."

"Well," said Tallow, "we live in hope. But this is really incredible. Thank you so much."

"You're welcome." Scarly grinned. "Would you like to be alone with your plant now?"

Tallow walked into the middle of the simulated living room. "For a couple of hours. Until you get the ballistics back on the Bulldog. Then I'm going to want to talk about paint chips."

"You wanna decorate?" Bat asked, raising his voice. Tallow was fairly sure he'd spent the past thirty seconds threatening the plant in a menacing whisper.

"I saw paints on things in the apartment. I want to know more about those paints."

"You sound," said Scarly, "like a man developing a case."

"I'm — no. Not yet. I'm a man telling himself a story, right now . . ."

Tallow found his voice trailing off as he looked around. He didn't see Scarly and Bat exchange a clever glance, just heard Scarly say, "We'll come and get you," as they both left for the elevator. They were already gone when he turned to thank them again.

He did a first walk of the emulation. There had never been a bed in this apartment, and the kitchen had been ripped out by his man long ago. There was nothing but guns. Looking down, he found the flintlock at the center of a large swirl of weapons. A goat's eye in the middle of a gunmetal sun.

The CSUs really had done an incredible, ingenious job. Everything was positioned correctly. Walking back into the living room, Tallow got a new perspective. The arc behind the front door had to be, and was, clear of weapons, otherwise the door

185

wouldn't open. If Tallow stood in the arc, he could see a space close to the middle of the room that could be reached by stepping into what were now obviously two gaps in the gun coverage, each big enough to accommodate a foot.

He tried it. Reached the central space. Sat down in it, cross-legged. The position had him facing the broad wall adjacent to the door. He sat and stared at the wall, hands in his lap. Scanned the mosaic of photos. Fought to see something in them beyond arrangements of guns mounted by a very careful lunatic who had been killing people in Manhattan and getting away with it for ten or twenty years.

Not a thing. Not a thing *yet,* he told himself, and went to retrieve his coffee. There was no way he could re-create the lighting, he knew, which was a shame. It really had had that churchlike effect on Tallow, standing in that apartment on Pearl Street for the first time. Maybe he could just play a CD of classically inspired ambient music, he thought, and smiled a little at it. Maybe find out the name of whatever Muzak they played in the lobby at Vivicy.

Tallow sat back down in the virtual space on the floor of the simulated apartment, gazed at photographs of murder weapons, and tried to understand where he really was and what they really were.

TWENTY

The hunter awoke gently from a peaceful sleep at the break of dawn, its rosy fingers softly touching his face as he slept beneath a great Central Park cypress by the water. He sat up, cross-legged, silent, breathing deeply as the rising sun warmed him. The hunter then stood, pulled some leaves from the cypress, crushed them in his hand to release their oils, and rubbed them under his armpits to minimize his odor.

Walking quietly around the park, he gathered cattail shoots from the water's edge, lamb's-quarter leaves, hen of the woods mushroom flesh, a little mountain mint, and wood sorrel, and he returned to his spot under the cypress to eat it with a piece of squirrel meat. He was always careful never to take too much from one plant. He was a hunter, and that meant he never knew when he might have to rely on foraging to live. The moment he allowed himself to believe that the movement of seasons was perfectly repeating and broadly predictable, he would be creating the conditions for his own death.

Having eaten, the hunter began to walk. He exited Central Park at East Seventy-Second Street.

Within a few minutes, the hunter was where he wanted to be: in sight of the Aer Keep Tower, a forty-four-floor glass spike sunk deep into the island. There was no strobing superimposition of Old Manhattan in his vision now. Something this viciously contemporary had him fully impaled in the present day.

The building repulsed him on a basic level. Nothing about it came from nature, not its alien glitter nor its computer-generated shape. It was a thing created in a lab. It had no place in his green world. It was the device of an invader.

He walked its perimeter. It was surrounded by high concrete walls, an urban blast bunker against the visual assault of the nearby public school, far too charmless and real for the unprotected eyes of the tower's inhabitants. The residents' view didn't start until higher up, where all the adjacent streets and buildings became nothing but distant pretty toys laid out around their feet. The comfortable perspective of giants.

There was no true pedestrian entrance. The only way in or out was through the underground garage. If you wanted to leave on foot, you had to emerge from beneath the building and walk the driveway to the main gates. The design obviously dissuaded the more adventurous rich from going on a walking safari. Far better to leave in convoys of black SUVs with tinted windows and discuss in gyms and bars how the possession of money made them prisoners of New York City.

Or perhaps not, thought the hunter, surveying the main gates. Perhaps they thought themselves a new wave of colonists, inhabiting an airtight biosphere and exploring the moon of Manhattan.

This was where Jason Westover lived. Jason Westover and his wife.

The hunter watched cars dock and undock from Space Station Upper East Side for a while, calculating his own trajectories.

TWENTY-ONE

The longer Tallow looked at the wall, the more it seemed that the guns on it interlocked somehow.

The gaps in the surface coverage were very much starting to appear as deliberate omissions, spaces awaiting the right shapes. An immense clock awaiting the right cogs, lying in the sleep of potential until the day the correct pieces were placed and all the wheels could finally turn.

A voice said, "John." He was so lost in the gun machinery that it took long seconds for him to both register the voice and understand that it was his name being called.

Scarly was standing by the table. Her face was drawn and he could see her pulse in her throat. She held a sheet of printout. "This isn't so funny anymore."

"What?"

"The .44 Bulldog. It's Son of Sam's gun."

"Seriously?"

"Same bullets they dug out of Donna Lauria and Jody Valenti in the summer of 1976. Those bullets went onto the ballistics database back when the DA in Queens declared the case reopened, in the late nineties. John, this is wrong."

"In all kinds of ways." Tallow stood up, knees protesting. He assumed, since Scarly was here, that he must have been sitting there for a couple of hours, but he had no sense of the time having passed.

"No, listen," Scarly said, voice low and urgent. "If someone had been killed with this gun, it would have set off flashing lights. The bullet would have been dug out of the body and processed, and the odds are that it would have matched one of the Son of Sam bullets in the database. There are plenty. Even the bullets that were so deformed they couldn't be fully matched to the weapon were scanned in and appended to the ballistics compilation on the gun. We don't have a body for this gun."

Tallow stretched, and regretted it instantly. Grimacing, he said, "So our guy dug his own bullets out of some poor bastard. Because, I'm telling you, there's no way that gun is in this apartment without there being a body on it."

"Our guy has a guy in the Property Office, John. And I don't mean the Property Office here in One PP. I mean the huge fucking storage facility. A guy in there, with access to thousands of fucking handguns. Even the ones that other people would be keeping a fucking eye on, like Son of Sam's piece, for fuck's sake — a guy in there who'll just boost them and give them to our guy to kill people with. And if the guns are too famous, he'll cut his own slugs out of the bodies and walk away. This guy, our guy, he's actually starting to scare me a bit now."

"A couple of hundred kills to his name didn't do that?"

"Meh. I dream about killing two hundred people every fucking night."

"You know," said Tallow, "whenever I'm in danger of forgetting you're a CSU, you always find a way to remind me. On the bright side, doesn't Bat owe you ten bucks now?"

"Tallow. Listen. I am not going to be the one who tells my boss that our fucking serial handgun ninja got someone to steal a famous gun out of an evidence barrel and did at least one person with it and recovered the bullet and so we have at least one completely fucking unsolvable case on the list."

"No," said Tallow, plucking the printout

from her fingers and grabbing his bag. "I'm going to talk to my boss about it first."

Tallow waited until he was outside the main building before calling the lieutenant. He dialed her cell phone. It was midmorning, and her movements weren't predictable at that time of day. Her phone rang. It rang long enough that he was expecting it to switch to voice mail. Then she answered with an uncertain "Hello?"

His brow creased. "It's Tallow. Where are you?" He could tell from the background noise that she was outside.

"Does it matter where I am?"

Okay, he thought. "Well, I'd like to sit down with you as soon as it's convenient. I have something on the case that I really need your input on before I take it further. Can I come by the office in a half hour or so and find you there?"

"Um. No. I won't be there for a while."

"I really need your help, Lieutenant. Where are you? I could meet you there, if that's easier."

"Oh God," she said.

"What's wrong?"

Tallow heard her take a deep, shaky breath. "I'm at Jim's funeral, John."

". . . What?"

Everything tilted, and Tallow's feet swam for purchase until his back met a wall. He stiffened his legs and pressed his back hard against it.

"I'm sorry, John."

"I don't understand."

"His wife . . . she wanted a quick funeral. And, well, I'm afraid she told me she didn't want you to attend. I mean, she's upset, obviously, and if she'd chosen to wait a week, I'm sure it would have been different."

All Tallow could think of to say was "We've never met. I've never met her."

The lieutenant's voice sounded somewhat strained as she said, "Yes, she told me that too."

"What did she say?"

"Don't, John."

Tallow let himself slide down the wall until his knees were drawn up and his backside was on the ground. "What did she say?"

"She said that she didn't want a stranger at her husband's funeral, and she didn't want to see the man who should have saved her husband, and she didn't want to see the man who should have died instead of her husband."

He'd asked her to say it. He'd badgered her to say it. But he didn't like her for saying it. And he didn't like himself for doing it and hating her. He didn't like anything. He covered his face with his free hand.

"John?"

"I wish people would stop saying that. Sometimes I wish people didn't know my name."

"John? What?"

"I was his partner. I was his friend. You tell her . . ." He caught himself. Gathered up everything in him in one fist and pushed it all down with everything else that was already down there. "No. Don't tell her anything. Don't mention me at all."

"Okay, John," the lieutenant said, uncertainly.

Yeah, he thought. *Talk to me like that. Talk to me like I'm a basket case. Talk to me like I'm an idiot. Talk to me like I'm already leaving the force.* He licked his lips like a lizard, his face tightening and hardening into sharp planes, relishing the anger that was starting to whip around inside him. He caught hold of that too, but he decided to push it out.

"You need to be in your office in one hour. I have Son of Sam's gun."

He waited just long enough to hear the start of her reaction, and killed the phone call dead.

Tallow walked to his car, drove out of One

196

Police Plaza, stopped at a store, and bought two lighters.

Homicide at Ericsson Place was empty when Tallow arrived. Everyone was at Jim Rosato's funeral.

The lieutenant was not in her office. Tallow entered her office, stood there, and waited.

He didn't move. Stared at the back wall of her office. Pictured the guns from Pearl Street there. Conjured them in his vision and continued to scan them for clues, evidence, sense.

Ten minutes later the lieutenant stalked into the room, angry and angular in a black wool Nehru-collared pantsuit with a sharply darted asymmetrical front closure. He wondered if this too was new. He also found that he didn't care.

"I do not like the way you are talking to me lately, Detective," she snapped, walking around her desk.

Tallow put down his bag, took out the printout, and tossed it on the desk.

"Did you hear me?"

"Read that."

"Tallow, do you want to be discharged? Do you want me to take your badge and gun right now and have you marched off

197

the premises?"

"Read. That."

"Tallow, you —"

"Lieutenant, I have a lot of respect for you. You have a hard job, in all kinds of ways, and you handle the pressure from all sides better than pretty much any boss I've ever had in the job. But you hung this around my neck, and you are just counting the days until it pulls me down and both it and me disappear from sight. I can understand that. But until what you put around my neck sinks me, you will treat me like a detective in the New York Police Department and you. Will. Read. That."

She looked at him for a long time. She then turned her gaze to the printout, but he could see her focus vanish, could see that she wasn't going to give it more than a glance before dismissing it, throwing it in the trash, and moving on to the far more present task of what to do about John Tallow. He directed his thoughts to anything that might be listening in the sky over Ericsson Place right then.

The lieutenant's eyes skidded off the page, and she pulled the paper off her desk, preparing to crumple it. She glared at him, and then looked at it again, her hand closing.

She stopped. Squinted at something on the page. Slid both sets of fingers around the sides of the page, holding it still and straight.

The lieutenant laid the page back on the desk like it was ticking.

"John?"

He was John now. She was jolted. It simply remained, he thought, to see where she was induced to jump to. His career could be over in the next two sentences, he knew.

"Yes."

"Are we sure this isn't CSU playing a prank?"

"Yesterday I met the CSU who did the test. A piece of the gun blew back and took off a chunk of his earlobe. They completed the processing a little over an hour ago. I think it's fair to say that their fear wouldn't easily be faked for the sake of a prank."

"Who else has seen this?"

"The pair of CSUs. Me. You."

She gave him a look that said she was reevaluating him. "You're sure?"

"Absolutely."

"Okay," she said. "Okay. Do you want to sit down?"

"Standing is fine." Tallow let a little bit of

ice into his voice when he said it. She caught it.

"About the funeral, John —"

"Forget the funeral. What about this?"

She pushed her hair back, worried, eyes darting around the page on her desk. "Tell me what you think it means."

"I think it means the owner of apartment three A on Pearl Street has or had a contact inside the Property Office and induced that person to steal this gun for a specific homicide. Knowing how incredibly identifiable this gun is, he then dug his own bullet or bullets out of his victim. So we have a gun we can reasonably assume was used for homicide by our man, but no victim to apply it to. It's my opinion that he used this gun because he believed it had some historical, thematic, or personal connection to the kill." At which moment, Tallow made a leap of intuition. Or a crazy guess. "Just like we'll find that Marc Arias, killed in Williamsburg in 2007, will prove to have some connection with the police."

The lieutenant's eyebrows shot up. "How do you figure that?"

"He was killed with a Ruger Police Service, a gun they made to sell to police forces, I'm told with not much success. Marc Arias is going to turn out to be a guy

200

connected to the police. Probably not a full-serving officer."

Tallow knew he was taking a huge, huge chance at this point. Tallow also knew that his brain was moving at speed, and thinking felt like it hadn't for years. He felt like a runner whose morning start had been hard and harrowing but who had hit the zone where the running was sweet and swift.

She turned to her computer. "You know what the police staffing the Property Office used to be called? The Rubber Gun Squad. Back in the day, they used only police who were on restricted duty or under disciplinary action."

He watched her input a search string into the networked database. He watched her eyebrow arch again as the Real Time Crime Center component spit back results instantly. She read it off the screen to him.

"Marc Arias, in 2007, was a discharged officer of the NYPD whose last posting within the force was . . . staff at the Property Office."

"Lieutenant, you shoved this into my hands when I still had my friend's blood on my clothes and told me to work the case. I'm working it. But I've reached the stage where I'm going to need your help. Are you going to help me, or do I stay out there on

201

my own?"

"Don't make it sound like you were the lone cowboy on the high desert there, John. But," she said, holding up a hand as his mouth opened, "I take your point. And while I think this is a little bit thin, and could be entirely coincidental, the fact remains that the gun should be in storage, not in an apartment on Pearl Street."

"What do we do about that, Lieutenant?"

"I need to speak to someone farther up the chain of command, and very quietly. This is not a news item that needs to be out in the world." She picked up her desk phone. "Get out of here, John. I'm going to try to get the captain's next free five minutes, and then ruin his day."

"I can go upstairs with you, help explain all this and how we got here."

"Go back to work, Detective. You don't have experience in explaining things to the captain in baby talk so that *he* can explain things to the assistant chief for Manhattan South and not sound like a senior citizen with a kilo of Vicodin in his system. Which he essentially is. This is my job now. You go do yours."

"Okay," Tallow said, picking up his bag and leaving her office. As he was passing through the doorway, the lieutenant said, in a small voice, to his back:

"I really am sorry about earlier. The funeral."

Tallow broke step for only a moment, and then continued off the floor and out of the building before all Jim Rosato's friends and coworkers returned from gently laying him to rest in the warm and welcoming soil of the mainland.

TWENTY-TWO

The hunter needed to obtain a weapon.

There were an unpleasant number of conditions placed on his forthcoming work. He needed the weapon by tomorrow. He was well aware of having a limited sum of money at his hideaway here in the south of the island. He could not bear to take the subway. And he knew that the response to his next hunt would be immediate and difficult.

The hunter kept walking west. The modern man in him understood that he was entering the part of New Manhattan called Hell's Kitchen by most, and Clinton by real estate agents' store-window ads, but he allowed Old Manhattan to wash up in his vision for a little while, and he contentedly followed the stream that the first Dutch on the island called the Great Kill.

His hand went into his bag, locating and producing first a pair of thin leather gloves, and then a ring. The ring was not the most beautiful piece of handcrafting he'd ever seen, or even that he'd ever made. It was wrapped wire, wide enough to accommodate the gloved index finger of his right hand, and in the crude but tight setting was a piece of quartz he'd found by the mouth of the Harlem River Ship Canal. The hunter had worked it carefully. It stood out just enough from the wire claws of the ring setting and was cut to such a sharp point that it made a functional punch weapon of last resort. The hunter had on one occasion used it to strike open a jugular vein, and on another to destroy a larynx.

The hunter slipped the gloves on, and then the ring.

Draining Mannahatta from his sight with reluctance, he began to pick his way through warehouses, gray-mud parking lots, and auto repair shops. It was, he felt, as desolate as this end of the island got.

He found the location he wanted: a five-story building whose frontage was a boarded-up pizzeria. The side door, which opened onto the stairs going up to the higher floors of the building, was, as ever, slightly ajar. One presented oneself in front of it, at which event the door would creak open to reveal a large man with a badly concealed gun standing in its lee.

And so it was that the door swung to show, in the gloom, a grotesque in a grubby orange tracksuit, dark hair growing patchily out of a head that appeared to have at some point fallen in, or been held in, farming machinery. It was as if his face were once a soft thing that someone had swirled with a finger before it had set.

"I want to see Mr. Kutkha," the hunter said.

"Ain't no Kutkha here," the grotesque said, predictably.

"Tell him a previous customer and distant old tribesman has come to visit."

"Got a name?"

"Tell him you asked for a name and that I told you I'm a human being."

The grotesque shrugged and walked up the short flight of stairs backward, keeping his hand on the gun shoved in the back of his waistband. At the landing, still keeping his deep-set eyes on the hunter, he relayed the information.

The hunter presently heard a laugh like bones being rattled in a tin, and then a harsh, snapping voice shouting, "Let him in, let him in!" The grotesque summoned the hunter up with a paw whose shape was lost to flab. On the landing, the hunter saw a second man, shorter than the grotesque, with a military haircut. His body was over-trained in the manner of the modern physical narcissists, speaking of a man who knew the names of most of his muscles. This one held out a hand for the hunter's bag, which he passed over easily. The hunter was silently directed to the door of the largest room on this floor, a room that hummed with the sound of machines. It did not quite smother a sudden composition of sounds from the next floor up: screams like a cat being dismembered, a deep thump that shook the ceiling, the noise of someone trying to cry while unable to draw breath.

The hunter showed no outward sign of having heard it. He allowed the man with the military haircut to pat him down.

The first thing the hunter noticed upon entering the room was a boy of sixteen, low-browed and broad-nosed, standing beside the door with the expression of a soundly beaten puppy. The hunter could not see the boy's hands, and so he moved to kill the boy.

Kutkha's voice stopped him. "Boy! You do not stand there when a true man enters a room! Do you want to die?"

Kutkha was thin like a switch, with a face flaked from flint. He sat with kingly aplomb upon a small, richly buttery sofa, flanked by two tall fans attendant on either side of his seat, with two floor-standing air-conditioning units on the floor before him like kneeling slaves. The hunter knew Kutkha of old: the man complained of being permanently hot, yet he loved clothes, and so he sat there in peculiar long shorts of fine cotton and white silk and an elaborately patterned waistcoat and nothing else, being delightedly hammered by the tundra gales of very new air-conditioning machines.

Kutkha was still cackling at the boy's frozen horror as he rose to shake the hunter's hand. "The human being himself! My distant relation!"

And then, to the boy: "A human being, see? He is of the Lenni-Lenape tribe. Do you know what those words mean? The 'Human Beings'! He and I, we are of the same blood. *Your* family?" He spat on the floor. "Your family are shit."

Kutkha turned back to the hunter. "My brother fucked a Muscovite. What can you do. Some people will fuck livestock if the animals stand still long enough. That family, they continue to send these little sperms up the B to beg me to make nice, come to Brighton Beach, eat kielbasa they made out of fucking dogs, and listen to them talk about how I can give them all my fucking money. Those people have been fucking my people for so long that you could look right into my very fucking DNA with a microscope and see someone from Moscow pissing on my genes and calling it summer rain."

Kutkha rounded again on the hapless boy. "Do you see? I am Itelmen! My people walked to Alaska and down into America and became *his* people! He is more my blood than you. You are like the things that fall out of my ass when I eat Italian foods."

Kutkha returned to his seat. There wasn't another chair in the room, but the hunter was expecting this. He knew Kutkha. He stood between the air-con units, a supplicant position before the throne. The hunter had harbored some small stone of regret about what would have to happen. It turned to dust in his heart as he stood there like a peasant between the rumbling little machines.

The Russian waved an airy hand at the boy. "You can speak in front of him. I am not even convinced he knows the language."

The hunter studied the boy briefly, and then decided to speak. "I need a gun. I would very much like a police gun."

"How so?"

"A gun associated with the police. With

use by the police."

Kutkha addressed the sullen boy. "He's a collector, see. Knows what he wants, knows what he likes. A man with an interest in history. You could cultivate that shit. Know where you've been and you'll see where you're going. You might be of some use to me if you could prove you could think. Or count. You do not have to go back to Brighton Beach and get jerked off by old men in piss-stinking *banyas.* I'll say that I can teach you things here in Manhattan that have been long forgotten in Brighton Beach."

The hunter said, "It doesn't have to be new. I'd prefer something in working condition."

"You know." Kutkha ruminated. "I'm almost positive I have a Colt Official Police. From the 1950s."

"What does the grip look like?"

"Checkered wood."

"And the barrel?"

"Six inches, I would say. I remember this because my specialist, he likes history like we do, and he saw this gun and made the little rocking motion that means he is happy, and told me many things about the gun until I had to say to him that I would shoot him to make him quiet again."

"I'll take that," said the hunter.

"A fine purchase. A weapon like that, it's like a good watch, from the days when they still had mechanical parts that people cared about. I could have maybe found you a SIG, but it's simply not the same, is it? The Colt comes with the original NYPD holster, but I'll not sell you that. If you want it, it's free, but I'll not take your money for it."

"Why?"

"It hasn't been used. It's a spare holster. And I will tell you a thing that I was told by my specialist, because it amused me. Policemen had to break in those holsters. They looked like leather but were just treated cardboard. So they had to force a Coke bottle into the holster for a week to loosen it enough to get the gun in. If you put the gun in there without breaking it in, you had to cut the gun out again. Or get shot. But breaking it in did so much damage that the holster would fall apart after six months. I am told this: In the 1970s, men of our kind could rip the Colts right out of the holsters. Just tear the holsters, pull the gun, and shoot the policeman. Those were sweeter times, if you ignored the clothes."

The hunter clamped down on the thoughts and actions boiling in his gut. "How much?"

"I will not accept more than one hundred

dollars for this gun," said Kutkha, chest swelling with pride in his own magnanimity. "It will come with twenty-four rounds of ammunition."

"That's very kind," said the hunter. "Thank you."

"The gun will have to come in from New Jersey. I'll make a call. Be here tonight around seven. It will arrive with my evening shipment. I will take it from the vehicle myself and ensure everything is correct."

"That is very professional and very timely. Thank you," said the hunter. "I'll be here with the money."

Which he most certainly could have been.

Kutkha did not stand again to shake the hunter's hand but instead picked up his cell phone and speed-dialed a number, looking at the hunter with the expectation that he was observant enough to know that his audience had concluded. The hunter nodded and left the Russian's little court. In the hallway, he took his bag from the military man, who watched him walk downstairs to the grotesque, who opened the front door for him and saw him out.

What the hunter knew was that there was the grotesque, the military man, Kutkha, the boy, and at least one additional man upstairs. All but the additional man or men

212

upstairs had seen him. When he returned, there would be at least one other, whichever employee from New Jersey had driven in with his gun and with whatever else Kutkha had previously arranged for his "evening shipment." Humans, the hunter presumed. In his bag there was the knife and some small tools for living in the forest. A pouch of tinder, a strike, some twine, a few other things. He had the ring on his finger.

He walked to the end of the block, ensured he was out of sight, and began to look for access to the rear of Kutkha's building.

On the east–west side of the block, five or six doors before a little food store, he found an abandoned hardware store, windows imperfectly whitewashed, the frames in the floors above mostly missing their glass. An official-looking sign had been pasted on the door, but weather had washed many of its words away. There was no one to see him put his knife to the lock and pry the door open. Inside, he closed the door with care and found a standing particleboard display unit to prop against it. The owner had apparently been forced to abandon the place in a hurry. There was still stock here, and many fittings. The hunter crouched in the gloom for a moment, listened, and inhaled. He could faintly detect human feces, but they were old. No one was currently squatting here. He searched what remained of the missing owner's attempt to live by the cheating laws of exchange in Manhattan. Whatever he took was fair. Mannahatta had been stolen from the Lenape in fraudulent barter. The hunter was no criminal. The spoils of the city on this island were his by right.

The hunter found, among other things, more twine and sliding trays of nuts and bolts that hadn't been worth the owner's time to pack and carry. A thought came to him, and he cut himself six feet of twine, gathered a handful of nuts and a few bolts, and looked for the stairway access to the upper floors and ultimately the roof.

Up here, he had an angled view on the rear of Kutkha's building and clear sight of its weed-choked loading yard and the access alley where cars could reach it. The windows on the upper three floors of the building had makeshift curtains tacked across them inside.

The hunter crouched behind the ventilation unit on the roof, out of direct sight of Kutkha's building, and began to tie nuts into the length of twine. He knotted the heavy bolts on either end of the string. Experimentally, he spun a foot's worth of string in his fist, the bolt at the end whipping the twine around in a tight arc. Good enough.

The hunter stood, faced Kutkha's building, spun the weighted twine until it buzzed, and flung it toward the top floor of that building. He watched it fly and then ducked behind the roof unit and watched from the best stealthy angle he could find.

The bolted twine hit the top window. Not hard enough to break it. With just enough force for it to make a sharp report and clatter down onto the window below on the fourth floor, and again onto the third, before falling away, landing in a thick patch of weeds in the yard.

One curtain was pulled away on the fifth floor. One on the fourth. Two on the third. Little bobbing heads trying to see what had made the noise.

Four more people. Also, whoever they were keeping up there. At least one woman being held. The hunter sighed, rolling back out of sight. This had gotten more complicated than it needed to be.

He wondered if the grotesque ever left his position for lunch. The grotesque did not have the shape of a person who was likely to forget about his lunches.

The shipment from New Jersey was obviously going to come through the access road to the yard, in dying evening light. It was a well-secluded space. Unless you were on an adjacent roof, of course, the hunter thought with a quiet chuckle.

His original plan had been to pay for the weapon, leave, return a few moments later, and kill everybody. There were now too many players, all too scattered, for that to work. The hunter needed to make the thing small again. He needed to isolate Kutkha. He did not want everything to balance on Kutkha having made a point of saying he'd take the gun from the car himself to check it over.

That said, the hunter had to admit to himself, that was the sort of thing Kutkha would do, and he'd done similar things in the past. The man did take steps, if not exactly pains, to act and present himself as a courtly criminal, operating in accordance with some mannered tradition that existed for the most part only in Kutkha's own head.

The hunter looked at the sun and calculated the phase of the day. He looked along the row of roofs, paused to count off his pulse, and matched his internal drums to a beat in his mind. The hunter then, staying as low as he dared, ran and leaped and ran over the roofs until he reached the corner he'd turned earlier. He committed the time elapsed to hard memory and crawled to the edge of this new roof. He had an oblique sliver of a view to the front door of Kutkha's building; enough that he'd notice someone leaving.

The hunter was very good at waiting. The roof became the gently curved crown of a foothill, and he was looking down into a gladed trail, the patchy blacktop so easily turning into shade-dappled ground that he smiled, broadly and genuinely, at its simple beauty. There were deer mice popping across the grass here and there, and the shadow of a sharp-shinned hawk orbited his head for a short and exquisite minute. There were patches of bladderpod, as lovely a pale violet as a summer evening sky, whose seeds were sacred. All was sacred, in this waiting time. Life was perfect.

The sun had just stepped to its noon summit when the hunter flinched from the wrenching uchronic sight of a twenty-first-century grotesque in a food-spattered orange running suit walking through a pre-seventeenth-century Mannahatta woodland trail. He almost threw up from the perceptual shock.

The grotesque followed the path the

hunter himself had taken. He turned the corner of the block. His only possible destination was the food store. The hunter, blinking back history, watched the man's walking speed, and as he turned the corner, the hunter ran for the roof he had come from, beating out the time in his head.

The hunter was on the ground floor and prepared within four minutes. He prayed it was enough. He moved the display stand and opened the front door. The street was still entirely clear. It wasn't, after all, a part of town you went to unless you had to. He stood behind the door, put it ajar, and waited again. This time, he was tensed. The grotesque couldn't possibly have bought food and made it back around the corner in four minutes. The creature just didn't move that fast. The street had to stay clear. Performing this hunt was risk enough.

The grotesque dawdled past the hunter's door.

The hunter counted off two more steps, to give himself more space to work in, and opened the door and moved.

A double loop of twine went around the grotesque's neck, and a vicious wrench pulled a complex knot swiftly tight. The hunter wound the twine into his left hand and yanked the creature backward. The hunter gave him credit for trying to reach for his gun with his right hand even as he tried to get his left hand under the loop. The hunter pulled him in close and drove his own right hand into the grotesque's temple. The hunter felt the bone give like struck eggshell under the quartz spike.

The prey's legs turned to mush. The hunter summoned all his strength and dragged the prey backward into the dark of the store. He pressed the prey into the wall face-first long enough for him to close the door as silently as he could.

The prey kicked.

The hunter was off balance and had not yet reached out for his knife, which he'd placed on the display stand. He fell backward with the prey on top of him, bucking like a wounded bull. In past years, the hunter could have throttled his prey by main force. But he had no ego about his age and was fine with jabbing his knee into the prey's back to increase the power he could put into the strangulation. In this position, the more the prey struggled, the quicker he choked himself against the twine.

The prey's heels skittered on the floor, and dug in. He paid for it. But the hunter realized the prey was making the space for what could be a successful grab at the gun in the back of his waistband. The gun the hunter had not yet had the opportunity to take.

The hunter heaved and threw the prey onto his belly. Still on his back, the hunter punched him four or five more times in the side of the head. Blood began to pump weakly from a jagged hole in the prey's temple, and he began to moan and flop. The hunter took the gun. He resisted the temptation to beat the prey to death with it. He had plans for the weapon and didn't want to damage it.

Instead, he stood and placed the gun on the display stand. He took his knife and turned to the prey on the floor.

The prey was up and going for him. One of its eyes had filled with blood. It couldn't speak beyond moans and croaks, and the foam in its mouth was red. It had urinated in its clothes. One of its giant hands, trembling spastically, went for the hunter's face and found purchase.

The hunter drove his knife in and up under its ribs. It made a sound between a choked scream and a whistle. The hunter drove the blade in again. The prey suffered a violent bowel movement. The hunter drove his blade in a third time, higher and harder, and felt down the length of it the resistance of meeting and splitting thick, dense meat.

The hunter twisted the blade.

The prey's open mouth became a still pool of blood.

It died, and dropped, and leaked, and was no longer interesting.

TWENTY-THREE

Tallow drove around the 1st for a while, until he was certain his brain was still ticking along smoothly. It was pushing noon. He knew he should attempt food. It also occurred to him that he should continue to hand-tame his feral CSUs.

People who didn't know John Tallow well were often surprised when he exercised some spending power, and even more surprised when they found out he lived on the island. Sometimes people assumed he was on the take in some mysterious fashion that didn't require his energy or interest. The simple fact was that Tallow didn't spend a lot of money, ever. He even did most of his laundry in the kitchen sink with cheap soap powder. He didn't go out much. He didn't eat much. He got his reading and his music inexpensively or free through the Internet.

Once in a very blue moon, John Tallow imagined his younger self standing down the timeline from his present life, bare toes curling in teenage beach sand, looking ahead to today and watching his future life collapse in on itself like a dying star. His future life becoming small and dark and dense, its gravity apparently grim and inescapable.

Once in a very blue moon, John Tallow spent some cash on a bottle of vodka and drank it at home within an hour.

He pulled up at a sandwich place he knew just before the lunchtime rush started, tucking his car in behind a brand-new SUV-type thing that, with its broad beam, gold, chrome, and huge tires, could have been a hyper-evolved version of a lunar rover. The place itself was little more than a hole-in-the-wall on a rolling six-month lease, and the selection was "minimalist," but the food was terrific, skilled, and considered. Tallow took out his phone and called Scarly.

"I hate this thing," answered Scarly. "It's like an ankle monitor you have to fucking pay for. Except for your hand. Shut up. What do you want?"

Tallow felt a little headache start behind his right eye, which twitched. "I wanted to know if you guys want me to bring you some lunch back."

"Hey. Bat. You want food?" Scarly yelled

without holding the phone away from her mouth.

While Tallow shook his head, he could hear Bat moaning in the call's background. "The bag hurts. Food is a trick on mammals. The bag is death, Scarly. Food is death."

"He doesn't want lunch," Scarly said. "But get him some anyway. Either he'll eat it and it'll kill him or he won't touch it and I'll just eat it myself. Where are you?"

"A place in the 1st I know. How about a cold sliced steak sub on fresh bread with a red onion marmalade they make with beer?"

"Hell yes. That sounds like real fucking food."

"Give me twenty minutes."

"Thanks, John."

"DEATH BAG," Bat howled in the distance.

John got out of the car, almost knocking down a tall, stringy man in a tan suede jacket and a guano-speckled bowler hat with three large turkey feathers sticking out of the makeshift duct-tape hatband. "Fucking filth," snarled the man. His teeth were the color of mud.

Tallow impassively badged him. "Te'bly sorry," said the man; he touched his fingers to the brim of his hat and shuffled on.

224

Tallow walked to the storefront. He'd read somewhere that in the Five Boroughs there were no fewer than four hundred thousand people reporting serious psychological distress, and God knew how many people on the street who didn't report to anyone and who slipped through the ragged net of the city's scarily named Division of Mental Hygiene and the myriad agencies it paid to supposedly get crazy people off the sidewalks and into the system. A lot of people got paid. Any idiot walking the 1st Precinct could tell you how few of them were actually doing the job. If you were crazy enough to store the guns you ritually prepared to kill people, then in New York City you could hide in plain sight. Tallow considered that for all he knew, the stringy man in the birdshit-spattered bowler could be his guy.

Inside the narrow store, there was a woman in a black, very architectural sort of jacket, turquoise jewelry, and unusual wedge-heeled boots that made her look like she was balancing on thick slices of gold. The two guys who ran the place, always in Williamsburg hipster uniforms of short-sleeved shirts and neatly trimmed beards that looked stuck on with spirit gum, paid, as ever, no attention to anything but the food and the money. Tallow imagined that every night they counted their money and prided themselves on having not made eye contact with anything human. New Agey synth music shot through with glitch and broken beats played softly from an iPod speaker station on the countertop.

The woman wore shades, and her hair was loose and framed her face, but Tallow could still see that she was pale. Not pale like the florist. This wasn't a woman who took in light. This was a woman who crumbled a little bit under it, whose skin was made dry and drawn by exposure to the world. Roll-on balm wasn't disguising bitten and blistered lips enough. He decided he was glad he couldn't see her eyes.

She paid cash, which was taken from a tooled leather cylinder held in the crook of her right arm, no bigger than it needed to be for a billfold, credit cards, phone, and car keys. As she turned, Tallow saw the brooch at her breast, a disc of rough animal hide on a gold mount, a gold image of an elk head in its center, framed by two gold feathers. She saw him looking, brushed it with compulsive fingers, false nails tapping on the gold, and left. He noticed her wedding band looked a little big on her finger.

"Three of the steak sandwiches, please."

"Coming up," said Beard Number One,

nodding to Beard Number Two, never once looking at Tallow. Together, they cut and smashed and wrapped the sandwiches in maybe twenty seconds. They'd gotten faster. Judging by the previous customer, Tallow thought word had really gotten around about the place. He imagined the pair training at night, listening to Animal Collective on repeat as they beat sandwiches into shape, racing against the same stopwatch they used to time their beard trimming.

Tallow paid his money, took his sandwiches under one arm, and heard the scream.

The woman in the black jacket was crouching on the sidewalk in front of the SUV and screaming as the man in the bowler hat stood over her waving his arms and wailing like a baby.

Tallow shifted the sandwiches to his left arm and shouted at the man in the hat to get his attention. The man turned and looked. Tallow very deliberately opened his jacket to show the man his gun. The man saw the gun. He stopped wailing.

"I just asked her for a light. She started crying. I figured crying was the thing to do today."

"Get out of here. I'm not making the offer twice."

227

The man ran down the street and away, clutching his hat with both hands.

Tallow sighed, looked around, and rested his sandwiches on the hood of the SUV. Good police never showed their guns unless they had to, he knew, but it was quick and easy and it worked. He'd bitch at himself later. The woman was rocking and sobbing now, wheezing, no air left in her lungs for screaming.

Tallow's empathy extended to reading a situation and not a hell of a lot farther. He had known that Bobby Tagg was in extreme distress and in the midst of a psychological break, but he very probably would not have been able to successfully extend comfort and calm to the man. Jim Rosato was a blunt object of a police, but people just naturally liked him better. It was why, Tallow thought, they'd made a good team.

Tallow had a sudden sour memory of the lieutenant suggesting that Tallow had been deluded about that.

He crouched down next to the woman. "It's okay, ma'am. I'm a police officer. He's gone. Can you tell me what happened?"

She folded her arms over her head and rocked, choking out the words "I thought it was him" over and over again.

Tallow said, "It's okay, ma'am," and

experimentally put his hand on her shoulder. She shrieked and jerked away with terrified revulsion, almost fell over, and started coughing as well as crying. Being strangled by her own throat muscles and fluids seemed to pull her out of the fugue. She wobbled on her haunches, those strange golden heels pushing around on the sidewalk for purchase. He touched her again, under her forearm this time, softly. She turned her gold-framed black shades to him, and she allowed him to gently guide and support her to a standing position. She started sobbing again, and fell into him. He put an alien arm around her somehow, and looked at the ground. Her cylindrical purse was on the sidewalk, unopened, next to her wrapped sandwich. He strained a bit and put out a foot to the purse, rolled it closer to him.

"I'm sorry," the woman said to his chest, sounding a million miles away.

"It's okay," he said.

"It's not," she said, scrabbling for an unconstricted breath. "He just asked me for a light. But I saw the, the feathers, and his clothes, and . . ." She broke into tears again, but the crying was cleaner now, more flowing, more purging. She was crying herself out, coming back to herself.

"What's your name, ma'am?"

"Emily." Her hands were shaking epileptically, and his arm was providing less emotional support than physical — he realized he was doing most of the work of holding her up.

"Let me get you sat down," he said, and shuffled her with difficulty toward his car. His spine popped as he reached down to unlock the driver-side door. He swung it open and lowered her sideways onto the seat.

"One second," he said, and swept up her purse and sandwich, reclaimed his own purchases, opened the rear door, and put his (and he had to ask himself, What was wrong with him that he was treating three sandwiches like fragile treasure?) precious food on top of the laptop bag. When he turned back to her, she'd fumbled her shades off and managed to stuff them in one pocket of her jacket. Emily did not have the eyes of someone who slept peacefully or often.

"Oh God," Emily croaked, "look at my hands." The veins on the backs were standing up like cables, and her hands were shaking so hard they almost blurred.

Tallow gave her her purse. She took it with difficulty, but held on to it. Tallow watched.

The shaking diminished, but it didn't go away. He hunkered down by her side, leaning on the car. "Can you take another shot at telling me what happened, Emily?"

He was oddly saddened to see deception crawl across her eyes like rainclouds.

"I, I don't really know," Emily said. "I haven't been, I guess, I haven't been well for a while. A, um, I'm not sure what you'd call it, an emotional problem, mental issues, I don't know, anything I say makes me sound crazy, right? Things just get on top of me sometimes. I get frightened easily, maybe? And that man. He just. Wrong moment."

She looked down at her brooch and plucked at it with hate, giving a laugh and a sob all in one horrible heartbroken sound. "And this stupid thing, it doesn't . . ."

She looked at him, and caught herself. ". . . doesn't matter."

Tallow indicated her purse. "You have your phone in there?"

She nodded, unzipped, and produced it. The phone was very new, a model he'd only read about: just a thin slice of flexible, scratchproof plastic with an artful streamer of antenna wire baked into the back.

"We get given prototypes by phone companies," Emily said, by way of explanation

231

or apology.

"What's your husband's name?" he asked, taking the phone.

"Jason. Jason Westover," she mumbled.

He opened the phone's contacts, found the name Jason, and pressed Call. The warmth of his hand activated something in the phone's structure, and it curled in his grip, taking on the curve of an old-style handset.

"Yes, Em, what is it," said a tired man's voice. Not a question; more a resigned statement.

"This is Detective Tallow, NYPD. Is this Mr. Westover?"

"Oh. Oh Christ."

"It's all right. Everything's okay. Am I speaking with Jason Westover?"

"Yes. Yes. I didn't —"

"It's all right, sir. I'm with your wife. She's had a bad scare, and I don't judge her fit to drive home safely. She's very shaken up. If you can let me know where you live and arrange to meet me there, I'd appreciate it."

"Oh. Oh, I see," Westover said. "Yes. Of course. Thank you. We live at the Aer Keep. I'll head home as soon as I can and meet you in the main foyer. What about the car?"

"It's locked and I have the keys. I realize it's inconvenient —"

"No, no, don't worry. I'll have someone come home with me, and I'll give them the keys and have them pick the car up. Where is it?"

Tallow gave him the address and listened to the scratching of Westover writing it down with a very sharp pencil on paper with a rich tooth.

"Thank you," Westover said. "Thank you for doing this. I'll start out for home now."

"We're heading to you. Thank you, sir," said Tallow, and ended the call.

Emily seemed more miserable. "Was he angry?"

"He was just glad you're safe. Now, can I get you to move over to the passenger seat? I'm not allowed to let you drive."

She almost smiled at that. But then, thought Tallow, it was only almost a joke. He helped her up, walked her around to the passenger seat, and installed her in it. Getting in the driver's seat and strapping in, he had a thought.

"I have to ask," Tallow said. "If you live in the Aer Keep, what were you doing all the way down here?"

She gestured at the storefront. "They have the best sandwiches," she said.

Tallow aimed the car uptown.

"It's really very kind of you to do this,"

Emily said.

"I couldn't leave you stranded down in the 1st, and I really didn't think driving was a good idea for you."

"The 1st?"

"1st Precinct. The NYPD breaks the city up into zones, precincts, and we're in the 1st Precinct right now."

"How funny," Emily said, without smiling. "Invisible walls for Wall Street."

"I suppose," Tallow said.

"Wall Street. Named for the wall the Dutch put up to keep the Native Americans out."

"You like history?" Tallow asked.

Emily went inside herself a little. "I've been doing a lot of reading in the past year or so. I don't really like coming down here. It's not far enough from Werpoes."

"Werpoes?"

"It was a major Native American village. Just by the Collect Pond. You can look at the little park there and almost imagine that you can see a bit of it. But I only went there once."

She was rubbing the brooch again, chin down on her collarbone and looking at it as if expecting a genie to rise out of it. No, sadder than that: as if knowing that, despite a story she'd been told, nothing was going to emanate from the device.

As they crossed Broadway, Emily asked, "Are we still in the 1st Precinct?"

"Just left it."

"This was an old Lenape walking trail. So one border of your 1st Precinct is the oldest road in Manhattan."

"Ghost maps," said Tallow to himself.

"What? Ghosts?" She sounded genuinely worried, eyes widening.

"Nothing," he said. "Thinking out loud. What made you interested in Native American history? Or is it just Native Americans in New York?"

Tallow couldn't tell if she was relaxing or coming apart again. She wasn't staring out of the windows as if expecting an attack on the car anymore, but her hands were trembling harder and her eyes were wet.

"Just something someone said to me once," she eventually said. "Did Jason sound very angry?"

"More like shocked."

"Don't look at me like that. He doesn't beat me or anything."

"I wasn't."

"Jason has a lot to deal with. More than anyone should. I don't like to make things worse for him."

"I see."

235

"No. No, you don't." Her eyes glittered at him like well water. "But you want to, don't you?"

Tallow had nothing to say to that. He kept his eyes on the road and continued to speed uptown. He could feel her look at him, and then look away, and then look back, as if keeping her eyes on him was safer than looking outside. Tallow started to feel like he should say something.

"Ghost maps," he said.

"What?"

"It's what I said to myself five minutes ago. You thought I said *ghosts*. Ghost maps. I had a meeting yesterday with a man who runs one of those big financial companies on Wall Street. You know, the kind you describe as a financial company but don't really have a clue what it is it actually does?"

Emily's smile was a ghost of its own. "I suppose it must seem like that," she said.

"Does to me. Anyhow. He was talking to me about how there's an invisible map of connections all over the financial district that do transactions at light speed, and how the map doesn't quite fit the territory? Something that's physically closer to the Exchange isn't necessarily . . . *information-ally* closer?"

"You're talking about low latency," Emily

236

said with a shade of surprise in her voice.

"I think so?"

"This was the sort of thing that was really taking hold as I was leaving the field," she said. "Ultra-low latency and algorithmic trading. Ultra-low latency means sending the trading information really, really fast. Algo trading is using specialized computer code to sort of break up every transaction into hundreds of little ones. You can almost think of it like rain, really hard rain hitting the windows of the Exchange. The rain's eventually going to form one big puddle, but you're not looking at that. You're looking at the rain. The big transaction's hidden in plain sight."

"You worked on Wall Street?"

"I worked for one of those mysterious financial companies. Vivicy."

"Never heard of it," said Tallow. "Why did you leave?"

"I met my husband there. Well, kind of. I met him through my boss. They were old friends. And after we were married, Jason said to me: Andy's kind of an asshole to work for, and the business is doing pretty good now, so why don't you work for yourself, like me? So now I'm an independent financial consultant, which means I can work from home with my dog and drive downtown for the good sandwiches instead of being one of Andy's wizards. I don't have to do the magic for him. But I can't learn the magic I need to know. *Fuck —*"

Emily started beating the dash with her fists, screaming *Fuck* over and over again. Tallow cast around with his eyes, twisted the wheel of the unit, and managed to pull over without causing a pileup. He reached across the seat and grabbed her wrists. She was still trying to punch the dash even in his grip. He yanked her arms toward himself and yelled, "Look at me!"

She jerked, and her eyes seemed to roll up into her head for a moment before they came back to his. "I'm sorry," she said in a small voice. "Please don't tell Jason. He worries so much."

"I've already told him all he needs to know. Anything else is between you and him."

"Yes," Emily said, but Tallow had the feeling that she meant something else. She sat back, and sat still, dread on her face.

Tallow pulled the car back out into traffic.

"Did Native Americans fish? Here in Manhattan, I mean," Tallow said.

Emily's eyes were closed now. "Yes, of course. They caught oysters too. When the Dutch came, they found huge mounds of discarded oyster shells and crushed them to pave —"

"— Pearl Street," Tallow said. "Right." He had the sudden strident sense of vast nets around him, so fine that they were invisible until the light caught them. He took out his phone.

"Scarly?"

"Lunch delivery is fail, Tallow."

"I know. I got into something, I'm going to be a little late. Listen. The paints. Every one of those guns was cleaned before it went up, but he must've put the paints on with his fingers. Before you do whatever it is to identify the paints, you've got to check them for DNA and anything else you can think of. Okay?"

"On it. Bring food."

"On it." Tallow killed the call with his thumb and checked Emily out of the corner of his eye to calculate her alertness. "Emily," he said, "do you know what Native Americans used for paints?"

She kept her eyes closed. "Ocher. Red ocher, around here, I think. It's mostly what you find on the East Coast. It's a clay-based pigment. They used it for all kinds of things, including body painting and staining their hair. Some people say that some of the first Native Americans to meet Europeans were

239

wearing it, and that that's where 'Red Indian' comes from."

Tallow knew his history. Not deep history, but certainly city history. He knew there had been mines all over the area. Staten Island, contrary to popular belief, wasn't built on landfill garbage. The Dutch had mines there early on. His mind was jumping around, looking for fingerholds.

"Anything else?" he said.

"Blue clay. Crushed clamshells for white. They'd sun-dry things, or burn them, to get the colors they wanted. Charcoal, obviously. Tree sap, berries. Why?" She opened her eyes and looked at him.

"Just keeping you talking," said Tallow. "You had a shock, after all. Where's your dog?"

"I have a dog walker for during the day. She took the dog out, I went for lunch. My husband walks the dog at night."

Emily seemed to be sliding into a state of . . . he wouldn't say emotionlessness, but certainly distance and apathy. Her voice came from somewhere deep inside her, somewhere dusty that was a long drive away from being present in the world. The same remote point that he had sometimes, in rare self-aware moments, heard his own voice coming from over the past few years.

The past two days had put Tallow back in the world. Two days ago, he would have pretended he wasn't police in order to safely walk past shrieking Emily and get in the car with his lunch. In the time before two days ago, he did everything differently. Which was to say, he did as little as possible. Cases got taken care of because nothing was hard.

He was back in the world, thinking energetically, engaged with people, and, he realized with a cold empty feeling in his gut, it was this that was making the scattered fragments of this awful, career-ending case slowly push together. His gut got icier and sicker as he kept thinking.

"So who was the man," Tallow said, quietly.

"What?" She was far away, and fear was suddenly spoiling the scenery out there.

"The homeless guy who scared you. Who did you think he was?"

"Nobody," Emily whispered, and turned her face from him.

Tallow steered into the Aer Keep. The front gate was a concrete checkpoint that wasn't shy about its Cold War look. Tallow showed his badge to the security guard there, noting that the woman was wearing the same Spearpoint insignia as the drones at Vivicy. The guard bent over and peered into his car. "Mrs. Westover," she said, "is everything okay?"

"Yes, Hannah, I'm fine. I felt ill, and this kind police officer said he'd drive me home. Is my husband here yet?"

"Yes, ma'am. Do you need anything? Should I send the building doctor up to your apartment?"

"I'm fine, Hannah, honestly. I probably just forgot to eat or something. But thank you."

The guard gave a smile that said she hoped she'd done enough because someone who controlled her employment would certainly be asking her that later, and the gate rose to accept the car into the Keep.

"You go down into the garage," said Emily. Tallow drove to the mouth of it, where it descended into the bowels of the Keep, and stopped. He wriggled his wallet out and took one of his cards from it. He slipped his notebook pen from his inside pocket and wrote his cell phone number on the card.

"Take this," he said, pressing it into her hand. "The number I just wrote down gets my cell phone, day or night. And I don't sleep much. If there's anything you ever want to tell me, anything that's ever worrying you, anything happening that you need help with, call that number. That number's

242

your new 911, okay? Even if you just want to talk about history. That number."

"Okay," she said. "Okay." She zipped the card into one of the peculiar vestibules of her jacket.

Tallow drove down into the island. It was lit down there, and Tallow thought of mines again. The roadway forked; he went right, which took them along a curve to the shining doors of the main foyer. There were more guards there, and one stepped to the car as Tallow got out.

"You can't park here, sir."

Tallow showed the man his badge. "Yeah, I can."

"Actually, sir . . ." he began, but Tallow was already walking around the car to let Emily out. The guard saw her; his features creased with frustration, and he was compliant in voice only. Tallow knew when someone was memorizing his face in order to do something medieval to him later, and the guard was taking a good long hostile look. Tallow gave Emily her purse and, with a smile, her sandwich. He took her elbow, gently, and guided her past the guard. Tallow took a good look at the guard too, and gave him a shark's dead-eyed smile, just for the hell of it.

The shimmering glass of the foyer front-

243

age slid open to accept Tallow and Emily. Just inside, a solid man a few inches shorter and a mile fitter than Tallow stood talking to an athletically slim younger man in a sleek black suit and a Bluetooth earpiece. Two steps into the foyer, Tallow saw the Spearpoint insignia on a discreet pin on the younger man's lapel.

Jason Westover greeted his wife with a warm, understanding "Car keys?"

Emily fumbled them out of her purse and passed them to Westover, who threw them to the younger man. The younger man nodded to Westover, discreet again in a small obsequiousness that stood in for the tug of a forelock, and left swiftly.

"You're Detective . . . Tallow," said Westover. Tallow's skin prickled. Something had just gone very wrong, and he wasn't sure what.

"That's right. And here's your wife, safe and sound."

"Of course," said Jason Westover, and reached a hand out for her. Not unlike someone who had just been informed that he'd left his cell phone on the table, Tallow thought. Westover was checking her over with the eyes of a man examining a bottle for leaks.

"Just curious, Mr. Westover. What business are you in?"

"I run Spearpoint Security. Founder and owner. Why?"

"Like I say, just curious. Lucky you could get away from the office on such short notice. But when you own the office, I suppose it's easier. Well, your wife's in one piece. Frankly, she's been terrific company, and it's been a pleasure to meet you both."

"You're very kind," Westover lied.

"I'm just glad I was there to help. Your wife had quite a shock, and I really was worried about the wisdom of her driving home afterward. I understand there's medical staff in the building? It couldn't hurt to have someone check her out. Shock can be nasty. It can sneak up on you."

"Yes," said Westover flatly, taking Emily's arm and turning away. "Well. Thank you, Detective. We appreciate it."

"Yes," said Emily, trying to keep her eyes on Tallow as she turned. "Thank you." He made sure she saw a smile on his face that said it was okay and turned to leave himself with a "Have a good day."

Tallow let the doors slide open so that the sound was in the air, but he stopped to watch Westover quickly guide his wife to the elevators. He was speaking tightly and insistently to her. Tallow saw the hand of her free arm twist into a fist.

Tallow went to his car. The guard was still standing by it. Tallow smiled again, and shook his head. "I was dropping off a resident," he said. "No reason to get uptight, okay? I'm heading out."

"We got laws in here," the guard said, straightening and expanding his chest.

"Laws?" said Tallow, laughing. "In here? You sound like this place isn't part of New York City, pal."

The guard, to Tallow's amazement, stepped to him. "It's not. Just happens to be standing on a piece of it. And it's my job to keep the laws in here. Pal."

Tallow stopped walking. The guard took another step toward him. "Listen," Tallow said, "you know what the difference between you and me is?"

"No difference," said the guard, "except that in here it's me telling you what the law is."

"No," said Tallow. "The difference is that sometimes you take off that shiny uniform with the Kevlar weave that some liar probably told you was bulletproof, and that great big gun that's never been fired at anything but a paper target, and you dress like a regular guy and take your days off and go out in the world like you're a normal person.

Right? I'm a New York City police officer. I don't live like a normal person. I don't take days off. Ever. So when you see me in the street, the way you've been dreaming of doing for the last five minutes, you think about that. You have a good long think about that before you ever take one step closer to me."

The guard took a step back.

"Enjoy the rest of your shift, sir," said Tallow, and he got in his car and drove away, as slowly as he could. He would never understand why everyone wanted to hand him whatever shit was in their baggage.

TWENTY-FOUR

Tallow turned the corner into Bat and Scarly's office to be greeted by a large plastic Japanese robot on the bench waving its arms and shouting, *"Say hello to my li'l frien',"* in an electronically processed voice as a small plastic penis repeatedly jabbed out from its groin on a short metal piston.

Bat emerged from behind the thing. "Don't judge me," he said. "I got bored."

"You don't have enough to do?" said Tallow, laying the three sandwiches on the bench beside the robot, which turned out to be wired into a flat cream-colored box sitting behind it.

"Hey, you never know when the future might need a giant Fuck You Robot wired to a hot-rodded motion detector. Also we got search results back on that ridiculous fucking flintlock."

"What did you get?"

"Did you bring food?"

"You hate food."

"The death bag has a mind of its own. Give me the food."

"It's on the bench. Talk to me."

"There's a reason why I set Fuck You Robot up."

"Talk to me or I will shoot you."

"Victim, Philip Thomas Lyman, resident of Rochester, New York. Funnily enough, he ran a security company, called Varangian. Worked out well for him then. He died in Midtown while on a business trip."

Tallow picked up one of the sandwiches and left the room, saying only, "I'll be downstairs."

Tallow paced around the emulation, eating his sandwich without tasting it, studying the fake room from outside, testing structures in his mind. Foundations of fact, scaffolding of speculation. Swapping out rods and plates, reassembling what he knew and what he suspected in different configurations. He finished the sandwich and tossed the wrapper, walking to the table. He pulled a couple of leaves off the tobacco plant, tore them up until the pieces were too small for his fingers to manipulate, and dropped them in the mortar. Tallow smashed the pieces with the pestle, hurriedly, still thinking, wanting to get this done. The oils released by the leaves tickled his nose. The scent wasn't right. He pushed the pieces out into the tin tray, tipped the tray, took his new lighter, and ignited them, waving and working the flame until the smashed green matter began to smoke.

He carried the tray over to the emulation and laid it down in the middle. The smoke rose. It climbed and twisted like a thin dark tree, and as it passed Tallow, he pushed curls of it up toward the ceiling with his fingertips, and he *knew.*

Tallow stood in the smoke, and inhaled it, and the scent was close to right, close to the dominant note he'd detected in the apartment on Pearl, and he slowly pivoted around and saw the guns wrapping around the room, forming shapes and partings for future shapes but wrapping, turning, revolving, and flowing around the apartment walls and over the floors.

Tallow knew that he'd met the man who'd fired all these guns.

"What are you doing, John?" asked Scarly. Again, he hadn't heard the elevator, and it felt like a warning: Be in the world. Don't get caught.

"Thinking," he said. "What have you got?"

"The paint. Pain in the ass, you are. The

white paint seems to be crushed clamshell and egg. Where the hell do you get clamshells to crush up for caveman paint?"

"Any dumpster on Mulberry Street. And it's not caveman paint. Anything else?"

"Clay. Blackberry juice, for the purple. That kind of thing."

"DNA?"

"I'm at least a day away from knowing that. And of course it's caveman paint."

"It's Native American paint. Our man thinks he's a Native American. Or wants to be a Native American."

"How do you figure that?"

"All this. And more. And also I met him."

Scarly stepped into the emulation. "What did you just say?"

"I think I met him. Yesterday. He was standing opposite the Pearl building when I went there to take another look at the scene. ECT wasn't there, it was a shift break, and the follow-up team was late. He bummed a smoke off me. Talked to me about Native American things. About tobacco, and smoke. It was him. The reason I was late back with the food is that I met a woman who I think is sort of sideways connected to the whole thing. Homeless guy walks past with feathers in his hat like a comedy Indian, she freaks out, and I hear her say, at

251

least once, 'I thought it was him.' "

"John, if you met this guy, seriously, he could have killed you. Hell, I don't know why he *didn't* kill you."

"You don't see it yet, Scarly? He couldn't kill me. He didn't have the right weapon. Look at all this. All this is the evidence of a man who matches his weapons to his kills according to some compulsive, insane logic. He killed a guy running a rent-a-cop agency in Rochester with the gun that committed the first murder in Rochester. We have his cache. He didn't expect to meet me on the street. He didn't have the right weapon to kill me."

"That's a hell of a guess."

"It feels right."

"I mean about the weapon." Scarly scowled. "He might have just decided you were an animal or an obstruction and knifed you."

Tallow sucked a stray strand of onion out of his left back teeth. "You are a little ray of sunshine, Scarly."

"You want to get with a sketch artist? Try a digital composite?"

"You're the one who called him a ghost. No. We have to hope he left some DNA in the paint." Tallow took another scan of the emulation. "This is about ghosts. And maps.

I'm going to need a map. A big-ass map of Lower Manhattan. And some more books."

"Is this working for you?" said Scarly, taking her own turn around the room.

"It's helping."

"I wish I'd seen the real place."

"Me too. You might have been able to identify some of the scents, if nothing else. And I still don't know how that door worked."

Scarly stepped to the photographs of the rear of the apartment's front door. "Yeah," she said. "Bat looked at these. He thought he might be able to puzzle it out if he could see it properly but that the photos didn't have enough information." She looked back at Tallow, eyes narrowed. "You really think you met the guy?"

"I really do."

"Fuck. Don't tell anyone else, all right? You don't want to be the guy who talked to his suspect and let the asshole walk."

"No," said Tallow, bumping back to ground level with a chill shudder. "No, I guess I don't."

Scarly walked past him to the elevator, punching his arm as she went. "Fucking correct."

"Thanks for having my back."

"You're all right, John. Also, you bring

253

good food. Even if it was a little late. Come on. We'll collect my pet retard from his robot-fondling session and you can drive us over to Pearl Street. We can take a look at that door. That is some high-end security shit, and if nothing else, *I'd* like to know how it works."

The words *high-end security* echoed in Tallow's head. One of the invisible supports in the last arrangement he'd conjured got a little more substantial.

They went to collect Bat, who was hunched over the bench looking at some paperwork and hugging himself.

"We got some more ballistics processing back. John, do you know of a guy called Delmore Tenn?"

"Del Tenn?" said Tallow. "Sure. He was once assistant chief for Manhattan South. Years back. There was some accident, he pensioned out . . . I want to say his kid got killed? Something like that. The poor bastard fell apart."

"Yeah," said Bat, not taking his eyes off the paper. "Stray bullet from a gang fire-fight. His daughter was shot through the head. But they never found the gun."

"Oh no," said Tallow.

"A Kimber Aegis handgun. There was

some weird rifling on it, like someone had been fucking around with the barrel. Would have been a snap to match bullet to gun. If they'd ever found the gun."

"Oh Jesus."

"You know what the worst thing is?" Bat said, his voice getting muted and flat. "The kid's name was Kimberly. No one would have thought twice about it at the time. Would have made a sick joke, at most. Kim getting killed by a Kimber."

Tallow didn't have anything to say.

Bat wrapped his arms tighter around his body. "What the hell are we into? What's fucking happening?"

Scarly walked around him to rescue a light coat that had slumped by the bench. "We're going to take a look at the apartment on Pearl."

Bat wanted to protest, or perhaps explain, but he visibly lost the energy for it even as he opened his mouth. Instead, he got up, went to a set of drawers with a wobbly column of paper and files balanced atop it, opened the second drawer, and took out a holstered gun. He silently clipped the holster onto his belt, picked up a grimy field bag from behind the bench, and then shouldered past Scarly and Tallow on his way to the elevator.

Scarly watched him go and then, mouth set in a little line, went to the top drawer, pulled out a holstered gun, and clipped it to her belt. She shrugged her thin coat on, arched an eyebrow at Tallow as if daring him to say something, and walked past him toward the elevators.

Tallow lifted and reseated his own gun.

"You didn't tell me to bring a fucking shovel," Bat said.

"Just get in the back of the fucking car," Scarly said.

"I would, but I didn't bring any fucking ropes. Seriously, John, how does your rear fender not just scrape along the fucking street?"

"Bat, just . . . I don't know, just give it all a shove."

"What if there's a landslide? I might never be seen again. Jesus, what *is* all this stuff?"

Tallow ran a hand through his hair. "You people work in the Collyer brothers' toilet, and you give me trouble about this? Push it all to one side. Get in."

"The Collyer who?"

"Ride in the back or ride in the trunk, Bat."

"Okay, okay. But I'm telling you, I think I see the Dead Sea Scrolls at the bottom of this, and I'm only getting in here because I'm afraid of what's in the trunk."

Scarly got in the front passenger seat, which was almost as strange to Tallow as the persistent weirdness of being in the driver's seat. "Who were the Collyer brothers?" she asked.

"Langley and Homer Collyer. First half of the twentieth century. Two hermits in Harlem, lived on the far-ass end of Fifth Avenue."

Tallow began navigating the car out of One PP.

"Weirdness ran in the family. Their father used to paddle a canoe to work, down the East River to Roosevelt Island. Somewhere around 1925, pop disappeared, mom died, and the two brothers were left this house. The locals thought they were eccentric and wealthy and started sniffing around the house, snooping, maybe trying to pop a window or two. But the Collyers didn't actually have a pot to piss in and were kind of crazy to boot. So they boarded up the windows, set up mantraps, and only went out at night. They'd sneak out, find stuff that looked useful or interesting or capable of being turned into a trap or weapon, and drag it home. Which is, you know, not a hell of a lot different from your office, except you get that stuff delivered."

"So this is what fills your car?" said a hunched Bat from the back, looking like the world's ugliest bit of origami. "Obscure New York history? Anyway. That doesn't sound so bad. I'd love to do nothing but collect shit all day."

Tallow gave a small dry laugh. "So in 1947, the whole block is suffused by this awful stench. The only people who aren't out complaining about it are the Collyers. So eventually people go in. And discover that every piece of trash that dropped on that block in the last twenty years was picked up and stored by the Collyers. A hundred and thirty tons of it. Twenty-five thousand books, fourteen pianos, most of a car, bits of people, uncountable newspapers and boxes. You could get around in there only through tunnels and crawl spaces. Homer Collyer was found dead of a heart attack brought on by starvation. His eyes had hemorrhaged out fifteen years earlier, and he had been completely paralyzed by untreated rheumatism. Langley Collyer was found in one of the tunnels. It looked like he'd been transporting food to Homer when he'd tripped one of his own traps and been crushed to death by a weighted suitcase and three massive bales of newspaper. He was actually the source of the stench. Blind old Homer had taken another week to die."

"Presumably wondering where his brother had gotten to with lunch," said Scarly. "This is why you need to call people when you're carrying sandwiches and taking a detour, John."

"Bits of people?" said Bat.

"Human organs in jars, stuff like that. Their father was a doctor, but he was ob-gyn. So I'm guessing it wasn't all heirlooms. Oh, and, of course, they also found a large cache of guns and ammunition. Had to knock the whole house down in the end."

"That'll be what our guy's second apartment looks like," said Bat, trying to get his knees out from under his chin.

"What?"

"Well, he wasn't sleeping in three A, was he? And he's not going to be sleeping on the streets. He's got a second apartment, and when we find it, it'll be full of gun magazines and clippings and shit. This guy knows his weapons and is at the very least capable of research. Otherwise he wouldn't have found out about the Rochester thing. Hell, he wouldn't have known anything about Son of Sam."

"The Native American thing," Scarly commented.

"Doesn't matter," said Bat. "The guy might think he's Geronimo or whatever, but he can't escape the evidence of his own eyes a hundred percent of the time. The asshole's too functional for that. Even the man who thought his wife was a hat knew where he was. Even if he's as nuts as he can possibly be on this side of the functional line — and that's, like, even if he spends six hours a day making little war bonnets for his own turds and sends them out into Central Park to attack Custer — then he's still aware of being in the modern world and he's going to study it in order to use it properly."

A bicycle courier darted alongside the car, trying to get his nose on the best angle of attack for the Brooklyn Bridge. Tallow tapped his brakes to let the cyclist go on ahead. He didn't acknowledge Tallow, but Tallow hadn't really done it for him.

"He checks his modern history," said Tallow, after thought, "but he doesn't live it. I know my modern city history, but he lives in deep history. I didn't see him, and he didn't see me, because we're moving through two different cities."

"When did you have time to get high today?" said Scarly. "And also, why didn't you smoke us out too? I thought you'd adopted us. Bastard."

"He didn't see you?" Bat said warily. "That means he *did* see you, right? You've *seen* the guy?"

"He *thinks* so," said Scarly, quickly. "And we're keeping that to ourselves."

To curtail further conversation on that subject for the moment, Tallow snapped on the police radio. All at once, horror tumbled out of it.

A ten-year-old boy shot dead in the South Bronx. The related chatter said the three assailants had been trying to hit his father. The father had been pushing a stroller. The baby inside was dead, preserved and painted, with packs of heroin inside its gutted stomach.

An elderly couple in Queens found dead execution style in their own bed. Someone had stood on the bed and fired down into their heads as they slept. There was fresh semen spattered over the entry wounds. Their son was missing.

One man hacked to death with a sharp spade by his neighbor in Brooklyn, reportedly the conclusion of an argument over a borrowed barbecue grill. The victim had been fixing his car at the time of the attack.

A building worker pulled off a nurse in a barroom toilet in Hell's Kitchen. The nurse might make it, said the responding cop, but the cop's own partner might have lost an eye.

One cop down in Briarwood, following the explosive discovery that a small restaurant was holding weapons and at least a kilo of coke in the back. They were stepping on the coke right there in the kitchen and sending out wraps with their food deliveries.

"Fucking hell," Scarly said.

The serial rapist that some wits were calling One Man One Jar had hit Park Slope again in the early morning. He completed his assaults by inserting a glass jar or bottle into the victim's vagina and then breaking it. Tension in the voices of police: nobody saw anything, nobody knew anything, nobody gave a shit. . . .

Someone had thrown a container of battery acid and ammonia in the face of a Port Authority cop, out by where Twelfth Avenue met Joe DiMaggio Highway. Attending officers were retching as they talked about how the man's face had basically turned into warm string cheese and stuck to his own shoulders and chest.

According to eyewitnesses, a man attempted to rob a Chase bank on Fifth Avenue by East Twenty-Seventh, then declared that he was a "disintegrating angel," went outside, shot a passing postal worker, pressed his gun into his own eye, loudly stated, "Disneyland was shitty too," and pulled the trigger.

"Man had a point," said Bat. "*Sesame Street* used to give me nightmares too. That thing that lived in the garbage can? I swear it was that that made me want to be police."

Tallow studied Bat in the rearview mirror for additional signs of mental illness. "You're kidding me."

"The thing lived in a garbage can, ate shit, and verbally abused people. How many crimes do you want? Turn that goddamn thing off. It's depressing."

"I like it," said Tallow. "You know, there was once a website that played ambient music under the LAPD radio band. I used to try that in the car, with a CD player. It was nice."

"Are you even allowed to have CD players in units?" Scarly asked.

"Not really. It's why my partner ripped it out. That and he didn't like the music. I wouldn't let him put a satellite radio in so he could listen to his retarded talk shows, so we called it even and just listened to the police band. Like I say, I got to like it. Flows of information."

"Flows of shit," muttered Bat. "I'd go insane, listening to that all day. It's just a river of 'Hey, this crazy disgusting thing just happened, and hey, here's another one, and another, and another, has your brain caught fire yet?' It's like disaster porn or something."

Tallow had to admit, if only to himself, that things did sound worse than yesterday. He shrugged it off as he brought the car in for a landing behind the ECT truck on Pearl Street. Getting out, he had to look around to see if there was a man in a heavy suede coat standing in wait nearby. When he'd assured himself there wasn't, he led the two CSUs toward the building.

The doors banged open before Tallow could reach them, and the two ECTs he'd met yesterday bumped and humped and bitched their way on to the sidewalk with their two-wheeled handcart piled with stackable plastic boxes. "Asshole," said one to Tallow.

"Nice to see you again too," Tallow said. "What's this? Lunch break or shift break?"

"Neither. We're out."

"This is our last load," said the other. "Our expertise has been redeployed to some other fucking location. Our expertise being wiping CSU's asses."

Tallow shot a look that tagged both Bat and Scarly, and it said *Do not.* They showed their teeth like ill-trained dogs being told not to eat the neighbor's baby. Tallow twisted back toward the ECTs, who were shoving their boxes into the rear of the truck.

"We're not done here," said Tallow.

"Oh," said the first, "we are utterly fucking done here. We got our orders. Why them orders weren't given two days ago when we started moving your little collection, I do not fucking know. But someone has seen the light, and we are freed."

The second was already getting into the driver's seat. "And you are screwed. But we don't care. What kind of asshole drops that kind of shit on the New York Police Department?"

"Your kind," said the first, pointing his finger at Tallow and stepping into the truck's passenger seat.

They drove off.

"What the hell is going on?" Scarly said.

Tallow took out his phone. "I don't know," he said, "but my boss can at least find out."

While he was placing the call, another truck pulled into the space vacated by the ECT vehicle. Tallow looked at it, registered what he was looking at, and canceled the call. The truck bore the Spearpoint logo on the side.

Tallow, in a taut voice, quickly said, "You let me do the talking. You do not say a word." They caught his tone, nodded, and stepped back.

The driver got out, an athletic woman in a Spearpoint uniform who had cropped hair and a rippled scar down one side of her neck that she did nothing to hide. She wore a strange, brutal-looking gun in a metal holster frame, one that was machined to release the weapon with a glide despite the odd fittings slung under the barrel. She glanced at Tallow as she started toward the back of the truck. "Please move along, sir," she said, not unpleasantly.

Tallow badged her. "Not just yet. Can I help you with something?"

"Oh!" she said, with a smile. "Yes! We're here to process a crime scene at this building here?"

"Really," said Tallow.

"Really," said the other Spearpoint employee as he got out of the passenger side, a man under six feet in height who very probably knew the names of most of the muscles in his body. He made the simple act of blinking look like he was burning hated fat cells. "There a problem here, Officer?"

Tallow saw that they were both wearing ruggedized touchscreen devices on their belts, Bluetooth earpieces, and odd touch-screen strips pinned to their chests where name tapes would usually have been.

"Detective," said Tallow. "And you know what? I don't know yet. I'm used to crime scenes being processed by the Crime Scene Unit and Evidence Collection Teams. So how about you tell me how you came to be here, and we'll work things out from there?"

The guy opened the back doors of the truck, clearly bothered on some base level that he wasn't allowed to rip them clean off and then eat them. "Our boss told us to show up here and collect the crap in apartment three A."

The woman had clearly decided to run defense, and she actually put herself between Tallow and her partner, even though Tallow hadn't moved. "Our boss called your boss, I guess. Everyone knows CSU's overstretched, right? That's why you created ECTs, and now ECTs are overstretched. Especially with a job like this one, from what we hear about it. So our boss called your boss and offered the use of . . . well, us."

"Well," said Tallow, "that's an incredibly kind thing to do. But we have processes we follow in a crime scene that are a bit more complicated than 'collect the crap,' which is

267

why this sort of thing isn't outsourced."

"We're trained," said the man, lifting out a black kit bag. "That's why the office sent us. We've completed courses and gotten certificates. Hell, we've probably got more on the ball than your CSUs. You know what those people are like."

Tallow did move, then, to put himself between the Spearpoint people and his CSUs. "I'm going to need to know who your boss spoke to."

She looked at her partner, sucking her teeth. He put down a complex chrome dolly, looked back, and shrugged.

"Okay," she said, and tapped the right end of the glass strip on her breast. She dipped her head, touched a finger to her earpiece, and said, "Ops, please."

"Oh my God," breathed Bat. "She has a Star Trek comm badge."

"No, she doesn't," said Tallow. "There were similar things being tested for use in hospitals a few years back, with voice control but a more basic technology set. I read about it in a magazine. We're just looking at the more up-to-date version."

"I want one," said Bat.

"You can take it off her corpse once I'm done with her," Scarly hissed.

"Behave yourselves," Tallow whispered.

The woman finished a short conversation and gestured at Tallow. "We've been cleared to operate through a Captain Waters at the 1st Precinct?"

Tallow swallowed the groan the name elicited, took a breath, and summoned a smiling mask. "That's my boss's boss. We'll head up to the apartment with you. Not," he said with his hands up, "to keep an eye on you. We were here to review the scene again."

She smiled with some relief and, on some impulse of reaching for a friend, stuck out her hand. "Cool. I'm Sophie."

He shook her hand, matching the strength of her grip closely. "I'm John. These are my colleagues Scarlatta and Bat."

"Bat?" She grinned at the CSU, who was studying her chest for technological purposes. "What's that short for?"

"Batmobile," he said.

"Behave yourself, damn it," said Tallow, moving to open the apartment building doors.

Sophie began to pick up the kit bag and grimaced. "Jesus, Mike. Did you put your car in here?"

"Hey, it's not my problem if you don't train as hard as I do."

Sophie lifted the kit bag. Watching her,

269

Tallow realized that although it was not too heavy for her, Tallow himself wouldn't have been able to get it off the sidewalk. Mike loaded collapsed plastic boxes onto the dolly, and Tallow held the doors open for them.

"Mike," said Mike, not looking at Tallow.

"John," Tallow said. "Nice gun."

Mike stopped as he got into the building's hallway and reappraised Tallow. "You noticed that, huh?"

"I did. I don't recognize the make or the fittings."

"You wouldn't, pal. These are made only for Spearpoint."

"You have custom guns?" said Scarly, interested despite herself.

Mike enjoyed noticing Scarly. "Sure. You want to see?"

"Mike," Sophie warned.

"Just being friendly," said Mike, standing the dolly up and drawing the weird gun.

"It's a SIG?" Scarly said, uncertain, bobbing up and down to consider the thing from different angles.

"SIG Sauer X911. Made exclusively for Spearpoint. See, it's badged on top and on the grip there. And check out the grips. That's African blackwood. That shit's so hard they have to machine it with tungsten

270

carbide. And tungsten carbide, *that's* the shit they use for mining drills."

"But what's that you've got slung under the barrel, on the rail?"

"Camera. When I clear the safety? The camera switches on, and it streams video back to the local Spearpoint ops room. And I swing this section around, and see? Switches on when it reaches the upright, and that's a night-vision screen right in front of the sights. The camera, it knows when it's dark, and switches to night vision all on its own. Laser sight in the front top there, see?"

"Jesus. This is insane. But doesn't all this make the thing nose-heavy?"

"All superlight materials. If anything, it helps the accuracy. I tell you, I've seen a new model being tested? A prototype? Fires rocket bullets."

"You're kidding me. Like the old Gyro-jet?"

"I dunno about that. But I've seen this baby being test-fired, and it's recoilless. Fires a .50-cal rocket bullet with no recoil."

"When you're done showing off the toys," said Sophie, trying to ignore that Bat was standing very close to her.

"I would very much like to marry your chest," Bat said.

"Bat. Back off. Now," snapped Tallow. And then, to Sophie, "He means your communications devices. Bat likes electronics."

"It's still not very appropriate," Sophie said, stepping away from Bat.

"He's a CSU," said Tallow with a smile that wasn't the evil smile he was smiling inside. "What can you do? You know what they're like." Tallow regretted his second of immature relish when he saw her mortified face. She'd tried to be civil to him, and he'd stepped on her. Tallow wished, not for the first time, that he was better with people. He'd never really had to be before he'd been to this place. He discovered then that he hated this building, this airless space with its sheen of human grime.

"Where's the elevator?" Mike asked, sheathing his weapon. Tallow felt a little better about telling Mike there wasn't an elevator and watching his face. But then Mike picked up the dolly, boxes and all, with one hand, took the kit bag from Sophie with the other, and started jogging up the stairs with "Third floor, right?"

"There," said Scarly, "goes a man who has names for all his muscles."

"I was just thinking that," Tallow said. "Serious gym rat."

"No, I mean he's named all his muscles.

272

That's a man who calls one of his muscles Steve."

Tallow waved Sophie on, saying, "After you," and then he grasped Bat firmly by the collar as he tried to follow. "Get it under control, Bat."

"I just want to touch her groin. Where the belt device is."

"I will touch you in the groin with my gun if you don't secure your shit, Bat," Tallow said, more quietly. "I want both of you to watch their every single move. Make like *they're* the crime scene."

"Do we get to complain yet?" Scarly said.

"When we get up there. But it's not like you're complaining, okay? It's like you're asking questions, learning their process, wondering if their clever company has good ideas. With me?"

"Okay, John."

The pair from Spearpoint were looking through the hole in the wall at 3A.

"Goddamn," Mike said, pulling off the fresh police tape. "This looks like it might be two trips."

"So," said Scarly, "what's your procedure, Mike? I mean, once you've processed the guns at the scene and loaded them up. You going to drive them straight over to me at One Police Plaza? We have good coffee."

"Nah," said Mike, hands on his knees, bent over and looking into the room. "Too late in the day. We're going to warehouse them tonight and drive them over tomorrow."

"You're going to . . ." Scarly began. Tallow put a hand on her shoulder. She brushed it off, but she knew what it meant. ". . . All right. I'm just going to say, that does put more links in the chain of evidence, which means more paperwork for you guys. It'd be a lot easier to drive everything right over to One PP."

"We have people to do paperwork," Mike commented absently.

"You have to remember," Sophie said, uncollapsing a plastic box, "that we're a lot more deeply staffed than you. Spearpoint's capitalized to the extent that we can do a job like this for the city pro bono."

"You're not billing the city?" Tallow said, genuinely surprised.

"Why would we? Bad business."

"I would have thought not getting paid was bad business," Bat said, failing to ingratiate himself by unfolding another box for Sophie.

"That's not how it works. You don't crush your competitors by charging more. You undercut, you make yourself useful, then

274

indispensable, and then you offer just one extra service for a little more money. And then another. And then another. And before the mark knows it, she's giving you all her money and all your competitors are dead."

Sophie realized what she was saying and gave an apologetic smile. "I know how that sounds, and I'm sorry. But private policing is the way of the future. It's not like there aren't already private police here, after all. Big Six Towers Public Safety in Queens. Co-Op City DPS in the Bronx."

"Aer Keep," Tallow said.

"Aer Keep! That's us, you know."

"Really."

"Yeah. So Spearpoint trains us in evidence collection, and crowd control, and that kind of thing. You know. Police work. Because it just makes far more sense for us to do it. And, you know, we're totally accountable, in ways you aren't. I mean, we can be sued for failure to provide services. You can't."

"So that's how Spearpoint became a big deal? It just killed all its competitors one by one?"

"I'm just saying," said Sophie, "that it's the way things are done. And it's the way of the future. Public services just don't have the budgets, you know? Look at this." She pointed to her belt device. "This thing here?

Because of this, Ops knows where I am at any time. It's got a biometric lock, so it only works for me. It's got environmental sensors. It's reading my vital signs. It's listening to the general area for spikes in the noise level. I'm on the Spearpoint net, and I'm on the Spearpoint map."

"The Spearpoint map," Tallow repeated.

"Sure. It's like . . . here I am, present in the city. But I'm also a point on a map that's overlaid on that. Our map. We get all the traffic data. All our people and units are moving points on the map. We have safe areas all over the city; they're not publicly signposted, so you can see them only if they're on the Spearpoint map. We have webcam take that ties into the map, through that . . . what's it called, Mike?"

"Ambient Security," Mike muttered from inside 3A.

"Right. Ambient Security. For some token fee, store owners get a sticker in their windows that says something like 'This Property Secured by Spearpoint,' and a webcam with a wi-fi memory card in it. And what it shoots, we call the take. The take gets beamed back to our servers and skimmed by an algorithm reader, which is a piece of software that's maybe as smart as a puppy. It sits up and barks when something

276

really unusual happens in its field of vision. But what's important is that Spearpoint has live cameras all over Manhattan, just sitting behind storefront windows and sending us everything they see. You couldn't do that."

"Of course we couldn't do that," said Bat. "That's your actual Big Brother shit."

"Maybe, if it's imposed by the state. But in this case it's a side effect of a transaction for property security. Protection."

Bat snorted. "Protection racket? But no. The property security is a side effect of getting your own private camera system laid out all over New York."

"What the fuck?" Mike said.

Tallow stepped into the apartment ahead of the others to find Mike with his fists on his hips, looking at the back of the apartment's front door. Enough of the guns in the area had been lifted by the ECTs that Tallow didn't have to tiptoe or stretch to get there now. "Yeah, I said something similar," Tallow said to Mike. "Any idea how the thing works? It's got me baffled."

"Sure," Mike said. "It's one of ours. How the hell did it get on here?"

Tallow had been feeling sick ever since he'd met these two. Now his gut was nothing but ice and acid. "Wait. You're telling me that this is a Spearpoint security system?"

"Sure as hell looks like it. Sophie."

Sophie was already there, standing behind them. "Yeah. I think that's the Spartan Wave, the seven version? Couple of years old. Very high end."

Mike was about as pensive as Tallow presumed he ever got, searching his memory with a degree of manual labor. "Sure. I saw one being installed one time. Some banker guy. We were putting one of these on the back of the door to his panic room."

"Tell me how it works," said Bat flatly from the other side of the door.

Mike rubbed some dust from the device. Scarly, in Tallow's peripheral vision, flinched.

"It's a magic-card system. What we've done is taken the original door here, and gutted it. Steel core, electric strikes —"

"I don't know what those are," said Tallow.

"Rods that push out from inside the door into the door frame and lock," Mike said. "And other stuff, but the important thing is there's a long-life battery in here that feeds a low-energy sensor. Where your skinny guy is, there, you stand there and wave your key card like a magic wand; the sensor feels it and wakes up the door. Power goes to the magnets and motors, and the door unlocks."

"So the card has a power source too?"

"Yeah, but it's like, you seen those sneakers kids wear with the flashing lights in the heels? They run on power harvested from running around. Same thing with the card. Wave it around a bit, and it makes enough juice to work the card and open the door. Without the magic wand? No one's getting in this apartment. You could fire a rocket launcher at this door and it'd still be giving you the finger when the smoke cleared."

"Magnets," said Bat. Tallow stepped away and looked out the hole to see Bat scrabbling around in his field bag, a worn credit card between his teeth. He came up with an old round tobacco tin that he'd done something to. Metal strips and wires were wrapped all around the tin. He opened it and produced a black metal puck with some occult electronics glued to the back. Bat pushed a little red-painted switch on it, and passed the puck from the left edge of the door to the middle. There was a clacking sound. He made several more passes, on both sides and at the top and bottom. Bat then put the deactivated puck back in its tin and put his credit card to the side of the door by the original lock. Within ten seconds, the door popped open.

"What the fuck," said Mike.

Bat stood in the open door and said, "I am a Crime Scene Unit detective from the New York City Police Department, you heinous fucking mongoloid, and there is nothing I cannot do."

"I think it's time to leave," said Tallow. "It was nice to meet you," he said to the Spearpoint people, and he went directly to the staircase, not looking at the place on the wall where everything in his friend Jim Rosato's head had splattered and slid.

Tallow didn't break step until he reached the car. The CSUs were ten seconds behind him, seething. "Get in," Tallow said. "I'll run you back to One PP. And then I'm going to see my lieutenant."

"You need to see your *captain,* apparently," Scarly growled.

"No. I need my lieutenant to handle the captain. Get in."

They got in. Tallow stamped on the gas. Scarly and Bat exchanged an awkward glance, but neither of them asked Tallow what the hurry was. Instead, Bat said, "How fucked are we? On a scale of one to ten?"

Tallow bit back his first response and chewed it over a bit. "I was going to say thirteen. But, honestly, we might have been at thirteen even before someone threw our evidence collection to the wolves. I've got nothing but connections I can't prove because, hey, there's no proof. We don't even know when our guy's most recent kill was. Profilers would laugh themselves sick at anything I had to say to them right now."

Looking in the rearview mirror, Tallow could see Bat fiddling with his tablet device and his wi-fi pod.

"Hey, Bat, you asked the question. At least listen."

"I am listening. Keep going."

Tallow found that he didn't have much farther to go down that road. "So unless you can get some DNA out of that paint, or the next set of processed guns gives us a kill from last week, the evidence isn't going to put us anywhere useful for a while yet. No. Let me add to that. Unless the guns give us some more kills that could paint in the picture a bit."

"Do you still want to talk to someone at the Property Office?" Scarly asked.

"My lieutenant wants to work through channels on that. But right now, it's enough just to know that he has a connection with it. Did you get to smell the air in the apartment, by the way?"

"Got a little bit distracted there, John,"

Bat said.

"Yeah, I figured," Tallow said. "Damn it."

"I wonder if anyone from Spearpoint had a little accident in the last couple of years," Scarly said, slowly. "Maybe an installation guy."

"Oh hell," Tallow managed to grit out. "You're absolutely right."

"So maybe our guy met a Spearpoint installation technician in a bar and said, Hey, for cash in hand and a hefty tip, maybe you could help me out. And a security door just kind of fell out of their depot into the installation guy's van, and on a quiet afternoon, or a Sunday, he put the door in. But the thing is, the installation guy will have seen our guy. Like the Property Office cop will have seen our guy. And that cop's dead."

"Varangian Security," said Bat from the back. "Founded in Rochester, New York, by Phil Lyman twenty-some years ago, providing private security services in the tristate area, its expansion curtailed by the tragic death of the charismatic Lyman in blah-blah-blah . . . bought out by and subsumed into Spearpoint Security two years later."

"What?" said Tallow.

"What what? I'm reading this off Wikipedia. Your tablet screen's fucked, by the way. It's like trying to read through a film of old semen. Anyway. Just working the evidence we've got, you know? Embracing the crazy."

Tallow stopped at an intersection. A bus rattled past, the digital ad down its side glittering. Apparently there was another musical based on an old Disney movie opening on Broadway. An animation flicked across the hexels: the prettiest, whitest "Indian" princess you ever saw, attending to the feathers in her hair before looking over her shoulder at Tallow, smiling, and winking.

Tallow drove on.

"While you've got the tablet on, Bat, look up *Werpoes* for me."

Bat clicked away. Tutted to himself. "Fucking autocorrect. *Wempus?* How d'you spell that?"

"God, I don't know. She said *Werpoes.* W-e-r—"

"Wait," said Bat. "Wait. Shit. Pull over."

"What?"

"Pull the fuck over."

"Damn it, Bat . . ." Tallow checked his mirrors and pulled to the roadside within an awkward twenty seconds.

Bat leaned forward and thrust the tablet device in front of Tallow and Scarly. He'd pulled from the web an image of beadwork of some kind, a broad strip of shell art featuring odd patterns and shapes and the occasional rippled angle.

"It's called wampum," said Bat. "Wampum belts."

"Oh fuck," said Scarly, seeing it immediately.

"It says the Native Americans wove these things out of beads to codify history and law, to mark social events, transmit information . . . they made them here in Manhattan, before the Europeans came. And when they did come, they saw how the natives prized the wampum and began manufacturing it themselves, as money." Bat tapped the screen with a jagged fingernail. "These things were art and book and device. John, wampum belts were *memory.*"

Tallow rubbed his eyes. Looked at the photo of the wampum belt again. He could see the similarities. The photographed belt of beads was finer work, and swirls were harder to execute . . . but then, whoever had woven this belt wasn't crazy. The similarities were striking. Their killer had turned the entire apartment into a memory machine, using guns.

They were both looking at him.

"All right," Tallow said. "We know why he did it now. His motivation beyond totem phase. It's one more piece of information. But it's not a case. Let's get you two back to One PP. I told you before — it's CSU that'll solve this thing. And so far I've been right."

"You are a lazy asshole, John," Scarly said, but she was grinning.

TWENTY-FIVE

Police-channel flow on the drive from One Police Plaza to Ericsson Place:

A dead man found folded into a suitcase that was left in the back of an empty building in Williamsbridge. First guess was that he'd been in there three months.

A dead woman found in front of St. Brigid's in the East Village. Police on scene commenting that they didn't know what she'd been drinking, but she appeared to have no stomach.

A dead man found in a Bronx apartment, stabbed to death within the past week, forensics complicated due to the corpse having been partially devoured by rats and a small pet dog.

An unknown individual blew him- or herself up at the Bushwick Inlet. One other fatality: the individual's arm had somehow been launched laterally at ballistic speeds, went through a parked rig's window, and broke its driver's neck.

Tallow killed the radio. He'd taken a slight detour on the way back to Ericsson Place, up Fulton, and now he wanted to concentrate. Driving slowly, he looked at the building frontages across the street from the Fetch.

There was a ripple of fear in his chest as he saw the PROTECTED BY SPEARPOINT SECURITY sticker on the window glass of a cheap shoe store not quite directly opposite the Fetch.

Tallow peered and calculated. The shoe store did not face the side of the Fetch that had the alley adjacent. There was a good chance that any clever camera located in that store window had not seen a thing.

He also noted that there was no police tape across the mouth of the alley, nor were there any notices to potential witnesses posted nearby.

Tallow drove on, well aware that his luck had been tested again.

His cell phone rang just as he was parking at Ericsson Place, and he fumbled it over the wheel trying to do two things at once when his mind was already in seven places at the same time. Tallow managed to keep the phone at his ear on the third try.

"Hello?"

"Detective?"

"Mrs. Westover?"

"Yes." Emily Westover gave a little laugh that disturbed him. "I just wanted to thank you again. You know, for looking after me."

Tallow listened to the ambience of the call. She was in her apartment. Her voice had that deadened quality that came with thick glazing, the kind that silenced the outside city and absorbed interior sound. There was music of a sort, playing in another room. Native American chants, he realized, but the authenticity was off. It was one of those nineties records, where ethnic audio sources were put to muted beats and electronic chill-out washes.

"You're very welcome, Mrs. Westover. Is there anything I can do for you?"

"Don't go to Werpoes," she said in a rush.

"What? Why would I?" Tallow said, thinking, *Let's see.*

"It's, it's just not safe. I worry that maybe I made you think about it."

"Your husband went back to work?"

"Yes. He doesn't know I'm calling you. I suppose he might when he gets the phone records, you know, the itemized billing. But I'm calling to thank you."

"Mrs. Westover, I meant to ask earlier.

That brooch on your jacket. What is it?"

"It's an elk symbol. It's . . . do you promise not to laugh?"

"I promise," he said, letting her hear the smile in his voice.

"It's protective. Protective magic. In Native American medicine, the elk protects you from the unknown."

Tallow felt a sudden crest of deep pity for Emily Westover. That brooch must have cost her five hundred dollars. She probably had a stack of CDs and a drive full of MP3s that were no more Native American than the pap she was playing right now. He couldn't help but think of Vivicy, of the mysterious wizards Machen hired but understood not at all, of the office that spoke of money without the basic grasp of aesthetic and arrangement that nature bestowed on even the common rat, and of the music that evoked some prefab heaven whose furnishers shopped at off-brand stores.

So there she was, living in a fiction, her wealth buying her nothing but pretty fakes, locked in a glass castle where all the guards worked for her husband.

"I see," he said. "Mrs. Westover, why don't you tell me what you're really worried about?"

She was trying to tell him, in her damaged way, that she knew. She had somehow found out that Westover and the killer were connected, and she was unable to do anything with that knowledge. It broke her. All she could do was learn as much as possible about what little she'd found out. She'd tried to learn about Native Americans. The sum of her achievement was that she was now scared of everything.

She gave that broken-glass laugh again. "The things I'm really worried about. Good God, Detective, I could be on this call all day. But then I think, you know, what do I have to be worried about? I'm surrounded by everyone I know. It's just that sometimes it feels like, well, I'm surrounded by everyone I know. If you know what I mean. I say that a lot. I worry that people don't always know what I mean, these days. I don't think I speak as clearly as I used to. Or think as clearly. But that's hard, because life was always simpler before, and there just weren't as many things to think about. It's like, walking through the city, on sidewalks, you only have to think about one thing at a time. But if you're walking a deep forest trail, you have to think about three or four things at the same time —"

"I've never walked a deep forest trail," said

Tallow. "Do you get to the countryside much?"

"I wish people could see what I meant," Emily said, sounding wistful. Her mood seemed to Tallow to be changing by the moment, and her voice was all but doing the scales. He thought of Bobby Tagg and clamped his lips shut against a surge of bile.

"We all say it, don't we?" she said. "We say, 'I see what you mean,' it's the metaphor for clarity. But sometimes I wish people could see the pictures in my head, instead of my having to describe them with words. Words are clumsy. I wish I could communicate in pictures."

"Like wampum belts," Tallow tried, experimentally.

"I just wanted a friend who didn't report to my fucking husband!" she screamed, and killed the call.

Tallow looked at the phone for a moment, debating whether or not to call her back, apologize for whatever he said or did wrong. He convinced himself that pretty much anything could have set her off. He'd think about it later. Her number was logged in his phone, and he added the number to a contact page and saved it.

The main office was full of people, none of

whom would look at Tallow as he entered. The lieutenant's office had all its blinds down. Tallow stood in front of his lieutenant's office door, and knocked.

"I said this was a private meeting."

"I wasn't here for that, ma'am. Sorry."

"Tallow? Is that you?"

"Yes, ma'am."

"Come in, please."

Tallow opened the door, feeling the eyes of the people in the outer office on his back. It was apparently safe for them to look at him when he couldn't look at them.

"You're awfully polite for a maverick cop on the edge, Detective," said the captain with a smile, putting out a fragile hand. His fingers seemed to move in the wind like brittle, vine-choked branches.

"The only thing I'm on the edge of is dinner hour, sir. Hello."

"John doesn't do the rulebook-chewing-mad-dog-cop thing so well," said the lieutenant from her desk chair. "Honestly? He's far too lazy for that."

"You're lucky I know she's joking," said the other man in the room. That man did not extend his hand. He seemed to be expecting something.

"Assistant Chief," Tallow said, offering his hand.

Assistant chief Allen Turkel was the commanding officer of Manhattan South, with ten precincts under his oversight, including the 1st. His two stars were very well polished. So well polished, in fact, that it looked to Tallow like he'd had to retouch the gold.

"Detective," the assistant chief said, with the barest incline of a nod and a weak, cursory shake. Tallow had the impression the man was holding out for a salute. He had the posture of a man who regularly sucked his stomach in. "I imagine you're here to talk to your lieutenant about your charming apartment on Pearl Street."

"Among other things, sir, yes."

Two plastic chairs were out, for the captain and the assistant chief. There wasn't a third one. They returned to their chairs. Tallow chose to stand with his back to the closed door, a position that had him facing their profiles. He clasped his hands behind him, reading the room.

The assistant chief chose to address the lieutenant. "You have a very smart lieutenant here, you know that, Detective? Smartest lieutenant of detectives in my whole borough. I like to think that one day she's going to be working with me at One PP. And then I think, *Why would I take my smart-*

*est lieutenant out of the line where she's do-
ing the most good?"*

He laughed. The lieutenant chuckled. Something like the sound of dry twigs snapping came out of the captain's mouth. The assistant chief's intended meaning escaped nobody. He checked his watch while everyone else dutifully faked amusement. Tallow eyed the watch. It looked like a Hublot, a Swiss device in brushed rose gold, and a bezel and dial in black ceramics, decorated in screws, grilles, and pistons that evoked the 1920s science-fiction constructivist aesthetic of the film *Metropolis*. The strap was black rubber. It wasn't a policeman's watch. It was a fetish object. Tallow had read that Hublots now came with electronic security cards so that you could prove on the Internet that you owned them.

"I appreciate that, sir," the lieutenant said. "And I appreciate you coming all the way over here personally. You didn't have to do that."

Tallow didn't smile at the well-planted stroke, but he wanted to.

"Oh, I did, I did," the assistant chief proudly faux protested. "It's my borough. It's my call. I just felt you were entitled to a direct explanation about all this."

"Well, thank you."

"Oh, no need, no need. I mean, you know, Charlie here" — indicating the captain — "knows that I'll give you anything you need to get a job done. But we also have to be attentive to the way of the future. And a case like this one — oh, yes, yes, Charlie, I know it's a nightmare — we have to be attentive to resources. Evidence Collection Teams were a good idea, and they help balance the load, but a case like this one completely knocks that out of whack."

The captain looked, to Tallow's eye, simply too weak to talk. He was only ten years older than Turkel, but he had thirty-five years on the job to Turkel's twenty-five, and the past ten had evidently bled the man in ways Tallow had never learned of. It was left to the lieutenant to negotiate the land-mines Turkel had scattered.

"None of us ever expected that ECTs would be tested like this, of course," she said. "And I'm not averse, in principle, to the idea of us receiving help from the public sector. I would like to know how the chain of evidence is going to work, sir."

"Oh, no need, no need. Just think of it as adding an extra link or two to the chain. I've known Jason Westover a long, long time. He really does understand our needs in this."

Tallow prickled.

"And he is . . . ?" asked the lieutenant.

"The founder and CEO of Spearpoint Security. We go way back." The assistant chief said it in that dismissive, it's-nothing way that meant it was not to be dismissed and that it was in fact very important for everyone to know he knew wealthy and impressive people.

"I met Jason Westover earlier today," said Tallow.

To Tallow, in that second, it seemed very much like ghost bombs were hanging from invisible threads above the room: like the cascade of circumstance had guided him into a trap when all the while he'd believed he was slogging his way toward the light. Like the hopeful sunrise at the end of all this turning out to be the glow of burning bodies and a house on fire.

"Really?" said the assistant chief, with a half-raised eyebrow of feigned half interest. Tallow could read the man. He was very interested.

"Yes. And his wife."

"Oh, yes, yes, Emily. She hasn't been well recently. I'm hoping it wasn't, um, a professional . . . ?"

"Not really a subject for the room, sir."

Turkel's face lit up. "Right. Yes. Thank you."

"So," said Tallow, "I have two people from Spearpoint literally loading my evidence into boxes and intending to drive it all to one of their storage facilities in two trips."

"They told you that?" the lieutenant said, wincing a little.

"Yes, ma'am. Right after they explained to me that the very elaborate security mechanism on the apartment's door came from Spearpoint."

"What?"

"That's right, ma'am. Which, in an ideal world, would lead us to sales and installation data at Spearpoint that would put a name on our man. But this is the real world, and I fully expect CSU to eventually match a gun from the cache to a dead Spearpoint employee who used to take on side jobs for cash. Just like we found a dead man from the Property Office when we looked for an explanation of how Son of Sam's handgun was in the cache."

Tallow discovered that the captain was looking at him, the expression on the man's face difficult to decipher. "What was your name again, Detective?"

"Tallow, sir."

"No. Your full name."

"John Tallow, sir."

"John Tallow. Okay. Carry on."

Tallow had no idea what that was about. "Well, I don't have a lot more to say, right at this moment. The assistant chief obviously couldn't know that the kind offer from his friend came from the same company that fitted the locks to our man's door. Perhaps that doesn't even matter. That said, the same company that had a security system walk out of its depot and affix itself to the door of a presumed serial killer is intending to look after almost all of our evidence overnight."

"Detective," warned the lieutenant.

The captain stirred himself. "I think John's just laying out the obvious concerns here, Lieutenant."

"Yes," said Turkel. "Well. It was a very kind offer from a company that wants to help serve this city and a police department already overstressed by case management. I don't think we can throw that kind of offer away on the strength of could-bes."

Turkel stood, adding, "The pursuit of this entire case is somewhat quixotic, in any event."

That escaped nobody.

Tallow decided to trip a trap and see what fell.

"By the way, Lieutenant," Tallow said mildly, "we got another ballistics match. Our man killed Assistant Chief Tenn's daughter."

The current assistant chief stopped moving.

The captain blinked slowly, like a lizard taking in the sun, and opened yellowish eyes on Tallow. "Del Tenn's kid?"

"That's right, sir."

"That was a stray bullet from a gang firefight."

"No, sir," Tallow said, speaking to the captain but daring to look directly at the assistant chief. "We have the gun in the Pearl Street cache. Our man simply waited for the most opportune time to make the hit. Gunfire, chaos. He hid his kill amid all the others. Just like every other kill he's made."

"Damn," the captain mused, sagging into himself in the chair. "You know what I liked about Del Tenn? He said to me once, Everyone tells me I can keep getting promoted and keep getting promoted till finally I'm not doing a job at all. I guard the south of Manhattan, where I was born and where my father was born. Why would I want another job?"

"I didn't know him," said the lieutenant.

"Lovely guy," said the captain. "Went to

pieces when his little girl was lost. At the funeral he said to me that it was like Manhattan had betrayed him. Never saw him again."

"Yes," said the assistant chief. "Well."

Tallow gave him an amiable smile without letting him off the cold hook of his gaze. "Quixotic, sir, yes. But as you can see, we're putting together a picture of our man. The way he works."

"Yes," said the assistant chief. "Well."

"The sort of people he deals with."

"Yes," said the assistant chief.

"Did you know Assistant Chief Tenn, sir?"

"No, Detective. Well. Not well. Marcus Casson took over from Tenn, and I took over from Casson."

"Yes, that's right," said the captain quietly, as if speaking from a distant cave. "Casson moved on to Transit as a bureau chief. After Beverly Garza died."

The threads of the net, thought Tallow, *are so fine as to be invisible, until the light catches them.*

"How did she die, Captain?"

"If you'll excuse me," the assistant chief said. Tallow was still standing in front of the door.

"I'm sorry, sir?"

"If you'll excuse me," he repeated, "I have

300

to get back to my office."

"Oh," said Tallow. "Yes, sir. You have to get back to work." He took a step to the side and opened the door for Turkel. "Thank you for coming over and explaining things to us. Very kind of you. I think we all know where we stand now."

Assistant Chief Turkel gave Tallow a hard look. Tallow saw a man without empathy. He'd heard of it, could fake it when he needed to, but felt nothing for anything himself. He looked at Tallow as if Tallow were a dead animal on the side of the road.

"You're working this case on your own, yes?"

"Yes," said Tallow.

"Shouldn't you be mandatorily off the street?"

"I was told we didn't really have the resources for that, sir. The whole system's out of whack, after all. So I was put where I'll do the most good."

"Perhaps," the assistant chief said, and left. Tallow closed the door.

"John Tallow," said the captain, "I did not know that you were a smart man."

"Jury's out on that," said the lieutenant.

The captain laughed a whispery laugh, standing with difficulty. "You know," he said, "if you'd been a smart man all this time, I would have heard about you. But I'll tell you a thing. When I was a detective, I was partnered with a smart lady. Very smart. So smart that she got promoted, up the chain and away from me. My next partner, God love him, he was so stupid that the squad room had to make up new words to describe him. It was like I didn't have a partner at all. And it was at that point, John Tallow, that I finally began to learn how to be police. You were probably a smart boy when you were assigned here. But I have a feeling that only just now did you start becoming a smart man."

The captain moved to the door, with some visible pain. Tallow opened it for him. The captain looked at him levelly.

"I can't cover your ass, John. I will leave this room and go back to approving the requisition of paper clips or some damned thing. Being the captain of the 1st doesn't even make me the most important office-supplies manager in the area. That'll be some Master of the Universe down on Wall Street. I've got no juice with anyone and a bunch of senior staff just waiting for me to cardiac out on the crapper one morning. I can see where you're taking this. All I'm going to say to you is, you better damn well *have* it."

Tallow said, "Captain, how did Beverly Garza die?"

The captain smiled, very thinly. "She was run down. Hell of a thing for the chief of Transit, right? But I'll tell you something. The pathologist swore up and down that he'd found gunshot residue on what was left of her head. Like someone shot her and then drove over her. CSU even turned up a mashed bullet on the scene. Nothing ever came of it, mind."

"Did you know her well?"

"Because I remember it so well, you mean? No. It stuck in my head because of that bullet. A .357, fired from a restored single-action revolver. The old night-shift boss at CSU, it was his personal project for six months. I remember it because he came up with the weirdest match. He thought it came from a Pinkerton pistol. The kind the railroad police used in the 1800s. But the old boss at CSU, he really wanted to come up with something. Now him, he was close to Beverly. Not me. I'm not close to anyone. Never was."

The captain left, no energy left for an acknowledgment to the lieutenant.

"Close the door, John," she said. He did.

"Sit down, John," she said.

"I'd rather stand."

"Sit down."

"You have really shitty chairs, Lieutenant."

She burst out laughing. "What did you just say to me?"

"Seriously. They hurt my ass. That's why you got them. So no one stays in your office too long."

"You incredible asshole," she said, still laughing. "How did you even . . . ?"

"The first time I had to sit on one for more than five minutes. It took the rest of the day for my backside to turn the right way out again."

"Are you waiting for me to fetch you a nice soft pillow, Detective?"

Tallow sat.

"Where *are* you going with this? Exactly how much more trouble have you made for me today?"

"Not as much as I think I just made for myself."

"Oh, the assistant chief made it pretty clear that he's going to look for ways to fuck you, yeah."

"That's actually not what I'm worried about," he said, and then paused. Tallow measured the fabric of his case in his head, and cut off the section he intended to show her. She didn't need to see the whole thing yet, he decided, and in fact, it might be counterproductive.

"Okay," he said, taking a breath. "By the end of today, with a little luck, I'll have more evidence to back up the idea that Spearpoint Security has an involvement in these killings."

"You said their security door on the apartment was probably a fluke."

"Probably. However, our man killed one of Spearpoint's competitors. Maybe that's a fluke too. But I bet you, I bet you the price of a nice ass cushion for this chair, that the assistant chief is on his cell right now, calling his good friend Jason Westover. And kindhearted Jason Westover will be wondering how quickly he can contact our man."

The lieutenant folded her arms. "You have no evidence that Westover knows our guy."

"No," Tallow agreed. "What I have is Spearpoint appearing in the conversation around the case too many times. What I have are too many questions. Why is this company Vivicy buying the building? Westover met his wife through Vivicy. His wife has a fixation with Native American culture, to the point where she freaks out in the street when she sees a homeless man looking like the worst-dressed Indian tracker in the cheapest Western you ever saw on TV at two in the morning. Our man has a fixation with Native American culture. I . . ."

Tallow stopped for a moment, looking for the words under the lieutenant's gaze. He then said, "Things hide in rain."

"I don't follow."

"Sometimes the rain is so heavy that we look up at all the raindrops when we should be looking at the shape of the puddle that forms from them. All of this has been rain. It's been rain for twenty years, and everyone was looking at the raindrops falling while all of these people have been moving invisibly. They weren't even traveling through streets we'd recognize. And the rain was so heavy, all over the city, that no one ever looked down and saw the footprints filling with water. I'm starting to see the shape of them now. I just need to be able to see the maps."

"Put your feet back on the ground for me, John."

Tallow ran his fingers through his hair. "Nothing is coincidence. We've walked right into a net, like a woodland mantrap. If our man had tossed his gun in the river after every kill, we would never have known a thing. I think our man is a directed killer. *Hired* may not be the right term. And he is so good, *so* good, that one or all of the people who directed him knew that his unsolved kills would eventually be sub-sumed in the annual unsolved count in an incredibly dense and crime-heavy metro-politan location. They knew that, so long as no one blundered into their very fine net, the whole operation would be invisible. The only thing we had on our side, it turned out, was that the killer was crazy and kept all his guns."

"Why? I want to know why he kept all those guns. Is it just some weird serial-killer-trophy thing?"

"Not to him. That apartment is visual language, the codification of a statement in pictures. Exactly what statement, I don't know, that's in his head. But when we've been taking guns out of there to process? We've been unweaving his life's work. Like unpainting a masterpiece or unpicking a tapestry."

"John. Seriously. How much closer are we to finding this guy? Because the captain just told you he can't cover for you, I sure as hell can't cover for you, and the assistant chief knows he has a way to pull you off the case and put you in your apartment for the rest of your life. And I'll be honest with you, I've thought about that more than once myself. If the assistant chief thinks he can make this whole thing go away — and you can be damn sure he's thinking about that, very hard — then he will. So I need a call from you. You've got no DNA, no nothing but some circumstantial tangle, a handful of processed guns, and some brilliant, fascinating, but mostly crazy-ass speculation. Tell me. How much closer are we to finding him?"

John Tallow closed his eyes, and took a breath.

"Probably not as close as he is to finding me, Lieutenant."

TWENTY-SIX

The hunter watched from the rooftop on the corner. The military man had a cursory glance around the block, and then went back inside Kutkha's place.

The auto repair shop across the street closed for a late lunch. The hunter found the access alley behind the hardware store, walked around the block, broke into the auto repair shop, and took a few things they wouldn't immediately miss, including a jacket and a ball cap that had been stuffed into a bag at the back. They stank of machine guts, but he wanted to be less obvious in his comings and goings over the next few hours, so he put them on in order to walk his wrapped spoils back to the hardware store.

In the cool shade of the abandoned store, the hunter began to make tools.

He carefully twisted long lengths of twine together and set them to soak in the can of gasoline he'd taken from the auto shop.

The dead thing was nothing but raw material now. The hunter cut many thin slices of its clothing off, having looked at it and determined there were plenty of polymers in the weave of its orange suit. The hunter soaked the strips in its blood. Once they were sodden, the hunter stuffed them into two of the three empty water bottles he'd found in the store's back room, along with the handful of Styrofoam packing beans he'd gathered from the floor.

The hunter couldn't find a decent hacksaw in the place, and it might have made too much noise in any case. He crept around the house in search of the weakest-looking copper pipes and spent patient minutes prying two of them from the walls as quietly as possible. He spent a short while grinding the tip of a bolt, and then used it to punch breathing holes down the lengths of both pipes. He then fed a length of twine down each of the pipes. He had to keep himself aware of the passage of time. This kind of work warmed and entranced him so wonderfully that he could have lost days to it. The preparation of tools was beautiful to him, even improvised tools such as these. The tying of a knot around a nut was an act of devotion and a preservation of sacred

310

crafts as much as the creation of a prayer tie from tobacco leaves. He mixed gasoline with the blood and fabric and Styrofoam, and looped the free end of the twine around the far end of the pipe so as not to lose it when he dropped the knotted end of the twine into the bottle.

He pushed three or four inches of the near end of the pipe into the bottle and made a seal with duct tape lifted from the auto shop. One end of the twine was inside the bottle, weighted by its nut; the other was still looped around the end of the pipe. He repeated the process with the second bottle.

He hefted one of his copper spears experimentally. The length was good. He then searched for things to weight the standing ends of the bottles, to give more predictability to the lift.

The front door of Kutkha's property was still a problem. Having weighted the bottles to his liking, the hunter prowled the building for more ingredients.

He came across an old broom, its shaft splintered, its imitation-horsehair brush balding and brittle. It solved a problem farther down his list. He slowly split it all the way in half — he didn't want the crack of breaking it sharply — and with his knife began to feather the top end of the wood into tinder as he walked the empty building.

Within ten minutes, the hunter had found a half-empty hand-sanitizer dispenser, a mostly full bottle of drain cleaner, a folded tube of strong glue, and a disposable lighter that looked to have five millimeters of butane in the bottom. The hunter took off his gloves and squirted a tiny drop of the sanitizer onto a fingertip. He sniffed it, and then rubbed it swiftly with his thumb. Alcohol based. Heaven alone knew what the attendant scent was supposed to be, he thought sourly. He knew he had a scattering of nails and pins downstairs. He took his knife again and dug into the walls of the room he was in until he found the lighting circuit's wiring and pulled several feet of it free of the plaster.

Downstairs, he put his tinder down and took up the gun he'd removed from the dead thing on the floor. It was a version of a Beretta 92, some newer iteration that he hadn't seen. It was a little lighter in his hand than he had been expecting given the make. Some parts were plastic, he saw on closer inspection. Unmistakably a Beretta 92, though, nine-millimeter and workmanlike. The slide was strong and smooth. He extracted the gun's magazine and pulled a bullet from it. The hunter sliced the top off the third bottle, poured the dregs of the gasoline can into it, unscrewed the dispenser arm from the hand sanitizer, and squirted that on top of the gasoline. He went foraging for nails. To his great pleasure, ten minutes' diligence saw him collect a substantial number of aluminum clout nails. In the bottle they went.

As the dead thing stiffened and then softened on the other side of the room, the hunter worked with his knife on the bullet and the wiring and other things, and his heart grew light.

It was late afternoon before he had completed his construction to his satisfaction. The hunter then turned, methodically, to the preparation of tinder. Moving as quietly as he could, he broke up the particleboard display stand and began to arrange its pieces. He feathered and shaved more tinder, ensuring he could easily reach it even as he began to gather more wood to it.

It would make a grand fire. A fire that would cook the dead thing down to a pile of black sticks, with the remains of its polyester clothes melted over them.

The hunter stopped then, took his last piece of squirrel meat, and took his time chewing it, considering every angle of what he had done and what he was going to do.

The sun came low. The hunter stood his weapons by the back door and went up to the roof to look around and wait. He had a reasonably good view from the rooftop at the corner of the block. He knew how to reach the side road and Kutkha's backyard from the hardware store's access alley.

The sun ticked down. The street grew silent.

The military man opened the front door, threw out two garbage sacks, and closed the door again with an audible click.

The hunter moved.

Five minutes later, and acutely aware of the passage of time, the hunter was unseen at the front door of Kutkha's property, pushing a nail into the wooden footboard of the front door, kicking a garbage sack — *What a gift!* he thought — in front of the door, and lowering a filled water bottle containing improvised partitions onto the bag. He extended the wires that hung out of the bottle and wound the end of one of them around the nail in the lower door frame. He pushed in another nail next to the door lock, wound the other wire around that, checked his work, and moved quickly away.

In the dark of the hardware store, the

hunter struck sparks. The pyre around the dead thing caught immediately. He took more tinder out of the back door with him in one of the small storage trays. Outside, he heard a car. The hunter stopped moving and listened, intently. He heard the car move down the access road, turn, negotiate the passage into the backyard, and stop.

The hunter struck sparks into his tinder and got fire. He lit the tips of the soaked twine where they stuck out of the ends of the two pipes and slid through the door in the fence that separated him from the access road. With five steps he remained out of sight of the backyard but had a clear line of sight to the rear of Kutkha's building.

He hefted his first spear and hurled it over the fence and through a third-floor window. He snatched up the second while the first was in flight, calculated a correction and the extra force, and flung the spear through a fifth-floor window. He could see little flickers of light through the breathing holes down the spears as the gasoline-soaked wicks burned toward the bottles. There was a flat report from the third floor, like a giant striking the ground with a cupped hand. Homemade napalm — clotted blood, plastics, and gasoline — erupted, and he was rewarded with shrieks from the third floor.

A fifth-floor window blew out as the second napalm bomb went off.

The hunter drew the Beretta and moved into the backyard.

There was a large seven-seater car parked there. The hunter made out the small faces of four small people in the rear of the vehicle, and saw that the doors were locked. Two men stood by the left wing of the car, their backs to the hunter.

He shot the first through the back of the neck. The bullet careened around the man's face and tore through the right joint of his jaw as it exited, so that the lower jaw swung around as if on a hinge toward the hunter.

He shot the second through the back of the head and heard the smack of a chunk of brain the size of a baby's hand hit the wall of the building.

Kutkha had a briefcase in his hands. Behind him was the idiot boy. Beside him was the military man, already moving for a concealed weapon.

The hunter shot the military man through the forehead. For a long second, the man refused to die. His eyes flashed with outrage. He opened his mouth as if to speak his mind at the intrusion, and half a pint of bright red blood fell out of it. His legs gave way and he fell to the ground in a coiling motion, like a clubbed snake.

The hunter snapped his gun down and shot Kutkha in the groin, accurately castrating him. He shoved the screaming Russian away and shot the boy twice in the brain, smiling as he told himself the second shot was in case he missed the brain the first time.

The third and fifth floors of the building were now fully ablaze. The shrieking had one or two voices fewer in it.

The hunter moved quickly to the heavy back door of the building, resting the gun in his left jacket pocket — it was too hot to push into his waistband now. He took a handful of short wires from his right pocket and pushed them roughly into the lock. He shot the last of the tube of epoxy glue into the lock after them, filling it as best he could. He drew his gun again and waited for thirty seconds, keeping one eye on the screaming, bucking Kutkha.

Someone inside tried to open the back door. But he couldn't get it to unlock. He heard scrabbling. Then nothing.

The hunter moved to Kutkha and stood on his neck as he picked up the briefcase. It was unlocked. Inside was money and, in two plastic bags, the Police Service and twenty-four rounds. The Police Service was a curiously lovely weapon. He stroked it through its plastic. It would serve wonderfully. It was the perfect tool for the next job.

He decided to take a brick of banknotes too. They had their uses.

"Why?" Kutkha gurgled. "Why? We do *business.*"

"I regret that, in this instance, I cannot allow myself to have been seen, Kutkha."

There was a loud explosion. Someone had opened the front door to the building, actuating the hunter's improvised explosive device. Drain-cleaning fluid had mixed with aluminum nails, alcohol gel, some water, and a little gasoline, lit by black powder and butane. The hunter did wish he could have seen this one. The fireball, and the hot rush of unburned caustic gas, the flaming gel, and the hail of burning nails. It must have been beautiful, the bloom in the evening shade. The garbage sacks would be burning now too. No one was getting out of the building.

Kutkha was crawling to the military man's corpse. Kutkha would have known where that one carried his gun. The hunter put his foot back on Kutkha. Kutkha sobbed, desperately. "We are the same blood! My tribesmen walked to America and became your tribesmen! We are the same!"

318

"No," said the hunter. "No, we're not."

He shot Kutkha in the back of the head. The angle was off. The top of Kutkha's head came away, and the damp matter inside the case jolted out onto the ground and skittered nine or ten inches away like a sea creature.

The hunter realized he was being watched. Four pairs of bright eyes inside the car.

The hunter sighed, drew his knife, and cut two swatches off of Kutkha's absurd shorts. He walked back into the access road and retrieved his tinder tray. The tinder was still burning, the plastic of the tray blackening and bubbling.

He carried it to the car, opened the fuel cap, fed the two strips of fabric into it, and lit them with the tinder. He tossed the tinder tray and the Beretta under the car and walked away, refusing to perceive the little fists hammering on the car's window glass, the muffled voices, the eyes.

The hunter was most of the way down the access road when the car went up. The hardware store was already burning. There were sirens, but they would not be here in time. They never were.

He walked to the shore, and sat by the water, and watched the Great Kill glisten in

the dark as the houses of his enemies
burned at his back.

TWENTY-SEVEN

Tallow drove his unit out of Ericsson Place, bone weary, abstractly disappointed, and feeling a lot less anchored than he'd let on to the lieutenant. He had no evidence. Just a theory that got wider and more sprawling and ungainly and borderline insane as the days went on. He tried to focus on one thing — other than his driving — and settled on the moments in which he thought he met the man who lived in apartment 3A. Tallow tried to summon up every detail of his experience of the man. The color of his hair and beard. His scent. His body language. The way he took the cigarette from Tallow. The way he pinched off the filter and put the filter in his pocket.

"The bastard," Tallow muttered to himself. It may have just been the act of a man who disliked a filter on his tobacco. But, Tallow thought, wouldn't it have been nice to go back and pick that filter up, with a nice clean print on the treated paper that covered it.

Tallow swerved, mounted the sidewalk with one wheel, stamped on the brake, and very narrowly avoided causing a pile-up. He didn't even hear the chorus of car horns Dopplering past him.

The man pulled off the filter. But he smoked the damn cigarette. He had to have left a butt. As careful as he might have been with the filter, he couldn't have just pinched off the burning end and pocketed the cigarette butt too. Could he? No. He didn't smell strongly. That would have stank, in his pocket, and Tallow didn't make him as the kind of man who'd want you to smell him coming. He had to have crushed out the butt. Or tossed it and hoped it'd burn out.

It was a wild and stupid hope.

Tallow rejoined the traffic and pushed hard for Pearl Street.

He parked across the street from the tenement. He pulled gloves, a ziplock bag, and a tweezers from the glove compartment. He stood where he had stood when he met the man. He looked around, and thought, furiously. He'd walked away before the man had finished his smoke. He shifted his feet into the position he believed the man had occupied. Put his hand in his jacket pocket, to simulate keeping the filter. The tweezers acted as his cigarette. He pushed imaginary smoke up from the burning end, as the man had.

He pretended he was finishing the smoke. The cigarette was burning down toward his fingers. That day, Tallow had already crushed his out. Tallow looked in the gutter. There were three butts scattered there among a few dead leaves, a little crushed glass, a penny, and a small potato chip bag, each butt crumpled and twisted by multiple encounters with things much bigger than itself. They all had their filters on. Tallow crouched and looked. One of them was the brand he had been smoking.

Tallow looked around, scanning for places he might jam a cigarette butt into without burning his fingers.

No.

He crouched to the gutter again. Picked up the potato chip bag.

Tallow looked up at the sky, took a deep breath, and quelled the shaking in his fingers.

Over sickeningly slow seconds, disappointment like a snake in his gut waiting to bite through his heart, he untwisted and peeled open the bag. Someone had taken it out of the gutter, folded it, tied it into a knot, stamped on it to make it look more naturally smashed, and tossed it back on the road to be ignored, run over, and swept up.

There was a cigarette butt in the middle of the knot.

Tallow laughed.

He extracted the butt, dropped it into the ziplock, and sealed it. Tallow returned to the car with it and the potato chip bag, which he awkwardly inserted into another ziplock when he got inside.

All I want, Tallow said to him, *is proof that you're not invisible too.*

Moving through the main lobby of One Police Plaza, Tallow, still in a mode of hyperfocused noticing, picked up bad air. People were looking at him for the first time since the case had begun bringing him to the place. Tallow picked up his pace, laptop bag in hand, and walked to the farthest elevator he could find.

He moved through CSU in long strides. Bat was mantled over the bench in his and Scarly's cave of crap and didn't even look up as he began speaking.

"Bae Ga," Bat said. "Twenty-four years old. Originally from Incheon, South Korea. Killed in the Kitchen eighteen months ago. Mathematician. The weapon used was a

Daewoo DP-51. Which is a South Korean handgun."

Tallow laid his bag on the bench with care. "A mathematician. Was he studying here?"

"He was working here. Some kind of financial job, for a company called Stratagilex. Mutual funds or something. I don't have a good grasp on financial stuff."

"Get me a name at that company. A boss. And a phone number. Where's Scarly?"

"Behind you."

"Jesus. Okay. I have something for you. Bat, you're just sitting there."

"It doesn't fit the pattern, John. It's a wild result. He faked a mugging on some Korean math whiz and shot him with a matched weapon, but the victim has nothing to do with anything else we've seen."

"I don't agree," said Tallow, opening the bag. "Scarly, look at this."

"What the hell have you got there?"

"I told you I thought I met our guy. I gave him a cigarette. He tore the filter off and put it in his pocket. He smoked the cigarette. He can't have pocketed the butt, because it'd stink, and he's careful about that. So he threw the butt into a potato chip bag being blown down the street, because who's going to be crazy enough to come back and check all the litter for a single cigarette butt that'd eventually be blown far from the site anyway?"

Scarly gave him a hard stare. "Who'd be crazy enough to think we could get anything off a cigarette butt that was probably hot when he threw it into the bag and therefore melted plastic onto it?"

"Me. Look. He left a long butt. He had to, right? There was no filter. And he wasn't enjoying it so much anyway."

Scarly turned her stare on the evidence. "Shit. We have two shots. Bat, get people the fuck out of the clean room and make sure the plasticware's been UV'd."

Bat was at the laptop, scribbling on the back of an old, unstuck coffee sleeve. He passed the thin cardboard to Tallow, walking around. "What have we got?"

Scarly was pulling latex gloves out of a pants pocket. "We've got cigarette paper to smoke for prints, and I want to trim the mouth end and try the fast EA1 proteinase method on it."

"The fast one?" Bat said. Tallow watched them click into professional mode.

"Yeah. I don't think we've got time for anything else."

"The trim's going to be problematic. We need a centimeter square of paper for the fast one, and that's going to cut into print space."

"No, we cut the end all the way around, gives us a total of a centimeter. We'll reserve the tobacco in case we somehow get more time."

"Slow up," Tallow said. "More time? Fast method?"

Scarly sighed. "My boss has been told by her boss that too many resources are being eaten up by the case. We're going to get pulled off this, sooner rather than later."

"And who do I get instead?"

"Nobody, John. I don't know what's going on, but we're not living in the same world we were two days ago. All our sins are forgiven, and the case is going to be sunk just as soon as some asshole finds a big enough anchor to hang on it. Possibly one just your size."

Tallow leaned against the bench.

Scarly's face hardened. "So. Yeah. We're waiting for the word. But in the meantime, we are still doing this. So we're going to use the fast method, and clear people the fuck out of the clean room, and get as much done as we can as soon as we can. All right?"

"All right. Go."

"I *was*."

Bat spread his wings and hustled her out

of the room. "The man's just trying to do his job, Scarly. Don't snap at him."

"I *wasn't.*"

"You were."

"It's not my fault, I'm fucking *autistic* —"

Tallow read off the information Bat gave him and dialed the number. Ninety seconds of fairly sharp conversation with secretarial interceptors brought him the voice of an executive named Benson.

"Ms. Benson, thank you for speaking to me. Let me make this very fast: I'm in the middle of a homicide investigation, and it just now looked like it had ties to the death of your former employee Bae Ga. The question is simple. I need to know what the nature of his employment was."

"Bae? Bae was so brilliant. Bae wrote algorithms for us." She had, Tallow thought, a voice like Lauren Bacall's, all cigarettes and brandy, enough age to know the way of the world and enough youth to still be capable of disappointment in it. "He was the new generation. He spoke excellent English — he came from a port city, you know, very international in outlook — and he was so brilliant, so gifted. And such a relief to work with. Before him, we had to use Russian physicists for algo work. Lunatics, for the most part. Bae was going to bring us to the next level."

"Are you talking about algorithmic trading?"

"Yes."

"Did anyone ever try to hire him away?"

"Everybody did." She laughed. "Goldman Sachs, Vivicy, Blackrock, you name it. But he wouldn't go. He was young enough to believe in loyalty, bless him."

"You liked him."

That laugh again. "I looked after him. I sometimes wondered what might have happened if I hadn't opened the closet door for him, as it were. He was going to a party in one of those awful new buildings in Clinton that night, you know, to meet his new boyfriend. He was a lovely young man too, an architecture student. I encouraged Bae to get out of his wizard's cave from time to time. I said, You found a lovely young man who wants to show off his brilliant boyfriend at parties, so go, go."

She paused. When she spoke again, her voice was lower and harder. "And then. Shot like a dog."

"One last thing. And this is just curiosity, but I'd like an answer. How did the loss of Mr. Ga affect your business?"

Ms. Benson laughed. "Andy Machen would be polishing my shoes if I still had

Bae today, Detective. He was, and is, irreplaceable. You only luck into one mind like that in a generation."

"Thank you for your time, Ms. Benson."

"If you find anything —"

"If anything new comes up, I will of course call you."

"Thank you. The business doesn't matter, you see. We soldier on, you know. But I miss him. And he didn't deserve what happened to him, not even a little bit."

"Thank you, Ms. Benson."

Tallow hung up and put the piece of cardboard into his bag before heading for the elevators and down to the map of a murderer's room in the basement.

Assistant chief Allen Turkel was standing in the emulation.

Tallow ensured that he didn't break step on seeing the man. "Sir," he said with a nod, and proceeded to the table outside the emulation.

"Detective John Tallow. This is an impressive piece of work."

"Thank you, sir. How can I help you?"

"I'm really not sure yet, Detective. I just wanted to see what you'd done down here, with this space you stole from my building."

Turkel was smiling, creating the suggestion that he was just ribbing Tallow. Tallow was still geared up. He saw the wear on Turkel's wedding ring. He was a man who took it off a lot. Not just to shower. It got slipped off and into pockets a lot. Turkel regularly paid someone quite a slice of money to cut his hair, and his teeth were fixed in preparation for a job in which he was in front of cameras and audiences often. His shoes were thrown from supple leather with a cultivated grain, a silver chain linked across the throat of each.

"Borrowed, sir. And I couldn't live in the actual crime scene. It would've slowed down retrieval of the evidence even more."

"Well, that's evidence of you at least giving half a shit about department resources, Detective. Tell me: Do you ever think about promotion?"

Tallow just looked at the man.

"It's just a question, Detective. Did you plan on staying a detective all your life?"

"In all honesty, sir, I don't plan for a lot. But if you're asking: No, I don't really think about promotion."

"I know cops like you," said Turkel, lifting his chin and smiling with the warmth of a man who thinks he knows where the power in a room is. "I always thought there were three kinds of cops. Police like you, who

331

think they're born to the job they've got, and they'll do it until it kills them or they walk away from it. And cops like your lieutenant, who want to be promoted because promotion is there, and they figure getting promoted is the job. Police like that, I have no real use for. Oh, your lieutenant's a good manager, and I'll make good use of her, but strictly speaking, she's not here to be a good police officer. She's here to be a good candidate for promotion."

Turkel paused, and Tallow accepted the cue with false graciousness. "And the third kind? Sir?"

"The third kind are police like me. Police who need to be promoted because they see what the real job is. A street cop sometimes finds it hard to see it this way, Detective, but police like me are the real idealists in this job. We're the people who actually have a vision of how the department can adapt and change and serve the city better. That's why I wanted promotion. Want it still. Because I want to change and improve your life."

"My life."

"The lives of the police under my command. Which is you. But I also have a responsibility to the people of this city. They are, after all, paying us, in a roundabout way. And one day they may be paying us directly. So I have to manage resources. Like this one. What purpose is it serving?"

"It's what the case is all about, sir," Tallow said.

"I thought it was about a lot of unsolved homicides you reopened."

"You really want to talk about this, sir? I mean, really talk about it?"

Turkel put a level gaze on Tallow. "Yes," he said, after a moment.

"All right, then. It's about the unsolved homicides, of course it is. To us. But to him, it's about this room. The killings were the means to this end."

"I don't understand," Turkel said. "The killings were the end. He just had to store the weapons afterward, so they weren't found."

"No, sir. This room is the point, for him. Let me . . ."

Tallow stepped into the emulation and looked at where Turkel was standing. "No. Stand over here. Face this wall. And then sit down."

Turkel frowned at him. "I'll stand."

"All right." Tallow stepped outside the whiteboard perimeter. "Focus on the middle of that wall."

". . . It's a shape."

"Yes, sir. Now pan across the room, heading left." Tallow walked around the emulation, feeling like an animal pacing just outside the reach of campfire light.

"All the way around?"

"Yeah. You'll see where to stop."

"Christ. It's patterned, somehow. It's like the guns all flow together, almost. There are gaps, but . . ."

"That's right, sir. There are gaps. Each of those gaps is a future kill."

"Oh. Oh Christ. Oh Christ. It wraps onto the floor."

"And there are more gaps, sir. And the great machinery of it all goes into all the other rooms, and around and back again."

Turkel's voice was very quiet. "What is it, Tallow?"

"It's information, sir. It's the work of a very methodical, very functional madman who is writing a book out of machines that kill people. It's an information flow, it's code, it's pictograms, mathematics that mean nothing to anyone but him. The work of a serial killer in permanent totem phase, permanently energized, permanently in the moment and permanently laboring to complete his message to history. That's what's been set loose in Manhattan over these past twenty years, sir."

Turkel looked like he was going to throw up.

"How long have you known Andrew Machen, sir?" Tallow said.

"More than twenty years now," Turkel muttered abstractedly, eyes still tangled in the gunmetal belt of the room. "Why? What?"

"Would you say you've known Jason Westover for the same amount of time?"

"What?" Turkel came back to himself a little, and looked around for Tallow. Tallow was circling the emulation. Turkel could glimpse the detective only between gaps in the whiteboards.

"Why do you think Andrew Machen bought the building, sir?"

"What? Where are you? Why would he buy the building?"

"For his little wizards, sir. For his algorithmic traders to continue making invisible maps all over the 1st District and make their money from hiding."

"You're talking nonsense. Stand still, damn it. Why would Machen buy —"

"See, that's what's been bothering me, sir. But it occurred to me, just five minutes ago, that you're all so busy making your invisible new maps of the city that . . . well, none of you can see the others' maps."

"What the hell are you talking about, Tallow?" Turkel was, Tallow thought, starting to sound a little unglued. The sound helped Tallow cancel out the internal susurrus of his own fear.

"Andrew Machen didn't see the maps the killer draws on the city. He bought the building on Pearl according to the needs of his own maps, without a clue that his own hired murderer used that building to store all the guns he ever used. I like to think that it came as quite a shock."

Tallow stepped into the emulation, behind Turkel. "It's all maps, sir. This is a map. A map of a room."

Turkel turned on Tallow, eyes juddering in their sockets, thinking as quickly as he could. "Are you saying Andy Machen hired this man to kill all those people? Are you really saying that? Where's your evidence? Where's *anything* to support that?"

"Are we still speaking honestly, sir?"

Turkel took a breath, straightened, and visibly found his courage. "Yes."

"And no one can hear us."

"That's right, Tallow."

"So you'd like to hear my sense of the case."

"Fuck you, Tallow. You won't be on the

336

case long enough for it to make any difference."

"All right, then," Tallow said, walking around the assistant chief in a slow circle. "Twenty years ago, you were probably a patrolman, Jason Westover was probably fresh out of the army, and Andrew Machen was, I don't know, selling old ladies' gold fillings on the street. And you all knew each other. Maybe coincidental drinking buddies. Maybe childhood friends. Who knows? I'll find out. And you were all young, and reasonably arrogant, and ambitious, and hungry, and a little bit greedy, and a little bit sick of how slowly things can happen even in the big city. And one night, one of you said, What if we could just kill all the assholes that are between us and the things we want? And each of you laughed, and had another beer. But the idea stuck, didn't it? You couldn't shake it off. And you — a policeman, a soldier, and a banker — couldn't help but start talking about how such a thing could possibly be done. What happened next? Did one of you know a guy? Did you go looking for a guy? Someone you could somehow place total faith in. Someone you could pay to be so dedicated to the job that he would remain, here's that word again, *invisible* in the city for as long as it took. And it always seemed to take longer than you'd thought, didn't it? There was always someone else who needed to be helped out of the way of your constant advancement. And you knew the stats, didn't you, sir? You knew how many unsolved homicides could be hidden inside the annual numbers. But what's brought us to this place here today, sir, are the things you didn't know. You didn't know your man was keeping all the guns and hiding them in an apartment on Pearl Street. Jason Westover certainly didn't know that the security devices whose disappearances he was turning a blind eye to were going to secure the door of that apartment. And Andrew Machen didn't know he was actually buying the complete revelation of the entire scheme."

Turkel convulsed and threw up.

As the man was down on his hands and knees emptying his guts, Tallow had to restrain a very strong urge to kick him in his heaving stomach. Instead, he stepped away from the stink.

Tallow had dropped at least three outright, extemporaneous inventions into his narrative, including the bit about Westover knowing about the security door on 3A. His instinct had told him that these three men were talking, regularly, and a little disinformation could work to his advantage in the long run. If he had a long run.

"What the fuck is going on in here?"

Turkel's energetic puking had managed to blanket the sound of the elevator doors opening. Tallow knew the voice, and he knew the face he'd see. A woman's face that had the constant appearance of having just taken a strong shot of Scotch whisky.

"First Deputy Commissioner," Tallow said.

She was flanked by two plainclotheswomen, and she moved in quick little stamps of steps across the room and past Tallow.

"Not talking to you. Al, get the fuck up off the floor."

"Food poisoning," rasped Turkel, coming up on his haunches, rummaging for a tissue.

"Good. Maybe it'll kill you so I won't have to. What the fuck are you doing, Al?"

"Wanda —"

"I'll tell you what you're doing. You're trying to fuck me out of my job. Don't think I don't know you, Al Turkel. I should grab the back of your head and fuck your eyes out right there on your knees. You want my four stars, you be a man and take them by fucking gunpoint."

"Oh my God," said the assistant chief, "what is happening."

"What's happening is you trying to bury the Pearl Street case in the same fucking week it opened, that's what. Trying to bury it and get away with it, knowing full well that if the commissioner got hauled up by the mayor or God knows who over it, he wouldn't shit down *your* neck, he'd shit down *mine,* because that's what a first deputy is for. Queen Shitrag."

"You're insane, Wanda."

"You want to know what's insane? The captain of the 1st, a man with maybe one ounce of juice left, which he's been saving to buy himself retirement with full benefits a couple years early, spending it today on this kid" — pointing at Tallow without looking at him and yet pinning him unerringly — "after he got the memo from your desk telling him to bury the fucking case."

Tallow rocked a little on his heels.

"I don't have to go to you to manage my borough, Wanda," Turkel said, clambering shakily to his feet.

"Your borough. My city. What the fuck are you doing?"

"It's insoluble. It's just a waste of resources. I'm having all the evidence gathered, and CSU will continue to process it in a non-prioritized work stream until a solid background is developed."

"Al, you fucking moron. Someone killed a cop with a gun stolen out of evidence that belonged to Son of fucking Sam. What do you think happens when that inevitably fucking leaks? Is it you that's going to be asked questions? No. Some happy shithead is going to be training a camera on the commissioner just after he's spent an hour fisting the mayor with handfuls of thousand-dollar bills — or whatever the hell it is the commissioner has to do to keep his job from week to week — training a camera on him and saying, Hey, I hear your department deep-sixed the case of the mass serial killer who stole another serial killer's gun out of your storage depot and used it to kill a cop, which was just one among the two hundred or so homicides you managed not to notice were connected. Any comment?"

"Wanda," Turkel said wearily, "aren't you supposed to be on medication for days like this?"

"Fuck you. Your order's been dissolved."

"You can't do that."

"Can and did. I know you want my job, Al. I know you want the commissioner's job one day too. And you're very good. Your mistakes are few, and you've risen up through the ranks pretty quickly. But I'll tell you this for free: You're thinking like a manager. You think that at your level it's still all about clearances and hiding the stats you can't clear. That's fine for CompStat and promotional reviews. But when you get to my level, Al Turkel, you need to see a bigger map. You'll take the hit on your stats, or else you'll be shot dead by the media and the politicians. And in this case, by every other cop in the department, who'll ask what happens if *they* get inconveniently shot by a gun you don't want to admit is out in the wild."

She actually spat on the floor next to Turkel. Tallow began to understand why the first deputy always traveled with security.

"Fuck you," she said to Turkel. "Be a police officer."

She turned on her heel and walked back the way she had come, past Tallow. Looking at him as she approached, she said, "You're John Tallow?"

"Yes, ma'am."

"You're an asshole," she said as she stamped to the elevator.

"Yes, ma'am."

Tallow kept his eyes on Turkel and listened to the first deputy leave. He counted off another minute in his head as Turkel cleaned himself up and pulled himself together, and then Tallow walked to the elevator himself.

Turkel said nothing as Tallow waited. After two minutes more, the elevator returned and the doors bumped and dragged open.

Tallow stepped inside. Turkel, not looking at him, spoke then, slowly and deliberately, with broken glass in his voice:

"I could have stopped this. You remember that, when you go home tonight. I could have stopped what happens next. But now I won't."

The doors closed with a jump and shudder. The electronics of the elevator car skipped out for a moment. For a few seconds, it all went dark in there.

Tallow spent fifteen minutes trying to scare up a janitor to clean the emulation, and when he did, he ended up having to bribe him with ten dollars.

"I don't believe I have to bribe you to do your job," Tallow said.

"And yet, here you are, paying me to do the job I already get paid for," said the janitor, snatching the banknote from Tallow's fingers. "The world of commerce is a mysterious and frightening thing, and not for the likes of you and me to ponder."

"I could have just told you to damn well do it," Tallow observed.

"Maybe you could have." The janitor smiled, pocketing the ten. "I'm sure there's some way you could have given the order that would have made me do it without your ending up ten bucks lighter. But we'll never know, will we?"

Tallow's eyes went glassy as he processed Turkel's words. "That bastard," he finally said, and moved.

His phone rang as he walked back to CSU. It was the lieutenant.

"It's only a reprieve," he said.

"What is?"

"The assistant chief's order got rescinded. But all that means is tomorrow he's going to release another order, one that's phrased differently, probably through another channel, and that'll be that. He's probably working out how to do it right now."

"Tallow, what the hell is going on over there?"

"I swear to God, I just watched the first deputy commissioner slap Assistant Chief Turkel around right in front of me."

The lieutenant gave an explosive, surprised laugh. "Oh my God. Was she wearing those crazy flat hiking shoes?"

"She was. Walking around like she was stamping on ants."

"I love her so much," the lieutenant said. "I really hope she makes commissioner one day."

"Turkel knows Machen," Tallow said. "Machen, whose company is buying the Pearl Street building. Machen, who's such good friends with Jason Westover that he introduced Westover to his wife. Machen, who tried to hire a Korean math wizard from another company and failed, shortly after which the Korean math wizard was found dead, killed by a Korean handgun."

"For Christ's sake, John," the lieutenant said, "give me some goddamn evidence, not more conjecture."

"Do you think I'm wrong?"

He heard her take a deep breath. "Not completely, no. But this is getting very big and very chaotic, very quickly, and you're not helping matters by seeing connections everywhere. Bring me something that can be seen by the naked eye. Because if you're right about one thing, John, then it's probably that the assistant chief will find another way to sink the case. It'll happen because you'll let him. You won't have anything concrete, and he'll latch onto the one thing that looks to him like it can be cleared —"

"Ah, hell," said Tallow. "And the first deputy handed it to him on a platter. She was yelling at him about the .44 Bulldog."

"Get me something. Soon. Because the captain just started putting his desk shit in a box, John. He's done, and just waiting to be told he's done. He threw himself in the path of one bullet for us. Don't let them fire another. Because I'm not taking it for you."

"Understood. But you do get how big this has gotten, don't you, Lieutenant? You do see how everything's connected."

"Don't talk to me like that, John. Or my ultimate conclusion will be that you're crazy and should have been on leave."

"All right. All right. I'll talk to you tomorrow," said Tallow, ending the call and knowing that might have been a lie. He knew in his bones that whatever he'd brought on himself, it would come that night. Considering that, with his phone in his hand, Tallow examined himself. It was a calm kind of fear he had, an emptiness in his chest and a flickering speed to his thoughts. He was still making sense to himself, though, and his hand wasn't shaking. A useful kind of fear, then.

Tallow was held in amber for a moment by a sense-memory: He was maybe five or six years old, walking home from school. His mother was waiting on the other side of a road for him. He could see it. A T intersection, where he had to cross the road that was the vertical bar of the T. Spring. The evenings getting longer, and the promise they brought of staying up later and doing more things and using the hours of warm gold light for excitement and joy or even just soft extended times of togetherness with his parents. The promise never seemed to come true enough, but in spring the promise alone was enough to make his heart light. His mother was judging the traffic. She lifted her arms to him. It was safe for him to cross. She'd told him that morning that she was going to the store, and there would be ice cream for him at dinner tonight. He ran to her. When there was a good evening ahead, with the sky still light, it was like you stole a whole extra day from the world.

He tripped. Tallow remembered it exquisitely. He tripped in the middle of the road and came down flat on his chest. If his head hadn't been so forward with the excitement of running to Mom and starting the evening, he probably would've torn his chin open or knocked his teeth out. Instead, he flopped down on his chest, palms smacking the blacktop, both knees hitting. He looked at his mother. His mother was looking at the VW camper van turning into the road. It was blue and white. He could pick the exact shade of blue off a color chart if one were shown to him right now. He could see the crawl of rust on the VW badge on the front of the van. A heavy woman was driving it; she had square-cut graying hair and a thick green sweater.

The fear was there, in his chest, that hollow horror of a sensation. His lungs were gone, vanished. His body told him there was no point in taking a breath because he had no lungs. His thoughts were a shaking procession, a praxinoscope of images and simple calculations and knowledge.

The camper van braked. Tallow's mother stifled a scream and ran into the road to pick Tallow up. Tallow could move just fine, but his mother gathered him up and took him to the sidewalk, waving and shouting thanks to the smiling woman behind the wheel. Tallow looked at the driver, and she seemed more grateful than his mother. Tallow remembered her stroking her steering wheel, releasing a shudder of a breath. The relief of a woman who had not, after all, driven over a little boy on the way home. Tallow had thought about that, in bed at night, all week. The woman was thanking her van for being good enough to have stopped when she told it to.

Tallow thought about that, himself at five or six years old, staring up at the ceiling where his father had glued plastic stars made from some glow-in-the-dark material in the rough shape of constellations. And he also thought about having known that, either despite the fear or because of it, he could have gotten out of the way of the van. He would go to sleep smiling in absolute certainty that he could have pushed himself up and clear of the van.

He had not been properly scared in a long time, John Tallow hadn't. Now he was, as vividly and coldly as he'd been that childhood day.

Tallow found Scarly and Bat's cave. Bat was in it, typing on a laptop.

"Where's Scarly?"

"Working the cigarette paper," Bat said, only half engaged. "She doesn't like me helping with that. The whole process makes me cough, and one time . . . well, we'd just had some shitty pizza, and I had stuff stuck in my teeth? And we were smoking something for prints, and I was coughing, and she was yelling at me, and I coughed, and this chunk of anchovy flew right out of my mouth and kind of right into hers."

"So she doesn't let you help."

"Not so much. I'm working on trying to pull some DNA off the trim."

"The quick method?"

"Not that quick," Bat said. "But I can manage it through the computer from here. With the best will in the world and all the luck there is, we're looking at at least an hour. And I have no luck and I work in the NYPD, you know?"

"Yeah," Tallow said. "So, listen, could I borrow you for an hour?"

"What do you need?"

"You. And some of your stuff."

"You sound like a man with a scheme, John."

"We're way past schemes and well into desperate-last-ditch-effort territory. Or maybe lying-in-a-road-as-a-van-drives-toward-you territory."

"Well, okay. Let me talk to Scarly first?"

"About what?" Scarly said, appearing behind Tallow. Her eyes were bright and her breathing was fast and shallow.

"What did you do?" said Bat, and then, to Tallow, "I know that look. She's done something. I know it."

"You're fucking right," Scarly said. "I got a print."

"Holy shit," said Bat.

350

"It's not a great print," Scarly said quickly, "but it's a print. And I think it's good enough that if our guy's been a previous customer of the NYPD, we should get a match. We got a fucking *print,* John. How the fuck did you even think of that?"

"What I'm thinking about right now is getting a print examiner in to confirm the latent if we get a match," said Bat.

"Don't piss on my parade, Bat. I got a print off a cigarette butt shoved in a potato chip bag. You should be paying me fucking obeisance right now and ordering me hookers."

"We don't need an examiner to sign off on it yet," said Tallow. "Get the print matched. We'll know the guy when we see him. I'm damned sure of that. I want to borrow Bat for an hour. We'll be back. We're going to lose the case tomorrow, Scarly, so we've only got tonight to develop something that looks like a theory backed with evidence. Are you up for that?"

"John, I've got a wife. I can't keep staying out all night."

"Hey. Scarly. What happened to five seconds ago when you got a fucking print?" Bat commented.

Scarly sagged and glowered at John from under a comically lowered brow. "All right.

I admit it. We're in too deep to stop now. But we're gonna need to eat, and I need to make sure I'm not going to get my head flushed down the crapper by the wife. Let me make a call."

"Make your call," Tallow said. "The print's being run now?"

"Yeah."

"Okay, good. Bat, I need some of your junk there."

In the car, Bat said, "You're just utterly fucking nuts if you think that's going to achieve anything."

"I am getting pretty tired of being told I'm crazy."

"Well, get used to it. I mean, I don't want to stick my nose all the way into your business, but were you like this before your partner died?"

"I thought Scarly was the autistic one with no social skills."

"No, no, I'm not unaware of what I'm asking. I realize that's going to still sting, you know? But it's a reasonable question. Do you feel like you're behaving differently than you would if you were working with your partner? Is there maybe just a possibility that . . . I don't wanna say you're traumatized or some I-need-a-hug bullshit, but . . ."

Tallow sighed. "You're asking if my seeing Jim get killed has made me a little nuts?"

"Basically," said Bat. "Only, you know, put more nicely than that."

A uniformed policeman walked into the road, signaling for the oncoming traffic to stop. Beyond him, a paramedic rig was parked on the sidewalk. There was a man burning on the street corner. Kneeling, engulfed in flame, quite dead, very slowly collapsing in on himself.

A guano-speckled bowler hat, with turkey feathers in the hatband, blew across the street behind the uniformed cop.

Tallow heard a voice in his recent memory say, *I just asked her for a light.*

"You're asking if *I'm* a little nuts," Tallow muttered under his breath.

"Yes, I am," said Bat. "This plan is a crazy man's plan."

"And yet here you are."

"Yes, I am. I didn't say I didn't *like* crazy-man plans. I'm saying it's not going to achieve anything."

"Look," said Tallow, "can you do the thing I'm asking for or not?"

"Yes. In fact, it will be fun. I just think . . . ah, hell. Injun ninja, no chain of evidence, his history-fu is stronger than yours, it's not solvable, et cetera and fucking so forth.

353

We've said it to you half a dozen times."

"History-fu," Tallow said, slowly.

"You know what I mean. Although I question why *history-fu* stopped you dead and *Injun ninja* just blew by."

Tallow took a deep breath. "All right," he said, on the shaky exhale, "here's the deal. My apartment building has three exits. Front, rear, and fire escape . . ."

The process took less than an hour, in the end. Bat got joyfully swept up in the execution of it and completed the work with a grinning hyperfocus that made Tallow wonder whether Scarly wasn't the autistic one on the team after all. Bat was still vibrating with glee on the drive back to One PP.

"You enjoyed the crazy-man plan, then," Tallow commented.

"Ha! *That's* why I got into this line of work, man. That was the shit right there."

"You became a cop because . . . you like building?"

Bat laughed again, wriggling in the passenger seat. "Nah. You want to know why I became a cop?"

"Sure."

"Cop shows."

"You're kidding me," said Tallow. He'd

heard that line before and had never bought it. If you were dumb enough to think cop shows were like real police work, Tallow reasoned, then you'd never get into the force because you were required to manifest enough intelligence to dress yourself.

"Nope. The Tao of cop shows, man. All those cop shows I grew up with, especially those in the aughties, say the same thing. If you are smart enough, and your Science, with a capital S, is good enough, and if you refuse to give up and just keep using Science on the problem, it'll crack and you can solve it. And the problem is always the same: the world has stopped making sense, and the cops have to use Science to force it to make sense. That's the heart of every cop show. Give yourself to a cop show for an hour, and it'll show you a breakdown in the ethical compact, and the process by which that breakdown occurred, and how it is fixed and made to never happen again. That's why everyone loves them. They speak to our sense that everything's fucked and then show you how to work to find out what really happened — simplify the world — and then deal with it. Because everybody knows that — listen, you ever cheated on a girlfriend?"

"Once," Tallow said, for the hell of it, even

though he hadn't. Not least because the opportunity had never presented itself.

"Then you know. You break that part of the ethical compact, the basic rule that says You Don't Do That, and it's only hard once. When the sun doesn't go out because you've been so evil . . . well, it's easier the next time. And the next time. So everyone who watches a cop show knows that the bad guy ain't going to do the bad thing just once. He has to be taken off the streets. That's what I wanted to be. I loved the idea of being the guy who could take that guy off the streets using nothing but his brains and his hands. I'll tell you a secret." Bat smiled. "I don't even tell people I'm a cop. I tell people I'm a CSU."

"Same thing."

"You know what? No offense, but I don't want them to be the same thing. I'm a CSU. I solve things. I hunt and build and solve things with science. You know what a New York City cop does? Beats protesters. Rapes women."

"Hey."

"You can't argue that, John. Remember that detective who raped that woman in the doorway of her apartment building in the Bronx? Remember what she said he said to her? 'I'm not as bad as those other cops who raped that other girl.' Remember how bad Occupy Wall Street got? Penning women up and then pepper-spraying them? Beating journalists with batons? Cracking the skull of a councilman? Dragging women out of wheelchairs? That's what a New York City cop is. We're not fucking heroes. So, yeah, I don't tell people I'm a cop. I don't like going out into the field. I like it on my floor of One PP, where we do science and just solve stuff without ever having to go outside and punch someone in the face for being in an inconvenient place and talking the shit that we so richly deserve —"

"You want to take a breath there, Bat?"

Bat didn't even bother to fake a dutiful laugh. "You know why CSUs hate beat cops and detectives? Because you remind us of where we work."

"Yeah," said Tallow. "Hunting the Injun Ninja."

That, Bat gave a little snorting laugh at, looking out of the window. "Hey," he said. "Where are we?"

"Taking a little detour. I wanted to look at something."

Bat peered around as if trying to track the random trajectories of a fly. "Is that Collect Pond Park over there? I thought it actually had a pond."

"It's been under construction for years," Tallow said. "There was a little pond added recently, and then they drained it and now they're re-excavating it or something."

Collect Pond Park was a dismal flagstoned square, so gray that the stacked yellow-painted fencing from some construction phase or other actually brightened it.

"That," said Tallow, "is Werpoes. A spring ran from Spring Street, through the stream that was dug out for the canal that Canal Street's named for, into a pond that was eventually called the Collect Pond. By 1800 or so, the pond was just a poison pit, so they dug out the canal to drain it out. Then they filled it in, and then they stuck Canal Street on top of the canal. And all of that used to be Werpoes, the main Native American village in Lower Manhattan, on the shores of the pond. What's left is, well, that. The pond basin, the remains of the dome houses of Werpoes, and any other sign that anyone was here before us are all well underground. Under that piece of park, and over there."

Tallow pointed in the other direction, and Bat followed his finger.

"The Tombs," Bat said.

"Yeah. The Manhattan Detention Complex is built over Werpoes and the Collect Pond. So's the criminal court. The original

Tombs complex was actually rotted out by the remains of the pond — the draining job was so bad that even when they in-filled the basin, the whole patch turned to marsh, and the damp crept up into the Tombs. So here's what I'm wondering —"

"Why your brain started receiving an NPR program on massively uninteresting history?"

"I'm wondering why Jason Westover's wife warned me not to go near Werpoes. Also, Bat, I'm going to remember that the next time you tell me my history-fu is much weak, because I did all the reading on this for that reason. The strong intimation was that our guy haunted Werpoes. But look around. The Tombs, the court, a park that a fat Chihuahua couldn't hide in, office buildings . . . where's a guy who stored his most prized possessions in a crumbling walk-up on Pearl Street going to live around here?"

"Lots of police too," Bat commented.

"Including us," said Tallow, pushing the car forward.

Scarly was in the office-cave she shared with Bat, lit by her computer monitor. "I made him," she said, without looking up. Her expression was oddly blank, in a way that made Tallow's stomach turn in some weird involuntary presage to fear.

Bat tumbled into the room, all flapping arms and nodding head. "You made him? You made who? Who's been made?"

"Our guy," she said flatly.

"I don't believe it," said Bat.

"Our guy became a customer of the NYPD right at the top of the introduction of DNA collection. His sheet's in the database. I got a match. I made him."

Bat looked over her shoulder at the screen and said something like "Shiiiiiiiiit."

"John," said Scarly, "you want to look at this." It was spoken like a threat.

Tallow didn't want to.

Tallow wanted to blow it off, tell them to get on with it, drive back into the 1st, get a coffee, and let the world go by. Not even watch the world go by. He remembered the days when the world was just a moving backdrop behind a stage occupied solely by himself, whatever comfortable chair he had found, and whatever thought or tune or paragraph it amused him to rotate in his head for the length of his shift. It seemed twenty years ago. He knew it was just last week, but he was unable to summon last week with any clarity. It seemed like an image of childhood summer — or, perhaps more apt, a photo of last week blurred and filtered and glazed by a digital application that stamped the patina of faded memory over it.

Tallow walked over and looked at the screen.

There was the man he met outside the apartment building on Pearl Street.

Twenty years younger, at least. Not quite so calm. Lean, but not quite as hard. Blood on his face. Not his blood.

There was a name on the screen. The name didn't seem to matter.

Tallow realized he could hear his pulse. As he swallowed and closed his eyes, Scarly's voice rose over the booming in his ears.

". . . ex-soldier. The doctor who looked him over has a note on the sheet saying he was probably schizophrenic. There's also a handwritten annotation on the scan of the paper. CTS?"

Tallow actually smiled. "You haven't spent too much time in emergency rooms."

"What does it mean?"

"It's ER medical slang. CTS means Crazier Than Shit."

"Great."

Tallow leaned in. His man had gotten pulled in on an assault charge, but the victim seemed to have somehow dematerialized. So all they had was a lunatic veteran wearing someone else's blood and cluttering up a holding cell. Given the general state of overcrowding and the general sense that there were more important things in the world to give a shit about, a supplementary note was written indicating that the arresting officers were wrong and that it was very probably his own blood that CTS was wearing, and since there was no visible crime or victim, the individual in question should be processed and tossed onto the street.

"The notes just say *former soldier*," Scarly said. "No idea if he was a vet or discharged before he was posted or what. Sloppy job. I'll bet it was just one person who decided to process him out properly, because he had *repeat client* written all over him. Probably the same CSU who would've been made to scrape the blood off him. I'd really like to pull up his service records."

"Can we do that from here?" Tallow asked.

"Probably," said Scarly. "But not right now. We've got enough to think about, and getting that information would take hours, and we have places to be." She shook herself all over, as if trying to awaken from a chill dream or trying to get cold rain off her skin. "Come on. Move."

"Move where?" said Bat.

"To the car, Bat. John can follow in his.

We're going back to my place, where my wife is going to feed us."

Tallow felt immediate revulsion at the idea. "I don't want to impose."

"John. This is a direct instruction. You are coming to our apartment and eating with us."

"I can grab something —"

"John," said Scarly, "I have been instructed. If I arrive without you, I will be punished. You don't want me to be punished, do you?"

Tallow was about to respond when he saw Bat, standing behind Scarly, shaking his head in short fast motions, very much communicating the sense of *No, John, no, don't mention that thing I told you at the bar that is making you want to say But you* like *being punished, Scarly, don't do it there will be consequences terrible consequences.*

"I just don't think it's a good idea," Tallow said, backing up to the door.

"John. We've been working late, and we still have a lot to talk about. So Talia offered to make dinner. It's not like we're trying to induct you into a cult."

"And," Bat said, "we also have stuff to do tonight. Right, John?" Scarly looked at Bat like he was a criminal. "Stuff? We have stuff to do yet?"

"John has a scheme," said Bat, smug in the warm glow of knowing something Scarly didn't.

Scarly stepped to John and screwed a surprisingly hard finger into Tallow's chest. "So it's settled. Bat rides with me. You follow us. Talia feeds you. And you tell me what you're hiding from me."

"I'm not hiding anything."

"It is not acceptable that Bat has knowledge of something that I did not already know first. Or at least that I could convincingly claim to have once known and then forgotten because I am so much more important than him." She was coming back to herself now. "Also I'm fairly sure he stole my Twine unit, and there's a jar of — never mind. You explain later. We go now."

"But —"

"There is no but. There is only go."

Tallow wanted to crawl somewhere and make himself die. The idea of this dinner was entirely antithetical to his life as he'd constructed it. The idea crept out like a spider and set off an autonomic repulsion. He just didn't want to be part of . . .

Tallow caught the thought in his head and made it pause before finishing. The thought went: *I just don't want to be part of people's lives.*

He had to turn that sentence around in his head, to view it from all angles and look for the traces that might suggest to him when it had formed into such concrete.

You're just utterly fucking nuts, said Bat in Tallow's memory. Tallow knew he wasn't. He could study that statement dispassionately and know that he was not crazy and it was right and good to stay the hell out of people's lives. He didn't need to see what they had, and they didn't need him hanging around. It occurred to him that he was never going to make anyone else understand this. He played people's arguments and shot them all down with logical efficiency.

It took one long second more before it occurred to him that that was actually probably what a crazy person would do.

"All right," said Tallow, "I'd like to meet your wife. Where are we headed?"

Tallow congratulated himself, very quietly, on having left all his options open. Perhaps he could just say hello and then leave. He told himself he wasn't committed to dipping himself into their lives.

The worst of the traffic over the Brooklyn Bridge was over, and, in convoy, they had a relatively straight shot off the island.

So preoccupied was Tallow with the looming threat of meeting other people and the worrying insight that perhaps he was indeed utterly fucking nuts that it took at least five minutes for it to leak into his perception that he'd snapped the radio on by reflex.

Multiple assaults in the Bronx after the head of a local Catholic school, fired after being found with a one-terabyte external drive stuffed with child pornography, escaped jail time.

A clerk beaten to death in a sex store on Sunset Park; crosses daubed on the counter and windows in the dead man's blood, approximately four hundred dollars' worth of apparently fairly brutal German pornography stolen. Murder weapon presumed to be a fifteen-pound rubber dildo.

In Williamsburg, a seventeen-year-old boy found naked on the street and bleeding out from more than three hundred cuts.

Queens: Landlord hacked an elderly tenant to death with a machete and then attempted to cleanly kill himself. He was still conscious when the emergency services arrived, despite his having turned himself into what one wit called "a human Pez dispenser."

Five gang members, all under eighteen years old, found stacked on a Watkins Street corner in Brownsville, in broad daylight, all dead, all castrated. Nobody saw anything.

Also in Brownsville, a sixteen-year-old girl slashed the throat of a thirteen-year-old girl, killing her within minutes. The sixteen-year-old had to be restrained from killing herself, since she claimed her intent had been only to scar the decedent in such a way that their mutual pimp would no longer be able to use her for high-end (twenty-dollars-plus) employment.

Man in Prospect Park found masturbating into the barrel of a nine-millimeter handgun. Upon being disturbed, he shot an Urban Park Ranger, a passing jogger, a dog walker, and a nanny before shooting himself through his open mouth up into his brain.

Some laughter over the crackling air: The Hell's Kitchen building used by a small-time gun dealer who went by the name of Kutkha but was better known as one Antonin Anosov was currently on fire. Many detectives across the Five Boroughs had met Anosov over the years, and there was generally a fond contempt for him. He was one of the few genuine eccentrics the local crime scene had produced in recent times, and while no one would be caught saying he actually liked him, he was certainly appreciated by most of those who dealt with him.

Therefore, there was a little flurry of jokes tossed around as to how his place of business had caught fire.

A few minutes later, there were reports of bodies at the site. A lot of bodies. The jokes turned to ash and blew down the radio waves and away. Smoke signals.

TWENTY-EIGHT

The hunter had time to kill.

He was experiencing a thing that he'd come to think of as the exhaustion of revulsion. The overwhelming, existential disgust that the modern world caused to roil and pustulate and burst inside him simply wearied him over extended periods. Being constantly, on some level, physically repelled and sickened by the alien world he had to interact with just drained him. He felt septic, and tired, and somehow old.

The exhaustion frightened him. It made him weak, mentally. He slipped deep into Mannahatta as he walked, so deep that he began to lose the ability to perceive modern light sources. Night gathered quickly, and traffic became the running of amber-eyed wolves. The hunter moved between the trees as best he could, holding his palms in his armpits to occlude the scent of fear in his sweat. No man was at one with the wolves.

Wolves ate even mighty hunters, for there was no honor or code among predators, and everyone's guts steam the same way when torn open on a cold night.

A car ripped out from the forest and almost gored the hunter on its chrome.

The hunter spun and clung to a red maple as the car sped past him and dissociated into a pack of silvered wolves racing away into the dark trees.

The hunter squeezed his eyes shut, and then slowly opened them in an experimental manner. He was rewarded with a blurry view that was perhaps 80 percent modern Manhattan, and with a pulsing headache. He could live with that: the pain would sharpen him for a time, before its persistence began to dull him further. Maybe it'd fade before then.

Food would help. He didn't dare risk Manhattan food. He had once, in a desperate circumstance, scavenged a half-eaten burger left in a brown bag atop a trash can. The meat was loaded with enough salt that he could feel his kidneys spasm as he chewed, and it had the signature flavor of having been cut from an animal whose own droppings had been a considerable part of its diet. The bun that wrapped it was, he supposed, some alien cousin to corn bread, except he could taste ammonia and chalk in it. Half an hour later, he threw up everything that had been in his stomach, painfully and protractedly. He threw up in colors he'd never seen himself produce before, and he was fairly sure, twenty minutes into the vomiting, that he saw the blackened stub of a baby tooth he'd swallowed when he was six. He'd lived off the fruits of this island of many hills for too long and just couldn't metabolize the machine-processed muck the new people survived on.

Now the hunter rummaged through his pockets and his bag and came up with half a handful of cracked black walnuts and six hackberries wrapped in a scrap of newspaper, all foraged from Central Park. He began walking again, eating as he went, chewing each bite thoroughly and methodically before letting himself swallow it down, alternating the rich, smokily vinous walnut pieces with the candied bursts of the hackberries. The morsels would give him the strength to get to Central Park and gather more food to get through the rest of this night.

He was abstractedly aware that he was crying as he walked but chose not to consciously acknowledge it. It was a thing off in the distance of his mind, in his peripheral vision, that he could decide not to focus on. Present, but not immediate: the sound of his own voice screaming in heartbreak that he was insane, hopelessly insane, and should find help, or jump in front of a car, because he was living like a demented animal and how did this happen to him and why is everything wrong and why are the street-lights smoking and why are the telephone poles breathing and please and please and please —

At a street crossing, the hunter noticed the modern people looking at him strangely. He ignored them. From the rattled expressions on their faces, anyone would think he'd been walking around crying and shouting. *And that,* he said to himself, *is not what a hunter does.*

He glided across the street to the fenced perimeter of Central Park and slipped between its bones like a knife.

TWENTY-NINE

It turned out that Scarly and Talia lived in the indeterminate urban foam around Park Slope: close enough to the district to reduce the cultural stress of two women living together, far enough from its declared boundary to make an apartment affordable. There was, to Tallow's amazement, both a public parking lot opposite their building and empty parking spaces in front of the building. As a Manhattanite used to at least a five-minute walk from parked car to apartment building, Tallow felt a little cheated, as if Heaven had been just across the bridge the whole time and no one had told him.

He parked behind Scarly and Bat in front of the apartment building, a wide red-brick home a scant four floors high.

Scarly and Talia made their home on the fourth floor, and Talia was waiting at the open apartment door for them. She was as tall as Tallow, and in infinitely better condition. She had an almost surreal copper-wire mane tied with rubber bands that made the back of her head look like a telephone cable trunk. She wore a gray wife-beater that showed off heavy, finely worked musculature, and black tactical pants that completed a picture of an off-duty SWAT officer. Her bare feet, as she stood on the rug by the front door, were callused to the extent that Tallow would guess her main training was in kickboxing. She wore no makeup; her skin was pale to the point of translucence; and she greeted Scarly's hug and kiss with guarded affection, one eye on Tallow the whole time.

"Thanks for this," Scarly said.

"No problem. Welcome home."

Bat came up, and Talia endured a peck on the cheek and a "Hey, Tallie." She smacked the back of his head, not completely fondly, sending him scuttling indoors.

Tallow stuck his hand out, making direct eye contact.

Talia pursed her lips, tested his gaze, and then shook his hand with brisk force. He matched it, and said, "I'm John."

There was the twitch of a smile at one corner of her lips, and she nodded as if to say *You'll do.* Tallow had put a little thought into creating his first impression on her, and

374

although, looking into her eyes now, he doubted that Talia was unintelligent enough to completely fall for it, he was content that she seemed to acknowledge the effort.

"Talia," she said. "C'mon in, John."

The apartment stood in stark contrast to the troll cave Scarly worked in. There was nothing in the apartment that was not beautiful, or useful, or both. Spare and spacious, but warm, a carefully and tastefully curated space rather than a chill minimalist plain. There was a sweet, rich cooking aroma in the air.

Ahead of them, walking to the kitchen, Scarly dropped her coat on the floor by a sofa.

"Scar*latta,*" Talia snapped.

Scarly froze, backtracked, picked up the coat, folded it, and laid it on the sofa.

"I'll let you get away with putting it there instead of in the closet because we have guests. You're not at work now."

"Well," said Scarly in a small voice, "I sorta am."

Talia turned and raised an eyebrow at Tallow.

"If I'm not welcome," said Tallow, "then, seriously, I'm okay with leaving. I felt like I was imposing anyway. It's fine, really."

"That's not what I meant," said Talia.

"What I want to know is where you get these magic powers that make Scarlatta happy, or at least compliant, about working one second more than her scheduled hours."

Talia stepped over, put one palm on Tallow's back, and began to propel him through the apartment. "I want you to sit at my table, John, and teach me of this magic, because I may be able to use it to make my wife pick up after herself and — who knows? — maybe even wash things. Although that might be testing even your wizardly abilities. And then after that, perhaps you might explain to me a little bit about this case that is causing me to feed you as well as put up with losing my wife for the night."

There was a howl from the kitchen. "Oh, *Tallie*. What did you *do*?"

"Whaddaya mean, what did I do?"

"Tallie, we can't afford this. What did I tell you?"

As Talia strode forth, Tallow stepped to the side and got an angled view into the kitchen, where, standing in unwrapped butcher's paper, was a stack of well-marbled sirloin steaks.

"What you told me," said Talia, "was that the only things you'd ever seen John eat were burgers and steak, which wasn't a whole hell of a lot to go on when it came to feeding him."

"Tallie, we have so many things to pay for
—"

Talia reached her and put her hands on Scarly's shoulders, making her appear even smaller than she was. "Yes, we do. But the butcher owed me a favor, and I went out to the stores at the end of the day. These cost pretty much nothing, and so did the ciabatta. It would have cost me more to make a pot of ramen. You need to not worry so much, Scarly. It'll put you in an early grave, and I'm not done with you yet."

Scarly gave in with a small laugh, and Talia kissed her forehead, slowly. "And I'll tell you another thing." Talia smiled. "No hipster runoff in some hole-in-the-wall tourist food shed in Lower Manhattan is gonna make better steak sandwiches than me. I just won't have it. John, are you a drinking man?"

"I'm a driving man," he said.

"I get that. But one beer won't kill you. I have some imported stuff you might want to try."

"Maybe I could split one with you."

"Deal. Sit, sit. Oh: How do you like your steaks cooked?"

Tallow sat at the oval kitchen table. It was old and well used, probably picked up at a sale or conceivably out of a dumpster. Someone had sanded down the various cuts and gouges, but just to the point where the edges were no longer sharp and raw. It had the feeling of having been smoothed by weather.

"Medium, I guess?"

"Medium? God, how boring. Middle of the road. Medium's for people who can't make choices. Rare or well done?"

"Uh . . . well done, then."

"Well done. You mean ruined. These are good steaks. I won't have it. You'll get it rare and like it."

"She only knows how to cook steaks rare," said Scarly.

"Shut up, woman," said Talia. "Since we have a guest, I'll make a special effort to do medium rare."

The sweet smell was onions caramelizing in a pan. A tray of chopped bacon and mushrooms was under the unlit broiler, and warmed, split ciabatta rolls were cooling on the oven rack below. Talia opened an oddly shaped green beer bottle with a green label reading ST. PETER'S SUMMER ALE and poured half the contents into a long glass for him. She toasted him with the bottle, a somehow ironic kink in her eyebrow, and swigged from it as she turned to the stove, poked at the onions with a pointed spoon, and poured some powerfully fruited olive oil into a broad, heavy frying pan.

Tallow sipped at his beer without tasting it, avoiding everyone's eyes for the moment. He watched the oil in the pan. It was slow to heat, because of the heavy bottom, but it heated very evenly. It raised little rolling patterns, like sand after the tide's gone out. He watched it grow a shimmer, and then glitter, with little scintillant wave crests of foam. The oil rippled and shone like the reflection of a harvest moon in a green pond. Talia took two of the thin steaks and laid them expertly in the pan. There was a great crackling rush as they seared. She pushed each of them lightly with the tips of steel tongs, to ensure they weren't sticking, and then studied them as they cooked. Tallow would have guessed it was precisely one minute before she flipped them. The marbled fat had rendered beautifully, but he did wonder how long Talia had been serving Scarly medium steaks and telling her they were rare.

Talia stepped to the oven, took two of the rolls and plated them, tugged the top tray out with the tongs and laid some of the bacon and mushroom on the cut side of the top half of each roll, and then picked up the spoon and pushed caramelized onion over the cut side of each bottom half. The second minute must have been up then: Talia plucked the steaks out, draped one on the bottom half of each roll, and pressed the sandwiches together before putting them down in front of Bat and Scarly.

"Ours next," Talia said to Tallow.

"Sure," said Tallow, who for no good reason found himself wanting to curl up in a dark corner and cry his eyes out.

This, he knew, was what he'd been avoiding. Seeing other people live lives. Something as mundane and utterly dull and ubiquitous in the world as watching one person cook for a loved one was crushing his heart in its plain little fist.

"You look miles away," said Talia, putting a plate in front of him and sitting to his left, between him and Scarly. Tallow looked up and realized he wasn't completely sure where the last two minutes had gone. But there was food in front of him now, and Bat and Scarly were both giving him that slightly scared look that in the past few days he'd learned indicated that he was being strange.

"Sorry," Tallow said. "Lots to think about."

"Try your food," Talia said, not unkindly.

He did. It was incredibly good, and he said so.

"There," said Talia, turning to Scarly. "Now, don't let me hear another goddamn thing about how John brings you the best steak sandwiches ever. *I* make the best steak sandwiches ever. Got it?"

"Got it." Scarly grinned.

Tallow tried the beer again, tasting it this time, and he found it to be equally good, big and hoppy, a well-chosen partner to the food.

"So," said Talia. "Tell me what you have to think about. And don't even consider saying that it's an active case and you can't talk about it, blah-blah. That doesn't work in this house, okay?"

"Okay," said Tallow and, between bites, gave her a rough overview of the case to date. Partway through, he noticed that Bat and Scarly weren't interjecting or expanding on anything. Talia ran the household. It occurred to him that he himself was falling into step and seeking her approval in some abstract way.

Even the broadest brushstrokes of the case, however, had a certain power, and Talia rocked back in her chair as she absorbed its kicks.

"Wow," she said, eventually. Looking at

Scarly, she said, "You're right. He's good. But I don't see where you go from here. He just said there's no investigative chain from the cigarette butt that'd stand up in a court."

"That's provided," said Tallow slowly, "that you think this'll end up in a court."

Talia's eyes widened a little at that.

"Here's what you don't know," Tallow said to Scarly. "Assistant Chief Turkel pretty much told me that I'm a dead man walking. If I'm right about everything, Turkel's never once gotten his own hands dirty. That means that our guy —"

"CTS," said Bat with a dark wry smile.

"— CTS, then. That means that CTS is going to be given a new job by Turkel. Which also supposes that Turkel knows where to find him. Which probably also means that Westover and Machen know where to find him. But shelve that for a second. It means that the guy we're coming after will soon be coming after me. Given the acceleration of certain aspects of the case, I think *soon* could mean as early as tonight. And let's be honest: it's not like Al Turkel doesn't know where I live."

"I'll make up the sofa," said Talia, and drained the last of her bottle.

"That's very kind," said Tallow, "but

there's no need. I'll be going home tonight."

Talia brought the bottle down on the table like a gavel. "No way in hell. After what you just told me? Look, I don't know you, but if these two say you're good, that's halfway enough for me, and you haven't exactly disgraced yourself tonight. And even if you had, it would not be fucking human to send you back to somewhere that's being staked out by some insane hit man."

Tallow then told them what he and Bat had done earlier in the evening. It seemed odd to him that no one seemed any happier afterward. Not even Bat, who'd done the work.

"Come on," he said, "it is at least a plan, right?"

"Coffee?" said Talia, rising and stepping to a forbidding chunk of technology on the far corner of the kitchen counter.

"Thank you," said Tallow.

"You haven't drunk it yet," said Bat.

"Bat, you have the digestive system of a runty, poisoned squirrel. John is clearly made of stronger stuff. Even if he is quite nuts."

"Why does everyone call me crazy?"

Talia, at the machine, said, "Has it occurred to you for just one moment that you could have spun this whole thing into promotions for yourself, Scarlatta, and probably even Bat?"

Tallow jolted forward in his chair. "What?"

"You could have easily just said to this assistant chief, Okay, I know what your game is — what's it worth to you to ensure no one finds out? You could have said, I want to be an inspector, or a lieutenant, and my good friend Scarlatta would like a supervisory role and a big fat raise. And Bat would like to lose his virginity. See to it, and all this goes away. You could have done that. Did you ever think of it, John?"

"No," he said, sitting back. "Not once."

"Now that you've thought about it," Talia said, "do you wish you'd done it?"

After some length, Tallow quietly said, "No."

"Crazy." Talia smiled. "But okay. You can still sleep over. I tell you, though, I imagine your life as a detective has been unnecessarily difficult over the years."

"Not really," Tallow said, mostly to himself. "Not until now."

His cell phone rang.

THIRTY

The hunter ate a little more, sat within a dark stand of trees in order to gather himself for a short period, and then slept for a while.

He awoke from troubled sleep with a shock, as if a dream had run him through with a spear.

Looking up and quelling some trembling in his hands, the hunter found a few stars and the moon to judge the time by, and he calculated that his appointment was imminent. He took his bag and checked through its contents — even with the gun and some things appropriated from the hardware store, he still felt worriedly undertooled — and then rose and began to walk, shaking the damp cold from his legs with some difficulty. Once his thighs and calves loosened up, he slipped into the deep growth abutting the designated meeting point, shifting to the slow and exaggerated steps of woodcraft training and approaching in silence and invisibility.

There were three people at the meeting point.

The hunter smiled. They still huffed and shuffled like three nervous boys in their early twenties. The meeting was obviously going to be more protracted than he would have liked, but it looked as if it'd make up for it in amusement.

He emerged onto the path, allowing them to see him. Their joint reaction pleased him to an almost guilty extent.

"Hello," he said. "The gang's all here, I see."

They all looked sick to one degree or another.

"It's been a very long time since we all stood in the same place," said the hunter. "I wonder why you have all arrived to make me feel so special tonight."

Westover slowly extended a hand, a slip of paper in his fingers. The hunter, regarding him with condescending humor, took it, slowly.

"That," Westover said, "is the name and address of the police officer in question."

"Do we know anything about his habits?" the hunter asked, noting that the location was a good two hours' walk away.

"No social life," said Turkel. "He spends

his nights reading and listening to music, apparently."

The hunter pocketed the slip. "Excellent. So, shall I be on my way?"

"I think we have to talk about how this ends," said Westover.

"How it ends? With the death of the man whose address you just gave me."

"Really? That ends all this?"

"That depends," said the hunter, "on what you mean by *all this*. What *I* mean is that I expect this man's death to hamper the investigation to such an extent that it effectively concludes it."

"I'm unclear on that," said Machen.

"If I may," said Turkel to the hunter. The hunter gave him a broad, mocking smile and bade him continue with a grand sweep of his hand. Turkel swallowed hard and continued. "Tallow *is* the case, at this point. He's submitted no paper report that I'm aware of. Tallow's death erases enough information to cripple further investigation. And, frankly, he seems to be the only one interested in pursuing it. I suspect he's mentally ill. There is another issue involving one of the guns removed from a storage facility, but investigatively it's —"

"A dead end?" The hunter chuckled.

"— going to be unproductive," Turkel

said, faint disgust in his face as it turned to the hunter.

"There we have it," said the hunter. "The death of this man concludes the difficulty in front of us. But I don't speak of an end to all this. There is work yet to be done."

"What work?" said Westover.

"My work. It has been undone, and must begin again. My keep has been breached, and my work dismantled and stolen. I strongly doubt that I will ever recover all the pieces, and in any case they may be too tainted to weave back together. I must begin again."

"If we're understanding you correctly," said Machen, "your . . . collection took the best part of twenty years to put together. But the work is done."

"Really?" The hunter chuckled again. "Have you all achieved your great ambitions? Dreams all come true? Is there nothing more you aspire to? I doubt that. I don't think that, for you three, greed was something you could don in your young winters and then shrug off like an overcoat in a warm room. Do you really mean to tell me that there is nothing left that you want? You, Mr. Machen. You could yet be running the great financial mill of this city. In twenty years you could be the mayor. Mr. Turkel here is not yet commissioner, is he? Mr. Westover — well, I shudder to think of what horrors he has still to achieve. Although, if I'm honest, I'm not greatly impressed by the security around his home."

"You don't want to stop," said Machen in a flat voice.

"I don't want to stop. I have a thing to finish. And since you three also have things to finish, I feel that it works out well for all of us."

Westover said, "What would it take to make you stop?"

The hunter laughed, surprising even himself.

"It's a serious question," said Westover. "It comes with the promise of substantial remuneration and whatever other facilitation you might require."

"We can begin in the region of half a million dollars in nonconsecutive used bills," said Machen.

"And, of course, a guarantee of safe passage out of the Five Boroughs, with provision of either a vehicle or a plane ticket," said Turkel.

"Well, well," said the hunter. "You've been talking among yourselves, haven't you? Three fat old men huddling in a park in the dark, wondering how to haggle their way out of the lives they chose for themselves. Fearfully hoping to buy off the agent of their success."

"We hired you, and we can —" Machen began.

"You hired me and so you can fire me? I work for you? Is that what you're saying? You idiots. You mindless, worthless, laughable slugs. I don't work for you. You work for me. I found three people so desperate to be somebodies that they gave me money for the work I already fully intended to do. You didn't give me purpose. You funded my purpose. I took the structure of your needs for my own use. You work for me, and I decide when it ends. All three of you are the same mediocrities you were when I met you. You simply own better shoes now. Look at you. You think I killed at your command to make you great. You're not great. You are nothing but the things that float to the surface when all obstructions are cut away. You can't buy me off because this was never about the money. It was about the work. You will continue to fund me as per the original arrangement, and you will continue to give me more modern people to kill, because it amuses me. Do you understand me?"

There was silence, and the stink of their fear.

"You never knew me at all, did you? You never understood a thing. Too focused on your own gain."

Westover opened his jacket.

The hunter's hand went into his bag, finding the grips of the gun he took from Kutkha.

Westover noted the movement, inclined his head slightly, and slowed his movements down. He withdrew an envelope from the inside pocket of the jacket and extended it to the hunter. "I presume you can drive," Westover said.

"When I have to," said the hunter, stepping back into the shadows to disguise any possible outward sign of the revulsion the thought caused him. He felt the envelope; there was something plastic in there, along with the rustle of folded paper.

Westover lowered his voice. "The envelope contains the details you would need to recover at least some of your weapons. The names therein are . . . expendable."

Turkel turned away.

"Well," said the hunter. "I have a busy night ahead. So I'll leave you gentlemen to the remainders of your evenings. I want to see you here tomorrow night. Just one of you will do. Choose among yourselves. Decide how we're going to move forward. We're all still young, and there's much yet to achieve here on this great island. Don't you think?"

Turkel was already walking away, his back to the hunter. Machen and Westover followed him. The hunter watched them go, moving position once a minute for five minutes until he was certain they'd all separated and were taking properly divergent routes. He then found a light source that was lonely enough for him to safely open the envelope and study its contents.

The hunter was not happy about traveling in a motor vehicle, but on this night, the speed of travel in a modern conveyance would undoubtedly be useful. He simply had to decide where Detective John Tallow fell on his to-do list tonight.

THIRTY-ONE

"Help me," Emily Westover said.

"What is it?" said Tallow, rising from the table, putting out a palm against the questioning looks he was getting.

"Jason's downstairs. Said he had to talk to one of the employees. He said he's going out tonight but he's not walking the dog."

"I don't know what that means."

"He goes out at ten forty-five every night with the dog, walks her around Central Park a bit. Every night. Tonight he says he's got to go out at ten forty-five but he can't take the dog."

"I'm sure it's nothing to be concerned about, Mrs. Westover."

"He's been taking calls from his two friends. I know what this is about."

"Which friends?"

"I shouldn't tell you."

"Mrs. Westover, with all respect, you shouldn't be on the phone to me either.

393

Now, you just asked for my help. I can't help you without knowing everything that's going on."

"You think I'm crazy."

"No, ma'am."

"Well, you should." She laughed. Giggled, in fact. The sound made Tallow go cold, for some reason. "I am crazy. But not so crazy that I don't know I'm crazy, and I think that's an important distinction. Andy Machen and that creepy bastard Al Turkel. He's been talking to them. Something serious is happening tonight. Jason told me that I know what it's about. Which means it's about what, what, what he did to get where he is. What they did. Do you understand?"

Tallow had walked into the other room. He caught his reflection in a small mirror on the wall and judged himself before speaking.

"Mrs. Westover, what are you afraid of at Werpoes?"

"Him. He lives there."

"Werpoes is buried and built on, and no one's hiding in that square."

"Jason told me to stay away from there."

Given that the cache on Pearl Street had seemed to catch everyone by surprise, did it make sense for them to believe that CTS lived elsewhere? No. They paid for the Pearl

Street apartment, and Westover himself was at least an accessory to providing a security door for the place. But then, CTS could not possibly have *lived* at the Pearl Street address, and he was unlikely to be sleeping outdoors all the time.

Tallow had missed something. His man CTS had to have more than one hideout. Possibly even several. Had anything gone wrong over the past two decades of his work, he would have needed other places to shelter. Perhaps places that his employers didn't know about. This would make sense if he expected that one day, one of them would get caught, or get sloppy. Or, perhaps, get an attack of guilt and talk to his wife.

"Mr. Westover told you to stay away from there because he lived in the area."

"He lives there. Jason doesn't know exactly where, but . . . Werpoes. He's there."

"Tell me how I can help you, Mrs. Westover."

"Save Jason. Please."

Tallow's words dried up in his throat.

"Please. You saved me. Save Jason. This is all too much for him. Save him. He's raised this thing, this awful fucking manitou from the dirt of Old Manhattan, and it's going to kill him. Please, John."

Tallow's mind was surging down parallel

tracks. He looked for a notepad and pen. The apartment didn't have a landline phone, so there was no table with scratch paper.

"I'm not sure how to do that, Mrs. Westover."

He ducked into the kitchen and furiously mimed writing. Talia pulled open a kitchen drawer and produced a notebook and pencil.

"I don't know. Talk to him. Promise him safety. Reason with him. Something. He wants out, I can see it in him."

Talia put the pad and pencil on the kitchen table. Tallow wrote as clearly and swiftly as he could, and spun the pad to face Bat and Scarly. They nodded, visibly shifting into professional mode. Bat pulled out a smartphone, thumbed it to mute, and began typing as Scarly quietly got up and left the room.

"I can get there tonight," Tallow said, "but not right now. Just sit tight. I promise I'll be there. Don't say anything to him. It would be best if he had no warning. Okay?"

"You'll save him."

"I promise you that I'll do everything in my power to save him."

"Thank you," she said, grinding out the words, audibly wrestling with a sudden appalling need to burst into tears.

Tallow killed the call.

Scarly was already at a laptop in the other room.

"That was the wife of one of the people we believe to have hired our killer," said Tallow to Talia, loud enough for everyone to hear him clearly. "She wants me to induce her husband to confess his involvement and save himself from the fallout. She also believes that Westover, Machen, and Turkel are meeting the killer tonight, in Central Park."

"Great," said Talia. "Send in the cavalry. Surround them and catch them in the act."

"Even if we knew which part of Central Park, which is a big-ass place and lousy to operate in at night, and even if we could summon the manpower, which is doubtful — my captain doesn't have the juice, my lieutenant doesn't believe me, and I don't have any friends — I don't think that'd work."

Tallow explained to them why he thought Emily Westover had been told to stay away from Werpoes.

"Christ," said Talia, finally. "So what do you do?"

Tallow sat down with a heavy sigh, and

waited a full thirty seconds before responding.

"I am kind of disturbed to report that I haven't felt this good in years, and that I know exactly what we're going to do. I just don't know if it's going to work. And I don't know if I haven't gone crazy too. The worst kind of crazy, where I don't know I'm crazy. I hear it's an important distinction."

"You're crazy," said Bat, not looking up from his phone.

"Thanks, Bat."

"Do we have to leave soon?" said Bat. "Because I'm going to need to use the bathroom, because *death bag.*"

"No," said Tallow. "I want to get all this sorted out first. You need to find what I'm looking for, and you also need to get some gear out of the trunk of Scarly's car. That's where I'm guessing you keep it."

"He keeps all his shit in the back of my car," said Scarly from the other room. "There's a pair of his underpants fused to my spare tire."

"Good. Also, check your weapons."

This time, Bat looked up at him. Tallow ignored the look. He was running through every eventuality he could conjure up for the next few hours of the future. The one thing he wasn't planning for, he told himself

with a small icy smile, was tomorrow morning.

THIRTY-TWO

There was a Spearpoint guard behind the wheel of the car. It was exactly where the note from Westover had told the hunter he would find it, not fifteen minutes' walk from the Ramble. The hunter spent an additional five minutes surveilling the car from four different positions before satisfying himself it was safe and approaching it.

The hunter walked past the car one last time, and tapped on the driver's window. The driver tried to pretend he had been ready for it. The car unlocked, and the hunter got into the rear passenger seat.

"Do you know where we're going?" said the hunter. He disliked the eager, excited gleam he could see in the driver's eyes in the rearview mirror.

"Yes, sir. Downtown storage facility B."

"Then start driving."

"Yes, sir." The driver grinned into the mirror.

"You weren't told not to look at me," the hunter stated.

"Oh. Yes, sir, I was. Sorry. This is all new to me."

"You don't normally drive?"

The car pulled away. The driver kept talking. "I, uh, I think I just got promoted? I usually work security at the Aer Keep. But I sent off a cop today, and I think I got noticed. So Mr. Westover told me, just tonight, that I have new duties and they're very important."

The driver was flushed with pride, and his eyes glittered with a new feeling of power and ascendancy. The hunter was displeased.

"Just drive," the hunter said, leaning forward and putting his face in his hands. The feeling of motion in a car was just a little too alien for him right now.

"Are you all right?" the driver asked.

"I am trying not to look out the windows," said the hunter. "And in general I would prefer not to be seen. Just drive."

"Yes, sir. Mustn't argue with a very important person like you. Must be up to all kinds of important business, to be given a personal driver at this time of night. Well, I'm up for that. You tell Mr. Westover, this is the kind of work I can do just right . . ."

The drive took too long. The hunter

wasn't able to closely follow the passage of time, but given the steady stream of noise from the driver, it was definitely too long. The ride was making him sick, and, even if he'd been in a more tolerant mood, he was unused enough to being trapped with human noise that the constant talking was driving him to blind rage.

Finally, they stopped in a quiet street. The hunter looked around and saw the broad shutter of the storage facility — essentially a place where a few vans could be offloaded and parked overnight.

"This is the place, sir," said the driver.

The hunter reached around and punched the driver in the neck with savage force three times, to make him die in a sudden flash of shredding agony.

The hunter waited until he stopped spasming, and then got out of the car and opened the driver's door to check the body for a gun, holding his breath against the stink of urine and excrement leaking into its pants. The weapon was a heavy, overly styled Beretta. From his library reading, conducted religiously on those days where he could face touching a computer, the hunter guessed it to be a Neos semiautomatic. He cycled it as quickly and quietly as he could: one in the pipe and nine left in the magazine. He'd have to be careful with it. It was the kind of gun that used the hot gases from a bullet's firing to cycle the gun and load a new bullet. The slide would kick back by a couple of inches of its own accord. He pocketed the stupid gun and closed the door.

The shutter on the storage facility was locked down. There was a pedestrian entrance next to it, in a recess. Inside the alcove was a card-reader lock. The hunter was having serious problems controlling his stomach. There was a security camera over the door. As Westover's notes had said, its telltale red light was off. Within the envelope was the plastic card the reader wanted. He took a breath and held it, willed his fingers to obey him, and slid the card through the reader's black lips. The door popped open with a sigh.

Inside, there was gray concrete, a single truck in Spearpoint livery, metal steps leading to office space upstairs, and two voices.

"Sophie," said a man's voice, "we have people to do paperwork. I just wanna go home. I missed a workout, I missed fucking dinner, I just wanna go home and sleep."

The hunter approached along the side of the truck. The voices were coming from behind it.

"For Christ's sake, Mike. It'll take two minutes. If I don't do it now, then it's going to take ten minutes first thing tomorrow when some desk drone decides he — and it's always a he, Mike — wants to justify his little job. Where are the keys?"

"In the ignition."

"For Christ's sake, Mike. You really are a giant asshole-muscle."

Sophie walked around the rear of the truck toward the driver's side door and right into the hunter. She gasped, mouth open wide, drawing in enough air for a shout or a strike. The hunter drove his knife through her hard palate and up into her brain and twisted. She died right there, and the only sound she made was the splashing of all the blood in her head falling out of her mouth and onto the concrete floor.

Mike looked around from the rear, smiling. The hunter skewered his eye, thrust deep into his head, put both hands to the grip of the knife, and lifted. Mike hung from the blade, a couple of inches off the ground, dying for a stubborn fifteen seconds. The hunter shucked his skull like an oyster and shook him off the blade. The body collapsed to the floor. A slice of wet gray brain oozed out of his destroyed eye.

The rear of the van hadn't been closed. It

was two-thirds filled with plastic crates. The crates were filled with guns. His guns.

The hunter was still for long moments, entranced by their destroyed beauty. All their true meaning smashed away by idiots who demeaned them, tossing them into ugly boxes like so many farming implements.

But they still had beauty. They could have meaning again. Even this raw amputated chunk of his machine would still have use.

In the envelope was the plastic lump he felt earlier. He took the key out and used it to unlock the shutter, which clattered up into the ceiling. The hunter closed the rear door of the truck and got behind the wheel. This was horrible to him, but it was necessary for the task. This was, as far as the hunter was concerned, now a rescue. He touched the ignition key, still in the small mouth of the car's workings, with an experimental brush. It buzzed under his fingertips with insect horror. The hunter clenched that fist, and then grasped the key and turned with determined commitment. The truck awoke, a vile, coughing parody of animal life. He summoned his memory of how it worked and gingerly operated the thing, edging it out of the garage and onto the street. There was a sour pleasure at having correctly recalled how to drive, something he hadn't done in years, if not decades. He parked ten feet down the street, stepped out quickly, pulled the shutter back down, and locked it.

The hunter drove his machine to John Tallow's house, the black branches of the Mannahatta forest clawing with hate at its glass and tin the whole way.

No car journey in New York City was short, even at this time of night — What *was* the time? he thought, for he couldn't see stars, and the dashboard held no clock — but he felt like he'd crossed the awful mathematics of Lower Manhattan in a reasonable period. He found parking on the street within sight of Tallow's apartment building, and consulted the envelope one more time. Someone — he assumed Westover — had been busy. A rough plan of Tallow's apartment's floor had been sketched out, with indications for placement and exits. The hunter stuck his head out the window and, with just a few seconds' difficulty, located north. Applying it to the sketch, he found he should be able to see Tallow's apartment's window.

Just as he discovered the correct window, the light inside Tallow's apartment went off.

The hunter got out of the truck, locked it up, and strolled across the street. He had time, intelligence, and the correct tool for the job in his bag.

As he approached the front of the property, he realized the main entrance was locked. But before he could reach it, a reasonably drunken couple in their twenties arrived and, laughing at their inability to make their fingers hold the key properly, took a useful minute to open the door.

The hunter stepped in behind them, the key to the truck in his hand, the metal protruding, his head down and weaving. "Thanks. Saved me the trouble of having to try that myself." The couple laughed, too wrapped up in each other to even look at his face as they headed for the elevator. The hunter angled away quickly, went through a fire door to the stairwell.

At Tallow's floor, he waited behind the fire door that opened onto the corridor for a minute or two. The fire door was propped open by his foot, creating a gap through which he could listen. He was hunting for the sounds of someone preparing to leave his apartment, trying to filter footfall and conversation from out of television noise and what he guessed to be some kind of video game. The same sounds that would make him so ill when he spent too long at the Pearl Street building. Only when he'd covered enough surfaces in gunmetal did the noise grow deadened.

This was the time.

The hunter found Tallow's apartment. He had two options at this point: silent entry and bringing Tallow to the door. Silent entry was always preferred but sometimes defeated by security measures.

The hunter took the card that opened the Spearpoint garage, flexed it, rubbed a little spittle on its short edge with his thumb, and slipped it into the space between the door and its frame. He worked it, gently and patiently and silently, until he felt the latch start to lift. With slow and precise applications of force, the hunter eased the latch behind the strike plate, maintained as much pressure upon it as he dared, and moved the door open. There were no chains and no dead bolts. John Tallow was evidently a very comfortable and unworried man.

The hunter drew the Colt Official Police from his bag. The grips met his hand with a warm and ineffable feeling of rightness. Everything was perfect.

THIRTY-THREE

Jason Westover opened the door to his apartment to discover he had visitors. Tallow watched Westover recognize him. Tallow watched Westover recognize the Glock aimed at him.

"Good evening, Mr. Westover. If you wouldn't mind carefully taking off your gun and your other weapons and laying them on the floor in front of you, I'd be obliged."

Tallow watched Westover's eyes flicker across to Emily, sitting down and getting over another crying jag, with Scarly standing over her, and Bat standing behind that sofa with his hand on the butt of his sidearm.

"There's no angle to play, Mr. Westover. Please do as I ask."

Westover met Tallow's eyes. Westover was a man who wore his pride like a shell. Pride in his own discipline, tough-mindedness, and practicality. All of that was in his gaze.

Tallow just looked at him.

Westover paled, and slowly took out a gun and a knife and laid them on the polished walnut flooring.

"That's good," said Tallow. "Now, why don't you sit on the sofa with your wife and tell me where you've been tonight?"

"I'd rather stand," said Westover with quiet venom.

"Fine. Tell me where you've been tonight."

"Why don't you go home, Detective Tallow?" said Westover with a thin smile.

"Do I appear tired to you?" said Tallow, centering the Glock's aim on Westover's heart. "Let me help you get started. You met Andrew Machen, and Al Turkel, and a certain other man whom Al Turkel discovered and presented to you some twenty years ago."

Westover's smiled broadened into something supercilious and infantile. He planted his feet and put his hands behind his back like a soldier standing at ease.

"Hands in front, please," said Tallow. "Don't test me, Mr. Westover. Nobody who's tested me this week has come off well. Including Assistant Chief Turkel."

Westover raised an eyebrow.

"Oh," said Tallow. "He didn't tell you? He tried to close this investigation. He wasn't banking on the fact that this investigation has become the only thing in life I'm really interested in. So I arranged for the first deputy commissioner to take him out behind the barn for a bit. Al Turkel's career is stopped dead. I've hung too much of this case around his neck. He might survive, but he's completely compromised. Tomorrow, he's going to be sat down in a small room and talked to by some very clever and fairly violent people. He mentioned none of this, right?"

Westover was motionless. Processing.

"I'm here tonight, sir, because your wife called me. She called me and begged me to save you."

"It's true," Emily Westover rasped, throat worn ragged by the crying.

"You can't save me," said Westover to Tallow. "You can't even save yourself. You certainly can't save me."

"Of course I can," Tallow said. "You haven't been listening. The NYPD have a rogue cop running an entire district. He's had other police killed. You were just starting your security firm when all this began. You had some of the money and materials Turkel needed to make his scheme work, but you couldn't possibly defend yourself against such a man."

Westover's eyes narrowed.

"Turkel's got a fat neck," said Tallow. "Plenty of space left to hang stuff around it. I certainly have no problem with telling people you were forced into the whole thing."

"Why?"

"She asked me to save you. Look at her. She's been one of the walking wounded ever since you decided to hurt her by telling her what your little life was built on. She's smarter than you. She has more imagination than you. So she feels fear and guilt more acutely than you. And I think you knew that. You knew it and you did it to her anyway. And she *still* begged me to save you. Do you get what that says about you? Even a little bit?"

Jason Westover could not make himself look away from Emily Westover. Emily Westover could look only at Jason Westover.

Westover whispered, "What do you want?"

Tallow lifted his phone out of his breast pocket and looked at the clock on the lock screen. "We're running out of time." He used the killer's real name and said, "Where is he now?"

Westover looked down, turned away. "On his way downtown, by car."

So that's how it is, thought Tallow, and

said, "Driving, or being driven?"

"Driving. I loaned him a vehicle."

"What's downtown for him?"

"I don't know. He said he had a place to hide. Wouldn't tell us where it was."

"Nowhere near Collect Pond Park?"

Westover scowled. "He wouldn't go there."

"Really? And yet you told your wife to avoid that area."

"He sleeps somewhere around there. That's all I know."

"So your meeting was to provide him with a car and . . . ?"

"Money. And to pursue the idea of providing him passage out of the NYC area."

"I see," said Tallow, who was experiencing the air in the room as thick and choked with the tangle of lies being puked out by both of them. Westover wasn't going to say one true thing to him. Or, worse, he was going to salt his lies with lonely little grains of truth, and Tallow would have to sift everything through the imperfect sieve of what he knew to be correct. He needed to get one useful thing out of Westover.

"Tell me about this Ambient Security thing of yours. Does it work on mobile devices?"

Westover frowned, genuinely thrown by

the new track of the conversation. "Sure. Why?"

"Give me twelve hours' access to it."

"Show me your phone," said Westover. Tallow did. Westover appraised it. "Isn't that a little pricey for a cop?"

"I don't buy a lot of clothes," said Tallow.

"No. No, I imagine not. Hold on, let me get my phone." Westover stepped to a nearby merchant's chest made from artfully distressed wood. Or, thought Tallow, possibly wood actually salvaged from an ancient shipwreck. Tallow looked up at the sound of a clicking.

Scarly had her gun on Westover. "If anything other than a phone comes out of that drawer, sir, I will put two in you, right in front of your wife."

"It's all right," Tallow said. "Mr. Westover's on our side now. Isn't that right?"

"Right," said Westover, coming away from the drawer with a phone held out for Scarly's benefit. "Switch your Bluetooth on, Tallow." After a few moments of tapping and fiddling, an app had been copied to Tallow's phone, and a registration code and password entered into it.

"There," said Westover. "On the standard setting, it's going to give you live feeds from whichever Ambient Security cams surround your GPS location. Tap that, and you go to the Forward setting, grabbing the live feed from the cameras ten to twenty yards ahead of your location."

"What's that for?"

"Pursuit," said Westover, looking at Tallow like he was an idiot. "Do you not understand what my company does? We're going to take your job, Tallow."

"I believe I've had the company lecture on that once or twice," Tallow murmured.

"Right. With Ambient Security, I can outsource *and* crowd-source the very concept of criminal pursuit in this city. The red button launches a speakerphone call to a live operator in the ops room. I don't need a bunch of cops and cars on the ground. I could chase and take down a speeding car with one operator using the Forward setting and a drone."

"Very clever. I'll be sure to tell the first deputy tomorrow. You'll need another advocate in the department once Turkel's gone, after all."

"Huh," said Westover, bluntly surprised. "I hadn't thought about that."

"Yeah."

"Yeah. You're right. Thanks. So what do you need access to Ambient Security for?"

"Well," said Tallow. "I want to take a drive

to Collect Pond Park before I head home, have a look around, and I figured that with this, I wouldn't have to get out of the car." He threw Westover a crooked, friendly grin and watched Westover relax just a little. "Also, I wanted to see if you'd cooperate. Ensure you're on board with all this."

"And there it is on your phone."

"And there it is on my phone. Just rescind my access to it in twelve hours, and I'll call that a sign of everything going well."

"Okay."

"Okay," said Tallow. "Time for me to go home. Officers." He meant Bat and Scarly by this, and they responded by marching dutifully to the door.

"Mrs. Westover." Tallow gave her the kindest, warmest smile he could find.

"Thank you," she said brokenly, and then looked down at her hands.

"We'll see ourselves out," Tallow said, and they left.

In the elevator, Tallow tossed his cell to Bat. "Westover put a password on that app. Change it."

"Why?" asked Bat, nearly fumbling it.

"Because if he knows the password he can rescind the app's access to Ambient Security."

"He could also just deactivate the registration code."

"He could, but it'd take him longer, because his own access to Ambient Security is on that code."

"That," said Scarly, "didn't go as well as it could have. Did it?"

"No," Tallow admitted. "No, he's decided it's a game to be played all the way through. Stupid. I feel sorry for his wife."

"I'm not sure I do," said Scarly. "Except that she's got all the classic symptoms of an untreated psychotic break. That, I feel bad about. Everything else, not so much."

"None of it's her fault, Scarly."

"You think? The way I see it, when she didn't up and leave him the minute he explained all that, it became her fault."

"You're forgetting," Bat muttered, tapping away at the phone. "If she'd up and left him, the next thing that happened, the absolute next thing, would have been him giving her name and general description to CTS. I wonder what kind of gun CTS would have chosen for her."

Scarly gathered breath for an outburst, which Tallow expected would involve judging and autism, but then she leaned against the elevator wall and deflated. "Yeah."

"Oh well," said Tallow, as the elevator opened up on the ground floor of Aer Keep.

"It's getting late. Time I went home, I guess."

THIRTY-FOUR

The hunter pushed the door just a little farther open, and stepped into the dark room.

An inhuman voice shrieked, *"Say hello to my li'l frien',"* there was a sharp flurry of detonation flashes, and the hunter felt multiple impacts on his chest and face. The lights came on, harsh and bright, blinding the hunter. He fired the Colt in front of him, but the hideous metallic din didn't stop, and now it was screaming, *"Fuck you fuck you fuck you."*

The hunter staggered back into the hallway, wiping his face. His vision was blasted and hazy, but he could make out vivid orange paint on his fingertips. The metal screaming wouldn't stop. The hunter ran for the fire door, fearing neighbors would be brought to the corridor by the noise. The hall creaked and tilted in his vision, becoming a dark tunnel, and he could see the sounds, suddenly, as pistoning metal tentacles, fucking their way through the wall and the floor after him.

The hunter hurled himself through the fire door and down the stairs. He had to stop at the next landing and throw up. The vomit spread through the floor and the walls, turning the stairwell into a wet red digestive tract. He kept running down the stairs, almost slipping twice on his own vomit where it coated the soles of his shoes.

The hunter burst into the hallway, still half blind, trying not to scream, feeling bruises bloom and stiffen his flesh where the thing had attacked him. Through the glass of the front door he saw a tall flapping creature, some black-winged half-human thing moving its long awful limbs and shouting words he couldn't decipher.

On the run, the hunter put two bullets through the glass and into the thing's chest, smashed through the door by main force and momentum, and didn't even break stride over the body on the ground as he sprinted off into the night.

THIRTY-FIVE

Packed into Tallow's car, he and the CSUs were five minutes away from Tallow's apartment when he said, "Kill the lights."

Bat took out his own phone and thumbed something into it.

"This is what you did with my Twine unit." Scarly sulked. "That cost me a hundred bucks."

"What?" said Tallow.

"The thing I wired into your lighting circuit. That lets me turn your lights off over the Internet."

"That cost a hundred bucks?"

"Yes. And I had to wait for it."

"Damn," said Tallow. "I hope he doesn't shoot it."

"You're not funny. I am also not thrilled about my paintball gear being cannibalized for this idiot stunt."

"Hey. Your office is filled with dangerous junk. Paintballs, dyes, detonator caps, God knows what else. You planned to use it all one day, right?"

"Well," said Scarly. "Actually, some of it's stuff that Talia won't let me keep at home."

Tallow blew stale air out of his lungs, wound down the window, and tried to get a chestful of something sweeter. "Our guy does two things. He kills people and he hides in plain sight. I want him marked. If he can't hide, he loses power. If we can take that from him, we finally, *finally* have an edge on him. We just have to be patient tonight."

"And lucky," said Bat.

"That too," said Tallow. "But both Turkel and Westover are pretty sure I'm going to get hit tonight. I wonder where Machen is."

"Jerking off inside his money bin," said Scarly.

Tallow found a parking space on the street that had the front of his apartment building in sight. The lights in Tallow's apartment were off. He pulled into the spot and turned the engine off. "Okay. I'll take the rear exit. Scarly will take the side escape. Bat can take the front."

"Why do I get the front?" Bat whined.

"Honestly? Because this is our guy, and our guy doesn't strike me as the sort of guy who usually takes the front door. He's a hunter. I'm expecting him to come in and out of the back exit, with the fire escape as a secondary measure."

"So now you're saying I can't handle CTS?"

"Make your mind up, Bat. Either you're upset because he might come out the front, or you're upset because I think Scarly is probably a better shot than you are."

"I can be pissed about both. I am very clever and a good multi-tasker."

"Get out of the car and check your gun, Bat."

"I already checked it."

"Check it again."

Tallow got angry at himself, at the nerves in his own voice. Bat didn't meet his eyes.

They got out of the car. Tallow locked it up and lifted and reseated his Glock, and they walked toward his apartment building.

"Wow," said Scarly. "You live in a shit-box."

"Take the side," said Tallow, just as his apartment window shattered and a gunshot smacked the air with a flat report.

"Move," Tallow said, and broke into a run. He was authentically terrified. He tried to count off imaginary time. He trusted that Fuck You Robot's motion sensor had lit off the explosive caps behind the dye-filled paintballs, and that the one gunshot was an instinctive squeeze of the trigger as the things hit his man. He would have quickly worked out that Tallow wasn't in the apartment and would be heading down. Tallow attempted calculations: How fast could someone run down that narrow stairway? Would his man have tried the elevator? Not while he was covered in fluorescent orange paint, probably, but if he made it into the elevator before anyone came out to see what the noise was — but it was a gunshot, and people tended not to come out from behind their doors to look for actively firing guns . . .

Tallow got to the rear exit, lit by a single overhead lamp and surrounded on two sides by cheap mesh fencing. Someone exiting that door could come only one way — right now, that was straight toward Tallow. He flattened his back against the wall next to the door, drew his Glock, and waited.

He counted off a minute. He was straining his hearing listening for the sound of another egress being used, but his own pulse in his ears was drowning out all other noise.

Tallow was jerked around by a double gunshot and a crash of glass.

"Oh no," he breathed, and then he ran. He was certain that the sound had come from the apartment building's front.

Tallow felt like he was moving through molasses, like he was in one of those nightmares where you could barely move even though something terrible was happening. By the time he got around the front corner of the building, Scarly was already at the smashed main entrance, and Bat was on his back with two seared holes in his shirt.

Tallow looked around. Someone was running down the street away from him, past his own car. As the man passed under a streetlight, Tallow could discern a thin cloud of orange powder around his head.

Scarly was tearing Bat's shirt open. "You *stupid* bastard," she was saying. "You *stupid* bastard."

Both rounds were buried in the Kevlar vest under Bat's shirt, one of the ones Tallow had insisted they retrieve from Scarly's car trunk earlier.

Bat coughed blood and then groaned. The groan made him convulse. Tallow guessed he had some broken bones. Scarly took out her phone. "I'm calling it in. Go and kill that fucker, John."

Tallow took off after the hunter. Reaching his car, he looked down the street to see where his man was running. Tallow then unlocked and got into his car, jammed his phone into the dash and launched Ambient Security, and twisted the ignition. He made the car sweep around in a wide circle, tilting with the anger of its turn, and then Tallow rammed the accelerator down.

THIRTY-SIX

The hunter didn't know what was happening. He knew only that he had to hide.

He ran down the middle of the street, zigzagging when he approached traffic lights since he knew of old that they often meant security cameras were close by. He could tell traffic lights by their three eyes, vertically arranged, and their long black bodies poised to strike, like cobras. One step was on blacktop, the next on dirt. Everything was wrong.

He knew where he was going.

There were still people on the street, and they were staring at him. The paint was everywhere, all over him, penetrating his clothes, gumming his eyelids together. He perceived a tiny flash, a red light, at the edge of his peripheral vision, and put his gun on it. There was no one there: the space between two trees resolved in his eyes into a storefront. He approached it. The red light flashed again. A box with black glass in it — a computer, he told himself — and an eye atop it. As he moved in front of it, the red light went off again, under the eye.

The hunter ran. Three stores down, he saw another light blink on and off.

There were eyes in every window.

He was trapped in the future, and everyone was watching him.

The hunter made the crosswalk. A bison, giant and dark and its fur slick with pond water, rushed him across the trail. On the run, he shot it between the eyes. It swerved unnaturally and struck a broad black maple on the corner, wrapping around its trunk and smoking as it came to rest. The hunter was already gone.

Tallow punched Ambient Security into Forward mode. The system started gathering motion-triggered webcam shots from the streets ahead. There was an arresting shot of a man demented by terror and covered in orange paint staring into the camera and realizing he was caught. It was three blocks in front of him. *You're a fast bastard, aren't you,* Tallow thought, and was glad he had taken the car. There was no way he could have kept up on foot, and frankly, he wasn't doing so well in the car. He matched the picture's location to the map, judged the traffic system, and made a turn, hoping to hell that he was guessing right.

He saw a car embedded in a lamppost, its windshield shot out.

A lynx tore past the hunter, making a noise like a riverfront storm. It had a human rider with a flat glass face.

The hunter was frantically trying to match landmarks to memory, but everything was shifting. He got a street sign to resolve through the twisting chaos of his vision, found his orientation, and sprinted down a conduit alley.

Tallow saw a blurred snap on his phone, flicked his eyes to the map, and knew where the hunter was going. He knew that alley, he knew where it came out, and he was now certain of the hunter's intended destination. Tallow figured that his man, in fact, was entirely too close to it.

The hunter emerged from the alley to see a pack of dogs come around the street corner to his left with a horrific squeal. The hunter shook his head, gripping his gun harder. The pack coalesced into a motor vehicle, one he knew.

The car mounted the sidewalk. The hunter could not stand and fight. He snapped off a shot at the car, turned, and ran for his life.

It was a good shot, and a good reminder for Tallow that the paint-spattered lunatic on the street was the most prolific and efficient killer he'd ever heard of. The windshield crazed, and the right corner of his seat exploded in shredded cheap vinyl and yellow foam. He was blind and had no choice but to stamp on the brake. His right shoulder burned, just at the top. He glanced at it swiftly and saw a neat notch seared at the shoulder of his suit jacket. Not important. Tallow elbowed out a hole in the windshield glass and tried to convince the car to move forward again. The car wasn't interested and made a sound like a sick dog gnawing on a branch.

The hunter had gone twenty or thirty steps before he realized he couldn't hear the car running. It was stopped, half on the sidewalk.

The hunter knew he should keep going. Half a minute of sprinting would put him entirely out of Tallow's sight. But the car wasn't moving. Perhaps he'd wounded Tallow. Perhaps he'd done some paralyzing violence to the vehicle's workings. He should run. But Tallow was there to be killed. He wanted to kill Tallow so much. A hunter didn't just leave prey sitting there. It would have been tasteless to walk away.

The hunter started walking back to the car, quickly.

The damned engine wouldn't turn over. Tallow didn't know why. Tallow wasn't good with cars.

Jim Rosato had always said Tallow wasn't good with cars. That's why he drove. Jim Rosato had always said Tallow wasn't a street cop like him, and that's why he went first in a street situation.

"Jim Rosato's dead," said Tallow as he wrenched the ignition and stamped on the pedals. The car leaped forward like an animal, spitting out a hubcap as it gained the street.

The hunter took a shot. He didn't trust his vision enough for a headshot, so he went for the biggest mass he could focus on.

The bullet slammed into Tallow's vest, right over his heart. It was like having the wind knocked out of his lungs by a baseball bat. His heart skipped six beats and the world went black and red around the edges. The car weaved, bumped up the opposite sidewalk, and took out a newspaper vending box before Tallow got it and himself back under control.

Another shot screamed across the hood. Flecks of hot tin torn up by the bullet's passage flew into the car and across Tallow's face. A sound like a roar came out of him as he aimed the car down the street with murder.

The hunter had no choice but to turn and run.

Tallow tried to keep the nose of the car on the hunter, but the bastard was threading between streetlights and mailboxes and any other damn thing he could put between himself and the car while running like a gazelle. Tallow swung the car out wide, making a guess. He was getting bright little spikes of pain across his chest whenever he tried to breathe.

The hunter angled left at the next intersection, firing another bullet without looking. The shell plowed into the front of the car, caromed around elements of the engine, and came out low by the driver's seat. Tallow yelled as a chunk of his right calf tore away. He swore and kicked his leg out to try to shake the pain. His face was wet. He wiped the sweat off it as quickly as he could, before it ran into his eyes, and saw blood on his fingers as they closed around the steering wheel again. He swore twice. The blood was making the wheel slick and hard to grip. His leg was full of burning grit, and smoke was leaking out of the car's hood.

Tallow had to drive across traffic to stay in pursuit. He missed a sideswipe by inches and had to mount the sidewalk again, clipping some signage as he barreled the wrong way down the next street, praying that no one would be driving toward him.

Ambient Security updates petered out. The storefronts were thinning out. The hunter was out of sight. Tallow had to trust to his knowledge of the city, everything he'd learned over the past few days, and his instinct. There was nothing else left.

The hunter had made it. He knew he was only seconds ahead of Tallow. He fumbled in his bag for the key, held in a loop stitched into the vessel's bottom. There was no one around: this face of the building, the rear, was always quiet at this time of night, and he had means of entry should he be challenged. But he needed the key. He only ever carried two. One for Pearl Street and one for this place. Both given to him. Both kept close and with care. He freed the key.

Tallow brought the wallowing car around on the rear side of the Manhattan Detention Complex. There were three entranceways, each just big enough to take a wagon from Correction, all covered in green shutters. On the far left of them, a single doorway in a recessed alcove. No police around. There was no traffic back here at night, as a general rule, and a patient man would wait out what little motion there was before going to that door.

The hunter was there, getting a key into the lock. If Tallow pulled up now, he had a clear shot. But a clear shot at distance, when his eyesight and his grip were both compromised. He'd have to aim for the chest if he wanted to guarantee a hit.

Tallow wanted to kill him.

For one second, he was at the top of the stairs in the Pearl Street tenement looking at the man who had killed his partner and becoming a mindless thing with a gun that just killed people.

The alcove was narrow.

Tallow gunned the car into it anyway.

The hunter turned and saw a burning black stampede with glowing eyes and smoke twisting off it and something covered in blood riding it toward him and he screamed to heaven.

The car rammed into the alcove at its best speed, crushing both its headlights, collapsing the ends of the grille, tearing off great swathes of the front fenders, and slamming the prow into the hunter, smashing him through the door.

The air bag enveloped Tallow in plastic clouds.

Tallow wanted to lie in it forever. He couldn't. The hunter had a gun. All he could think was that the hunter had a gun. He beat back the air bag and got the driver-side door open. It took some force, and he had to put his shoulder to it, which hurt. He stepped out of the car and fell right over. His calf wasn't doing some piece of work essential to standing up. Tallow grabbed hold of the door, pulled himself upright, and braced himself before pulling the Glock.

The hunter was lying on his back in the debris of the door, motionless.

"No," said Tallow.

Tallow clambered over the remains of the front of the car, cutting his thigh on a jutting length of bodywork and barely even noticing it. He wasn't worried about the hunter's gun anymore. All he could think was *Don't you* dare *die.*

The hunter wasn't moving. And then there was a painful, juddering intake of breath. And then another.

Tallow could hear sirens now. Moments later, there were voices within earshot, and the clicking of guns. Tallow held up his badge, told them who he was, and told them he needed medics here five minutes ago.

"This man does not get to die. He doesn't get to escape."

Tallow stepped away. The hunter's gun was in sight, which pleased him. So was the hunter's bag. Tallow picked it up and looked inside it.

Folded in the bottom of the bag was a small black wallet containing a New York Police Department detective's badge.

THIRTY-SEVEN

It still wasn't much of a case, but they built it anyway.

Bat insisted he had gotten more bandaging than Tallow because he was hurt worse. When informed, not with kindness, that Tallow had also had a calf wound packed and wrapped up, that his hands were bruised for God knew what reason, that half his shoulder was black with bruising and burns, and that he looked a bit as if someone had emptied a nail gun into his face, Bat started bitching about how someone had stolen Fuck You Robot from Tallow's apartment. With additional poison, Bat further noted that Fuck You Robot must have been the only item of value in Tallow's apartment, as nothing else had been stolen.

"What are you, autistic?" said Tallow. Scarly laughed and Bat told him never to darken their door with his bullshit again.

Assistant Chief Turkel was, these five days

after Tallow had driven his car into the back of the Tombs, on administrative leave. This was, officially, due to the loss of one of his oldest and dearest friends, Jason Westover, and also Jason's beloved wife, Emily. It had occurred under such tragic circumstances — a murder/suicide pact, among such people, in such a place as Aer Keep! — that Turkel had declared that he was unable to serve while suffering such grief.

Unofficially, Turkel had stood firm for two deeply unnerving days. Turkel had not been aware that Tallow had ridden with the hunter to Beth Israel and had put off his own treatment until he'd found a doctor he could convince to start pumping anti-psychotics into the bastard. Two days later, the hunter started making a degree of sense and explained to attending officers that the key and the badge had come from his good friend Al Turkel.

Tallow got himself attached to the team directed to search the less used basement regions of the detention complex. It had turned out that there was an informal system at work in which tired cops between heavy shifts were allowed to grab sack time in disused cells out of sight of the main workings of the complex. Tallow felt faintly aggrieved that no one had ever told him about it.

Three hours of poking around (which was hell on Tallow's leg) turned up a cell down in the guts of the place that showed signs of more regular use. Someone had been finger-painting on one wall. Swirls. Scarly matched the paint to that recovered from Pearl Street, and they were off to the races.

At this point, Turkel started talking for his life, explaining that he'd been forced at gunpoint to take the shield of a dead detective with no family and give it and the key to the hunter so that he could use a cell at the bottom of the Tombs as a hideout. Tallow thought it must have been very pleasant for the hunter, being able to hide so close to the buried surface of Werpoes. He could probably have pretended he was sitting in a teepee or whatever in the village at night.

Machen, who'd accidentally started the whole thing, was long gone. He'd gotten on a plane to Mexico a little over an hour after his meeting in Central Park, and his where-abouts were currently unknown. The where-abouts of a considerable quantity of Vivicy currency were also being questioned. Tallow doubted very much that he'd ever see Andrew Machen again.

Turkel's stories crumbled as the hunter

kept talking. He talked like a man who hadn't spoken to anyone in a very long time and was determined to make the quantity up in as short a period as possible. Tallow, Scarly, and Bat could provide evidence in support of enough of it that the administrative-leave story was cooked up, and Turkel was essentially placed under house arrest.

Today, the case had ascended out of Tallow's hands and into those rarefied Olympian heights at One PP where the police gods decided how to correctly handle the affairs of foolish mortals and limping detectives.

Tallow was due to attend his lieutenant's office at Ericsson Place to officially sign off on seven days' leave. A leave that he was assured he would be able to return from. But he was on Baxter Street, parking a new car — new to him, anyway, though it drove like something out of *The Flintstones* — and then walking across to the Tombs.

"Asshole," muttered a sergeant as Tallow signed in.

"Where is he?" Tallow said. "Same place?"

"Don't know who you mean, buddy," the sergeant said.

Tallow sighed and read the sergeant's name tag. "Okay. I'll be sure to give your name to the first deputy commissioner when she asks me later how the Tombs are running today."

"Fuck you," said the sergeant. "He's in the same place. Just got back from court. Asshole."

"Thanks, Sarge," said Tallow brightly, and limped off.

The hunter lay alone in a holding cell, reading a book. He didn't have much choice about the lying. His crutches were propped by his bunk, his legs were mostly plaster, and he was in a back brace and a neck brace. The trauma team told Tallow that the hunter had gotten off lightly, considering, and most of the damage had been done by his being put through the door rather than his being hit by the car, due to the walls absorbing most of the kinetic energy when the car struck them. Someone had dressed the hunter in parts of a cheap suit. His shoes were off.

"Hello, Detective," the hunter said. "Excuse me not standing up. It takes two other people for me to do it, at the moment."

"Hello." Tallow still couldn't bring himself to use the man's name. It lessened the man, somehow, and Tallow didn't want him lessened.

"I just returned from the courthouse," he said, not looking up from his book. "It turns out I'm going to live a long and productive life."

"I heard," said Tallow. The fix was already in. In return for cooperation, and to save haggling around the vexing question of whether an unmedicated schizophrenic can be held responsible for his actions across twenty years, the hunter would get life imprisonment without possibility of parole in a maximum-security facility, probably Sing Sing.

"So," said the hunter, eyes still on his book. "Are we doing more questions today?"

"Just one," said Tallow. "What were the guns on the wall *for*? Was it wampum?"

The hunter's eyes flew to Tallow with delight. "Wampum! You knew it!"

"A wampum belt wrapped around an entire apartment?"

"Very close, Detective, very close. It was wampum. And wampum is information. Just as art is information, and song is information, and music, and dance. You can imagine it — and, hell, now *I* can imagine it, with the amount of medication swimming inside me — as a giant machine. A great big apartment-size machine, like the early computers that filled a room, running its own code."

"But it wasn't finished, was it?" said Tallow. "When I walked around inside it, I could see blank spots. Missing elements."

"That's right. I wasn't done yet. Every piece had to be just right. Every piece had to have its own little bit of machine magic, its own piece of code."

"What was it for?"

"What do you know about the Ghost Dance, Detective?"

Tallow frowned. "That's older history than I'm usually good for. I know it was a Native American thing. Something magical about killing all the white people."

"In one interpretation. The history is more complex than I really have the strength for. But the gist of it is that the Ghost Dance was a complicated ritual dance, rich in information, which, if completed correctly, would lead to several things. The removal of whites and all their evil from North America. The restoration of the native dead. And the renewal and replenishment of the land, free of all the structures imposed by the white man. Do you see where I'm going, Detective?"

"I don't know," said Tallow, slowly.

"I was building a ritual machine that, when completed, would do the work of the

Ghost Dance. When it finished and ran, or danced or told itself or whatever, it would restore Manhattan to old Mannahatta, the island of many hills, and my people would return."

"You're not actually Native American, are you," said Tallow.

"Not even a little bit," the hunter agreed.

"And you built a machine out of murder weapons to destroy New York and replace it with the Happy Hunting Ground."

"In my own defense, I was completely insane." The hunter smiled.

"So I've heard," said Tallow. "Sing Sing, then?"

"Yes indeed," said the hunter, wriggling a little on his bunk. "My very own cell. Lots of books and paints. Probably some limited interaction with the state's other guests, which I imagine will grow somewhat looser before too many years pass. Do you know where the name Sing Sing comes from, Detective?"

Tallow did know this one, but he shook his head anyway.

"It comes from the word *Sint Sinck*. The Sint Sincks were a tribe of Mohegan who lived on the coast there. Neighbors to the Lenape. Sing Sing is actually built on Native American ground."

The hunter's smile widened, to show his teeth.

Fifteen minutes later, Tallow was outside his car, patting his pockets for the keys. There was a crinkling in his jacket, and he withdrew a crumpled pack of cigarettes, untouched for a week. He looked at them and thought for a minute. He selected a cigarette, and tossed the pack in the gutter. He tore off the filter and lit the cigarette.

John Tallow, with his bruised fingertips, pushed a skein of smoke up into the sky for Emily Westover, and another for Jim Rosato.

John Tallow pushed a curl of smoke up toward someone else's heaven for himself too, and then crushed the cigarette out and left for the 1st Precinct.

ABOUT THE AUTHOR

Warren Ellis is the award-winning creator of graphic novels such as *Fell, Ministry of Space, Planetary,* and *Transmetropolitan* and the author of the novel *Crooked Little Vein.* His graphic novel *RED* was adapted into the #1 box office film of the same name. He lives in London.